Books by Barbara Michaels

*Available from Harper

Greygallows

ELIZABETH PETERS
WRITING AS
BARBARA
MICHAELS

HARPER

An Imprint of HarperCollinsPublishers

This is a work of fiction. Names, characters, places, and incidents are products of the author's imagination or are used fictitiously and are not to be construed as real. Any resemblance to actual events, locales, organizations, or persons, living or dead, is entirely coincidental.

HARPER

An Imprint of HarperCollins*Publishers*
10 East 53rd Street
New York, New York 10022-5299

Copyright © 1972 by Barbara Michaels
ISBN: 978-0-06-082863-9
ISBN-10: 0-06-082863-3

First Harper paperback printing: February 2007

HarperCollins® and Harper® are trademarks of HarperCollins Publishers.

Printed in the United States of America

Visit Harper paperbacks on the World Wide Web at
www.harpercollins.com

10 9 8 7 6 5 4 3 2

To Peter Weed with thanks

PART ONE

LONDON

Chapter

1

THE BLACKENED SHELL OF THE HOUSE STILL STANDS on the edge of the moor. Ivy has crept over the rough stone, veiling the ugly marks of fire, blurring the stark squares of emptiness that once were doors and windows.

In other times and other places there would be nothing left to mark the site except a roughness on the coarse, veiling grass. The stones would have been carried away by the villagers, to mend their walls and build sturdy byres for livestock. Cut stone of such quality is rare in the North Riding; but the walls of Greygallows stand untouched save by the elements. The wild animals of the moor shelter there—foxes and birds and badgers. Their calls and the sighing wind are the only sounds that break the silence. The villagers shun the spot. They call it accursed; and who am I to say that they are wrong?

* * *

I have always avoided books that begin "I was born." But here I sit, about to commit the same literary sin. I can plead some excuse, for in my case the phrase is not merely a conventional opening. It is significant that I was, in fact, born in the year eighteen hundred and twenty-six, seven years after the birth of her Majesty and eleven years before she ascended the throne of England. In the year of my birth, almost half the total land area of the realm was owned by five hundred nobles. Naturally the franchise was limited to members of the landowning classes. In 1826, it would be a quarter of a century before divorce was obtainable by any means other than a special act of Parliament; sixteen years before English law rescued tiny children from the lightless pits of the mines; and half a century before the Married Women's Property Acts were passed.

Such great impersonal issues might seem to have little bearing on the life of one young woman of good birth and fortune. Yet the bizarre fate that befell me was the result of the legal and social conditions of that time.

I was happily unaware of these portentous matters, as I lay in my cradle sucking my coral and uttering infantile cries of protest, or later, as I sat my first pony under the fondly critical eyes of my father. I scarcely remember him, except as a tall, lordly form surmounted by a luxuriant crop of whiskers. Mama is an even dimmer memory— only a sweet scent and a silken rustle of skirts. They both died in an accident when I was seven.

I was thrown from the carriage, or so I was told; I have no memory of the accident or of the days that followed. When I was restored to life, after weeks of illness, it was to find my familiar world turned upside down. My home, my nurseries, and my fat old nurse were exchanged for a cold, narrow room shared with three other little girls; and to take the place of Mother and Father, there was Miss Plum. Even my body had suffered a change. One of my lower limbs had been hurt in the fall, and though it healed with scarcely a scar, I could not walk without limping.

My first weeks at Miss Plum's school in Canterbury were a nightmare. Rebellious, sickly, bereaved, I fought all efforts to console me. Later, though, I came to love the school and its mistress. It was a good school, as schools went in those days; perhaps it communicated little in the way of knowledge, but it was a comfortable, kindly place, and that was not always the case. As for Miss Plum . . .

I can still see her in my mind's eye, a rosy dumpling of a woman, almost as broad as she was tall. Her face was round and pink and usually damp with perspiration, for the good old lady loved rich foods and roaring fires. Her heavy opulent clothing added to her girth. She panted like a fat old spaniel; it was impossible for her to spy on us girls, for we could hear her coming yards away, gasping and wheezing and dragging her enormous petticoats.

Not that she was ever a harsh mistress. Quite the contrary; she was too fond and sentimental to be a good disciplinarian, and she spoiled me abominably. I was a pretty child, with brown curls and dark eyes, and an unusually pale, translucent complexion. Miss Plum dressed me like the big china doll I rather resembled. There was plenty of money for clothing or for any delicacy I fancied. I took that for granted; it was many years before I realized that my status as Miss Plum's pet depended to some extent on my position as an heiress. Orphaned and alone, I never left the school, not even for holidays. Miss Plum pitied me for that, and for my infirmity; instead of urging me to exercise and walk, she coddled me with warm fires and teased my feeble appetite with her favorite rich foods.

It is no wonder that under this treatment I soon became a spoiled little prig. My schoolmates detested me as heartily as Miss Plum doted on me. I took no notice of their dislike until one day, my tenth birthday, when it was brought forcibly to my attention by one small guest whom I had been teasing in my usual fashion until, driven by exasperation, she threw her jam-filled cake straight into my face.

Speechless with shock, I began licking jam off my spattered countenance; and suddenly the expression on Miss Plum's face awoke a hitherto dormant sense of humor. I began to laugh, and the guests followed suit. I was more popular with the girls after that, especially when I was able to persuade Miss Plum to spare little Margaret the punishment she was scheduled to enjoy. It was not difficult to dissuade Miss Plum from whipping a student; no doubt we would all have been the better for it if she had resorted to corporal punishment more often.

At sixteen I was the oldest student in the school; I had seen my friends leave to take their places in their family circles, or to make the marriages that had been arranged for them. It was in May of that year that Mr. Beam made his appearance.

He was my father's solicitor and one of my two guardians, my aunt being the other. Miss Plum had often mentioned his name, since it was through him that the arrangements for my fees and allowance were made; but he had never done me the honor of calling on me before, and my first sight of him was somewhat daunting. He was a tall, elderly man, as neat as a wax figure; every grizzled hair was in place, every fold of his old-fashioned garments looked as if they had been glued down. He was the kind of man whom it is impossible to visualize as a little boy; if he had ever had an emotion, it had died and been buried years before.

Not until later, when I came to know him better, did I realize that under his stiff manner he was as uncomfortable with me as a great dignified mastiff would be faced with a kitten, or a butterfly— something small and insignificant and hopelessly frivolous. But he knew his duty; he sat for an hour in Miss Plum's fussy, overheated parlor, interrogating me like the lawyer he was. Apparently he was satisfied with my progress, though he never said so; some weeks later came a letter from my aunt announcing her intention of removing me from school, since my education was complete.

After nine years of comfort and love, I should have been reluctant to leave the school. At least I should have regretted leaving Miss Plum. Such, I am ashamed to say, was not the case. Sixteen is a selfish age, and I had outgrown my nest. The basket which is a cozy fit for a kitten will cramp a grown cat. For the year before my sixteenth birthday I had been aware of restless stirrings of body and of mind.

Yet my emotions were not unmixed. My aunt, who was also my guardian and sole surviving relative, was an unknown quantity. Twice during the early years she had come to visit me. Her visits caused a great bustle in the school, for she was a lady of title. My memories of these events were not wholly pleasurable. They were mercifully short, for Lady Russell, the fashionable widow of a wealthy landowner, had more important things to do than call upon a gawky young niece. Her gilded coach would come dashing up amid a great jingle and clatter; the big footman, his white-stockinged calves bulging, would leap down to open the door and hand his mistress out. She was like the coach, gilded and jingling. She filled Miss Plum's little parlor. I thought her quite beautiful, however, with her bright golden hair and whitened face. When she took me into her arms her scent almost overpowered me. Yet the embrace was not the soft, scented thing it should have been; under her ruffled garments was stiff hardness, and her hands were painfully strong. Another disconcerting feature of these visits was that she seldom looked at me directly. She sat nodding and smiling and sipping with poorly concealed distaste at Miss Plum's home-made wine, while Miss Plum described my progress in the arts of embroidery, music, and Italian. Lady Russell was clearly bored by the whole business; after a decent interval she would rise, enfold me in another of those hard embraces, and sweep out as magnificently as she had come.

So, as I sat in the parlor that summer day, waiting for my aunt to bear me away into the world, I had an uncertain future to contemplate. The two people who would henceforth control my life were strangers to me, and neither seemed to have a very high opinion of me. Mr. Beam, being a man and a bachelor, could not be expected to regard me with much favor. I was only another professional problem to him. But my childless aunt, as alone in the world as I was—might she not be expected to dote on her only niece, to visit her often, and shower her with affection? She had not done so; I could only conclude that there was some terrible flaw in myself that made me unlovable.

It was no wonder, then, that my hands were damp and my heart was pounding heavily. Miss Plum's training triumphed, however; I sat stiff and prim, showing no sign of my inner alarms. At least, I consoled myself, my appearance could not be criticized. Miss Plum had bought me a new traveling dress and bonnet, and had brushed my hair till it shone. If only the room were not so hot! Miss Plum must have a fire, even in August; and my aunt was late. When finally the coach could be heard approaching and I prepared to rise to greet her, a wave of dizziness came over me. I would have fallen if I had not surreptitiously caught hold of the heavy carved back of my chair.

Then the remembered figure swept into the room and I stared, forgetting my nervousness in surprise. Where was the radiant beauty who had awed the little girl of ten? This was a wrinkled, fat old woman, with rice powder caking the lines in her sagging face. Her bright golden hair was obviously false. Her dress was cut too low, and the ample shoulders thus disclosed looked as pink and puffy as a sofa cushion. She was heavy, but not tall; I towered over her by several inches.

Her little black eyes hardened as they met mine, and I realized that I was staring rudely; I swept into a quick and inelegant curtsy. When I rose from it she was staring at me, and her expression was decidedly unpleasant.

Then a smile reorganized her wrinkles and she came forward with a great swoop of skirts and plumes.

"Dear child!" she exclaimed, catching me in her arms. "You have grown up. What a great girl you are, to be sure!"

Her stays bit into me as she squeezed me. Her scent was as sickeningly sweet as I remembered it, but it did not quite conceal another, more natural smell. Clearly Lady Russell agreed with Miss Plum on the dangers of too-frequent bathing.

"So," my aunt went on, turning to Miss Plum, "are we ready? Her boxes are packed, I trust?"

"Yes, my lady, of course," said Miss Plum, fluttering; one would not think a woman of her size could flutter, but she did. "As you directed, my lady. But will you not take some refreshment after your journey? My currant wine—"

"Dear Miss Plum," said my aunt, with a grimace that was probably meant to be a smile, "I am in such a tear, you would not believe. I have canceled three engagements to come to collect my little friend, and I must return in time for Lady Marlborough's ball tomorrow night, she depends on me. So you must excuse us. Lucy . . . your boxes . . . ?"

The bustle and hurry were welcome; they left me no time for tears or prolonged farewells. When I looked back out of the coach window, I saw Miss Plum standing on the steps of the school. She was waving a white handkerchief, and the front of her dress was darkened by tears.

A slight pang went through me; but my inclination to weep was checked by my aunt's appearance. She had relaxed in the privacy of the coach and was sprawled across the opposite seat, her ruffled skirts filling it entirely. One beringed hand rested on her ample bosom, as if she were short of breath; and indeed she must have been, after compressing her girth into the iron-bound stays. The look on her face was unnerving. It was no more hostile than it was kindly; it held instead a cool appraisal, the sort of look I had seen on Miss Plum's face as she tried to decide which dress material to purchase.

After a long moment my aunt nodded slowly.

"I suppose something can be made of you," she said. "Your fortune, of course, will be a vast help."

"My fortune," I repeated stupidly.

"Come, child, don't look so vacant. You must know you are an heiress. You should have known, from the way that fat old woman fawned on you."

"I knew there was enough money," I said, resenting the reference to Miss Plum.

"Enough!" My aunt's laugh was like a dog's bark, sharp and explosive. "Ten thousand a year is enough for most tastes, certainly."

"Ten thousand," I said. "It sounds quite a lot."

"Indeed," said my aunt, with a snap of her teeth, as if she wished to seize on the ten thousand like a bone. "Enough to enable you to be choosy. You can buy yourself a pretty husband in today's market, with that amount."

"Buy—"

My aunt emitted another barking laugh.

"Bless the girl, must you repeat every word I say, like a parrot? Why did you think you were taken out of school? Why am I, do you suppose, inconveniencing myself to sponsor you this winter in London?"

"I am too old, now, for school," I said. "I thought perhaps you wished to form a family circle, since we are the only ones left."

If I had ever harbored such an illusion, I no longer did; every word, every look, of my aunt's made her feelings painfully clear. I cannot say the realization came as any great shock to me, but deep in the back of my mind a wisp of hope had lingered through all the years of her neglect. I could not help wishing there were one person who loved me.

To show my hurt would have been stupid. I was actually more angry than hurt. Though a boarding school is a comparatively innocent place, it is not without malice, and I had learned some things not in the course of study. I said, in my sweetest voice,

"Now that you are elderly, Aunt, I had hoped to be a dutiful niece to you in your declining years."

My aunt contemplated me with an unchanged face.

"It is truly remarkable," she said softly, "how much you resemble your mother. My dear late sister."

Despite the softness of the words and the voice, a little shiver ran through me. My emotion must have shown in my face, for my aunt smiled maliciously.

"No, my love, our present association is for your benefit, not mine. That old busybody Beam proposed it, but I must confess he was probably right; it is dangerous to put these things off too long. The possibility of scandal . . . Lud, there's that vacant look again! You can't be that innocent, surely; have there been no elopements, no flirtations, at that school of yours?"

Chaperoned as we were, there had been flirtations. The tall, older girls walked at the end of the line when we went out. Thus placed, far from Miss Plum's observation, they had opportunities for exchanges of glances and notes. But I had no intention of admitting these encounters, or of mentioning Margaret's unfortunate affair with the

curate. My aunt's avid, amused expression filled
me with disgust. So I remained silent, and after a
time she went on,

"Well, well, be innocent if you like, it is a desir-
able quality in a young girl. But you must have
some suspicion of what goes on between men and
women? You have heard tell of the institution of
marriage? Don't put on airs with me, miss; you
must know the future intended for you, it is the
only one possible for a girl of fortune and family. I've taken a house for the winter, in the West
End—you won't know it, provincial as you are,
but it is *the* fashionable district—and if we can't
manage a spring wedding, it won't be for lack of
effort on my part."

"Your part," I repeated; and felt myself flushing angrily as she grinned at me. "I have nothing
to do with it, then?"

"Not a great deal," she said indifferently. With
a frown she studied my new frock, which Miss
Plum had selected so carefully. "To judge from
what you are wearing, your wardrobe must be
frightfully *démodé*. But that can be remedied. Not
that your appearance matters, except to me; I cannot be embarrassed by appearing in public with
a frump. You might be a blackamoor or a hunch-
back, or both, but with ten thousand a year—"

"I am coming to hate those words," I interrupted rudely.

"You would be very stupid to do so. They rep-
resent your position in the world."

"My father's position."

"Not at all." My aunt chuckled. I preferred her

barking laugh; her chuckle was fat and cruel. "If your father had not regrettably passed away in his prime, you would have very little left. Fortunately for you, he died before he could squander the prize money he had won in the war, not to mention your mother's sizable inheritance. You inherited also from your father's elder brother, whose children all died in infancy, and from your grandparents. Yes," she said, with ghoulish deliberation, "you are rich because many people died untimely deaths. A pretty thought, is it not, to found your fortune on a dozen graves?"

II

In that year of 1842, there were only a few hundred miles of railroad in all England, and people of fashion shunned the trains because of their dirt and discomfort. It was a long day's drive by coach from Canterbury to London. The drive was not so unpleasant as I had feared. After her burst of spleen, my aunt relaxed and proved to be an entertaining companion. She regaled me with anecdotes about the great city and its inhabitants. Some of the stories were funny, some were dramatic; but all were malicious. I pretended a vast sophistication, which amused Lady Russell very much, but secretly I was shocked at some of her tales, especially those that criticized the young Queen.

Miss Plum was devoted to her Majesty; the parlor was overcrowded with lithographs and sketches showing the sovereign's pretty pouting face and dainty little figure. When she married her handsome cousin, Prince Albert, our school-girl hearts fluttered romantically, and we all swooned over the Prince's delicate moustaches and tall, manly form. We welcomed the birth of each royal child with loyal enthusiasm. No one could say that the Queen shirked her duty; there were already two infants, one for each year of her marriage.

After Miss Plum's adulation, my aunt's remarks struck me as blasphemous. She admitted that the Prince was a well-made fellow, but claimed he was a horrible prig. The court was already suffering from his dull, sanctimonious habits. As for her Majesty—I realized how carefully Miss Plum had censored the reports that filtered into our secluded world. For the first time I heard the nasty rumors about the Queen and her minister, Lord Melbourne. There were horrid little verses about "Mrs. Melbourne." Other verses accused the Queen of being fat; of wearing the "britches," as they put it; and of other qualities my aunt did not quite dare voice aloud. She repeated the lines, but camouflaged their significant words with a mumble and a leer. I can still recall one relatively innocuous couplet which concerned the effect on the Queen of those beautiful moustaches of Prince Albert's:

> ". . . that dear moustache which caused her first
>   to feel,
> And filled her bosom with pre-nuptial zeal!"

I restrained the indignant comment that came to my lips, but my aunt saw my look of outrage, and it re-doubled her mirth. She guffawed till she was breathless.

By midafternoon the effect of an ample luncheon overcame her enjoyment of baiting me, and she fell into a doze. She really was a hideous sight as she snored, open-mouthed and asprawl across from me. I concentrated my attention on the view from the window, but it was not until evening that I saw a sight that made me exclaim. My cry woke my aunt, who thrust her head out the window to see what had excited me.

"Yes, yes," she mumbled irritably. "It is St. Paul's. Thank God we are almost there. I am half-dead with fatigue. Now, girl, don't gawk. It is not modish."

I couldn't have stopped myself from gawking if I had cared about being modish. I had heard of London for so long, from the lucky girls whose parents lived there, and who visited them on holidays. The metropolis of two million souls, the largest city in the world; with its amazing gas-lit streets and fine buildings, with pleasure gardens and palaces and magnificent churches. There were lions and tigers in the Surrey Zoo, and a tortoise so gigantic it could carry children on its back. I was too old for that now (there was a pang of regret in that admission); but I yearned to see the panorama that showed the Great Fire. Amelia had seen it; she had cried out and tried to run away, it looked so real, but her papa had laughed, and held her. And the Queen. Perhaps I might see the Queen. . . .

I must have spoken aloud. There was a vulgar snort from my aunt.

"You'll see her Majesty and your pretty Prince. And all the royal whelps as well. Lud, they say she is breeding again."

She condescended to comment on some of the sights as we passed through the crowded streets. The rattle of the wheels grew deafening as we passed from country roads to cobblestones, but it was the roar of voices that dizzied me. Everyone seemed to be shouting. I had never seen so many people together in all my life. And such people! There were servants in gilded liveries; young men with muttonchops whiskers and tall hats; workmen in shirt sleeves and little paper caps; vendors crying their various wares; beggars . . .

I pulled my head back in the window, and my aunt, following my repelled gaze, laughed aloud.

"You'll see worse before you've been in London a day. What, are there no beggars in Canterbury?"

"His face," I whispered. "That great red . . . And his eye—the one eye—"

"All false," my aunt said cheerfully. "The scar washes off at night, you may be sure; if the fellow washes, which is not likely."

"And the man with no legs?"

"Tucked up under him on that little platform and strapped tight to his body. Don't be so gullible."

She pointed out a tall, melancholy-looking man in a blue swallow-tailed coat and tall hat and trousers which had once been white. He was harassed by a crowd of grinning urchins, whose comments I could not make out.

"One of the Blue Devils," my aunt remarked. "Lud, girl, haven't you heard of Bobby Peel's boys? He had great plans for putting down crime in the streets, but you can still have the shoes stolen right off your feet walking down Oxford Street."

I went back to my gawking. The streets were handsome, with beautiful houses and tall trees. The air rang with a din of hammering and pounding, and buildings were going up everywhere. When I commented on this, my aunt snorted. Every change in the city was a source of aggravation to her.

"More and more people, more and more dirt and crime," she grumbled. "The city was well enough fifty—that is, some years ago. Now they are destroying all the old landmarks just to make a mess. They've torn down the old Royal Mews for this new square, with Nelson's Column, as it's to be. The shops are fine, but—faugh, girl, get your head in and put up the window. The stench is enough to make you sick."

I obeyed without demur. We had come into a section of narrow streets whose old houses leaned on one another like crippled beggars. The smells were concentrated and remarkable. Miss Plum's drains were not the best in the world, but I had never encountered anything like this.

Gathering dusk and the dusty window made it hard to see out now, and after my initial glimpse I was not eager to do so.

"Why do we come this way?" I asked my aunt, who was waving a bottle of scent fastidiously before her nose.

"Oh, these sections are all around," she said indifferently. "One can hardly avoid them."

"It is so dark. Where are the gaslights I have heard so much about?"

"You don't suppose they would waste them in this street, do you?"

"This sort of street is where I would suppose they are most needed," I retorted. "Crime flourishes best in darkness, surely, and the wealthy and wellborn do not commit crimes."

The dusk was deepening; my aunt was only a lumpish shadow across from me. I heard her laugh.

"I must present you to my Lord Ashley," she said mockingly.

"A pretty husband, to be purchased for ten thousand a year?" I suggested, with equal asperity.

"It would take more than ten thousand a year to buy the Earl of Shaftesbury's heir, even if he were single," my aunt replied coolly. "Lower your sights, my girl; our family blood is not distinguished enough for such gentlemen. But you would get on with him; Ashley is a fiery reformer, always ranting about the rights of the poor."

"I am no reformer."

"I trust not. It ill becomes a woman of breeding to take any stand on politics, much less such an unpopular stand as radicalism."

With a suddenness that made me blink we emerged from the dark alleys into a broad avenue.

Here were the famous gas lamps; I had never seen anything like them, they made the night bright as day. And the shops! Great glass windows displayed a profusion of wares that made me stare greedily. Smaller gas jets within the show windows illuminated the products on display: bonnets and gowns, magnificent jewelry, rolls of India muslin and cashmere, gloves and shawls and white satin slippers for evening. . . . There were other commodities, of course; but these were the ones that caught my eye.

"Regent Street is a fine sight," said my aunt complacently, her civic pride touched by my exclamations of delight. "The shops and these new plate-glass windows, I own, are a kind of change I do not regret. Don't fall out of the window," she added, not unkindly. "You will have ample opportunity to go shopping."

With that promise, and the glittering sights before me, I thought London must be the finest place in the world. I had forgotten the foul alleys. I did not recognize them for what they were: a portent, and a warning.

Chapter

2

THE FOLLOWING WEEKS WERE A BUSTLE OF MILLI-ners, dressmakers, and shops. I enjoyed it heart-ily. My aunt was in excellent spirits. She acquired several new frocks herself, and a cloak lined with fur. She even took me to see some of the sights of the city. We visited the zoo and the Tower, and one evening, escorted by a toothless old beau of hers, we went to watch the spectacles at Vauxhall. My aunt drank punch, but would not allow me to do so; she and Colonel Parker became very merry as the evening went on, and exchanged jokes that were incomprehensible to me, but at which they laughed very much. Many of these jokes seemed to refer to the young ladies who strolled along the leafy paths arm in arm with various gentlemen. They were lovely ladies, ruffled and jeweled and very pink of cheek. When I commented on their healthy complexions, and remarked that they must take much exercise, my aunt laughed so hard she fell into a fit of coughing, in the course of which she tumbled off her chair. She had to be helped to her coach by the Colonel, who was not in much better condition himself. By the time we arrived at our door the Colonel had fallen asleep and was snoring so loudly that the interior of the coach shook. My aunt was in better case by that time; with the assistance of the stalwart young coachman she made her way into the house, directing the driver to take the Colonel home and put him to bed.

I had heard of gentlemen being the worse for wine, but it had never occurred to me that a lady might take too much to drink. That naïve ideal, like so many others, did not survive long after my arrival in London.

When I was invited next morning to see my aunt, the room was in profound shadow, yet not so profound that I failed to note her color, which was very odd indeed. I was prepared to offer sympathy and tender ministrations; but she wanted none of that. She had summoned me for only one reason, to caution me not to speak of our Vauxhall visit to Mr. Beam. We were to pay a visit to the lawyer that afternoon. Neither of us was looking forward to it, and I suggested that perhaps we ought to put it off, if she felt so ill.

"Curse the girl," said my aunt violently. "Don't you understand, Miss Innocent, that I would avoid the old fool if I possibly could? But we have overshot our allowance with all the things I was forced to buy for you, and we must have more money."

"Do you mean that Mr. Beam gives us money?" I asked. "I thought the money was mine."

My aunt groaned, and the maid handed her a glass. Lady Russell gulped down the liquid, shuddered violently, and sat up a little straighter.

"That is better. The money is yours, but naturally you have no control over it. By the terms of your father's will, Mr. Beam must approve all expenditures until your husband assumes that task. Hence our visit. For pity's sake, guard your unfortunate tongue when we are with him, and let me do the talking. And in the meantime, go away, so that I may fortify myself for the ordeal."

Mr. Beam's office was as gloomy and ancient as the man himself, but it was not nearly so clean. The stairs were very dark, and a peculiar musty smell pervaded the place. The outer office was almost as dark as the stairs, owing to the fact that the narrow windows had not been washed in goodness knows how long. It was filled with high desks and stools, each of the latter occupied by a stoop-shouldered man bent over a huge book and scribbling away for dear life. The scratching of the pens made an odd sound, like Miss Plum's chickens scrabbling in the yard.

An elderly man hopped down from his stool and addressed my aunt by name. To my surprise—for he did not seem the sort of man who would impress my aunt—she simpered and smiled at him.

"My dear Lucy, let me present Mr. Beam's chief clerk, a very competent clerk indeed—a man upon whom Mr. Beam *depends*"—with a significant glance at me—"Mr. Harkins."

Mr. Harkins bowed.

"Mr. Beam is expecting you," he began, and was about to continue, when the inner door burst open and a young man emerged.

Perhaps "emerged" is the wrong word; he stopped where he was, in the doorway, his back turned to us, and continued a harangue which the closed door had hitherto kept us from hearing.

". . . one law for the rich and another for the poor! You, sir, and your fellows in the law, are like Belshazzar. The writing is plain upon the wall, and you cannot read it!"

Harkins trotted across the room and tapped the speaker urgently on the shoulder.

"The visitors, Mr. Jonathan," he exclaimed. "The ladies! Your language, Mr. Jonathan, if you please!"

I could not observe that Mr. Jonathan had said anything very shocking; I concluded that Harkins knew him well enough to anticipate the next part of the speech. The old man's admonition was successful. The young man stopped speaking and turned, with the same violent energy that had marked his speech.

He seemed the tallest, thinnest young man I had ever seen, with a head too large for his body and a shock of unkempt black hair. If his head was too heavy for his thin frame, his features were too large for his face: a great jutting beak of a nose, bristly black eyebrows that, like his hair, needed trimming, and a mouth which, being still open in the midst of his interrupted tirade, showed teeth as large and white as a wolf's.

My aunt, unperturbed and unimpressed, let out a loud, haughty "hem!"

"Announce us, please," she said; and, as the young man made no move to do so, but stared fixedly at us, she struck the floor sharply with her stick. "Sir! You stare!"

A heavy tread sounded from within the inner office, and beyond the gaping young man I saw Mr. Beam's grizzled head. He was scowling hideously, and my heart lurched; then I realized his anger was not directed at me.

"You do indeed stare, Jonathan," he said brusquely. "Where are your manners, sir? Step back at once and let the ladies come in. Lady Russell, I believe you have met Mr. Scott. Miss Cartwright, allow me to present my assistant, who is not always so ill-bred as he presently appears."

I think that with the speech Mr. Beam administered a sharp jab in the ribs to his assistant, for Mr. Scott started nervously. To my amusement, a wave of crimson rolled up from below his wrinkled cravat and swept grandly up his face, till it disappeared into the untidy jet hair on his brow. I had never in my life seen a man *blush*. But then I had not seen many men.

Lady Russell swept forward, wielding her stick like a whisk broom and pulling me with her, passing me from her right hand to her left with the skill of a juggler. Clearly I was not to be contaminated by the slightest contact with Mr. Scott. He had withdrawn himself as much as possible; he was standing on tiptoe against the doorframe, with his chin pulled in and his shoulders pressed to the paneling. He looked so ridiculous that I couldn't help giggling as I was dragged past; and I was delighted to see a second, even darker blush trace along the path of the first.

He followed us into the office and, at Mr. Beam's request, closed the door. He had regained something of his composure and in an attempt to make amends tried to set a chair for Lady Russell. She snatched it out of his hand and sat down, with a thud that shook the papers on the desk.

After that inauspicious beginning, the interview did not go well. My aunt's request for money was received with what would have been, in any other man, a cry of outrage. With Mr. Beam it took the form of a long rumbling sound and a series of alarming movements of his mouth.

"You have already exceeded your allowance for the entire quarter," he said severely. "You must cut expenses."

"Just like a man," said my aunt, fluttering her scanty lashes at him. "Sir, I vow, you do not know the condition of this child's—er—belongings. It was necessary to replace every item! And the house—and the servants—"

"And the carriage," Mr. Beam interrupted rudely. "And the enormous amounts of food and drink, madam—enough for a family of twelve. Do you entertain so much?"

I had not realized that Mr. Beam went over our household bills. My aunt did not care for the reminder; her eyes narrowed wickedly, but she held on to her temper.

"But of course I entertain. What is my function, after all? And what is the purpose of all this, but to entertain and be entertained?"

Mr. Beam started to speak and then checked himself, with a glance at me.

"Jonathan," he said. "Miss Cartwright would like some refreshment. Take her into your office."

Mr. Jonathan's room was smaller and in greater disorder than that of his superior. Such a chaos of books and papers and dust you cannot imagine; he had to clear a chair and wipe it with his pocket handkerchief before I could sit down. Leaning against the desk, with his hands shoved into his trouser pockets, he paid no attention to me but stood with his head cocked as if listening. Naturally the door was open. The door to Mr. Beam's room had been firmly closed by that gentleman as we left, and I could hear only a murmur of voices from within. It was that sound which held Mr. Jonathan's attention, and the sobriety of his expression suggested that he expected some difficulty.

Since he was not looking at me, I felt quite free to observe him. In repose, his features were not so displeasing as I had thought. I came to the conclusion that his was the sort of face that would improve with maturity; his features were too severe for his age in life. Having reached this decision I had nothing more to do; and finding the silence tedious, I ventured to remark,

"You appear, sir, to expect something to happen. Will my aunt and Mr. Beam come to blows, do you think?"

"Mr. Beam would never strike a woman," said Jonathan. "But in the case of Lady Russell, the provocation is extreme."

"You are speaking of my aunt."

"And you, of all people, must be aware of how provoking she can be."

I could not help smiling. Jonathan's mouth twitched, but instead of returning my smile, he burst out.

"It is all so stupid! Putting you out of the room as if you were an infant! It is your life they are planning in there, your fortune which is being spent."

"But it would be foolish of me to remain," I said. "I have no understanding of business matters."

"Why not?"

"Why," I said, surprised, "why, because I do not . . . because I am . . ."

"Young and ignorant," said Jonathan. "But these defects can be cured."

"Really, sir," I exclaimed. "I don't want them to be cured! Business is tedious. I should never understand it. And why should I, when I have Mr. Beam—and you—to handle my affairs for me?"

My flagrant compliment had no effect. Jonathan regarded me with disfavor, his hands still rudely in his pockets, his heavy brows drawn down.

"You should understand your affairs because you are the one whom they concern. At least Mr. Beam is honest. Not all your advisers will have his integrity. And even he—"

He checked himself, sensing the impropriety of criticizing his employer before I could have the pleasure of pointing it out.

"He must have my interests at heart," I said, hoping to bait him.

I was successful; he was easily provoked.

"How can he possibly comprehend your interests? He is a crusty old bachelor, with a very poor opinion of your sex. How can he understand the feelings, the emotions, of a beautiful young—"

He was rescued, just in time, by the appearance of Mr. Harkins with refreshments. I was disappointed. I had prepared an exquisitely cutting retort, which I never had the chance to utter.

Before long we were joined by my aunt and Mr. Beam. I concluded that the interview had been successful; my aunt had the smug look of a cat with a dish of cream, while Mr. Beam looked more forbidding than usual. My aunt, in high good spirits, declined refreshment and swept me out.

In the carriage she settled back with the air of a general who has just emerged from a victorious battle.

"Lord," she exclaimed, fanning herself vigorously, "what a trial it is to haggle with that old wretch! He hates women. And he allows that young man far too much freedom. I hope, Lucy, you were distant with him and his impertinences."

"He was not impertinent," I said, and then wondered why I had said so. Mr. Jonathan had certainly been free with his opinions.

"No?" My aunt shot me a keen glance. "He

gawked at you like a lovesick calf. Of course he knows you have ten—"

"No," I said sharply. I don't know why the implications angered me so; imperceptibly I had come to accept my aunt's tacit assumption that my fortune was the only thing that would attract a man to me. But in this case . . . I tried to master my annoyance. I was learning the necessity for concealment, and my aunt was watching me keenly.

"You were attracted by him?" she asked softly.

"Oh, desperately. You know how I adore bony young men with bad manners. Don't you think he would make a pretty sort of husband?"

"Your jokes are in poor taste," my aunt grumbled; she was clearly relieved by my contemptuous tone. "His family is good enough, I admit, but there is no money at all. His father was an improvident wretch, who left his mother penniless; were it not for Mr. Beam's charity, in taking on the son without the usual fees, he would have no chance for advancement. He will only be a solicitor, after all; hardly a fit mate for ten thousand—"

"I may expect a lord, no less," I snapped. "What is the price in today's market for a title, Aunt?"

"That need not concern you. And for the love of heaven, don't speak so immodestly when we are in company. You shall have as good a husband as I can find for you."

"Delightful," I muttered; then, as my aunt's face settled back into its smug lines, I asked curiously, "Were you able to persuade Mr. Beam to advance more money? I don't understand how it is paid. Is there a fixed allowance, or does he—"

"Good heavens," my aunt said, in honest surprise. "What has gotten into you today, to ask such absurd questions? It is really none of your concern. Oh, I almost forgot; we must stop by the dressmaker's. Lady Arbuthnot's ball is on Friday and your gown is not ready."

She leaned forward and gave directions to the coachman. But even the thought of my new gown, which was of pale-blue satin trimmed with rosebuds of pink silk, did not rouse me from an odd discontent. Mr. Jonathan's rough words had found a crevice in my mind and lodged there. Was it really so absurd that I should want to have some decision in how I spent my money, and my life?

In the growing activity of the season I forgot that brief doubt. Ball followed ball, and the days were filled with calls, dinner parties, and drives. Our lives fell into a pattern; normally I slept late, after the fatigue of evening parties, and had a languid breakfast in bed. My aunt and I entertained for dinner, or went out, almost every day.

On the days when we had no engagements I remedied the flaws in my education. My aunt had reviewed my accomplishments and declared herself satisfied with almost all. I knew enough Italian and German to translate the little songs I sang, and my drawings and needlework were good enough to display to the uncritical gentlemen who nightly filled our drawing room. But my music! That, according to my aunt, was an essential accomplishment. How else was the company to be entertained but by the performances, on pianoforte and harp, of the unmarried girls in the group? I had my little repertoire of songs for the pianoforte, and sang them in a pleasant enough voice, but my aunt was sadly disappointed by my performance on the harp. As she remarked, the harp was such a splendid thing for showing off graceful arms and soft white hands; the piano was nothing to it. I must have more lessons, and at once, so that I could use the great gilded instrument she had rented—at enormous cost, as she frequently reminded me—which occupied a prominent position by the long windows in the drawing room. Against the heavy crimson velvet drapes, my white hands and light gowns would look elegant as I bent gracefully over the string.

That was how I met Ferdinand.

He said his name was really Fernando, but he did not look at all Italian. He reminded me of the Prince, with his dainty moustaches. I fancied he had the same handsome mouth as his Highness. He was not so tall, but he was divinely slim and graceful.

I told him, naïvely, that I thought all Italians were dark and swarthy. He explained that he came from the north of Italy, where many people were as fair as he. From the first we found it easy to talk together; only too easy. It must be confessed that my skill with the harp did not improve as rapidly as my aunt desired. How could I concentrate on notes and scales with Fernando's fingers brushing over mine as he bent over me to correct my touch?

I did not see him often; our lives were too busy. As November wore on, we began to prepare for the greatest social event of the season. With great difficulty and slyness my aunt had managed to get an invitation to a ball at the palatial home of Lady S——, one of London's noblest ladies and most distinguished hostesses. The invitations were prominently displayed, and my aunt went daily to rearrange the card tray to make sure they were visible.

My gown was new, and so lovely I didn't mind the tedious hours of fitting necessary. It was of rose-colored silk, lavish with lace and cut daringly low to display my shoulders and a good deal of my bosom. I could hardly wait to wear it.

Two days before the ball my aunt called me into her room. That morning, contrary to her usual custom, she ordered the curtains to be opened, and as the bleak winter sunshine shone into the room I thought she looked like a frog that had been too long under a stone, with her protuberant eyes and yellow, pouchy face.

Her expression, as she studied me, was critical.

"Good Lord, girl, you look like a fish. I thought last evening that you were pale. This will never do. A certain degree of languor is not unbecoming, but with her Majesty getting plumper and pinker every week, pallor is not in fashion. How long has it been since you went out?"

"Why, only yesterday, Aunt. We called on Mrs. Sherbourne, and left cards with—"

"Yes, yes, I recall. They say a good brisk canter

in the park is good for the complexion, but I have never favored these modern notions about fresh air. In any case, it is too late for such remedies. A little paint will do as well. But, however, it will not hurt you to take more air. Mr. Pomeroy has asked us to go driving this afternoon."

"I have a lesson."

"The harp can wait."

"I detest Mr. Pomeroy," I grumbled.

Actually I had nothing against that unfortunate young man except that his face and figure showed the effects of too many sweets. He was inordinately fond of bonbons, and brought us a box whenever he came. The fact that he ate most of them himself did not annoy me; he was so tongue-tied in my presence that he had to do something with his mouth to conceal the fact that he had nothing to say.

"You had better not detest him," said my aunt. "He is an only son, and his father is sure to be knighted one day."

"The fact that he has no conversation and no wit and altogether too much figure has no bearing on the case?"

"None at all. Do you prefer Sir Richard?"

"Oh, Aunt, he is at least sixty! And I know he pads his calves. Why will he not wear pantaloons, like the other gentlemen?"

"He had a fine figure in his youth," said my aunt, with a malicious grin. "His legs were much admired."

"At least he is more interesting than Mr. Fox," I

admitted. "When *he* calls he will not sit for fear of spoiling the fit of his trousers, and he does nothing but suck on the head of his cane."

"Mr. Fox has four thousand—"

"Ginger hair and no chin," I interrupted. "Why should I care how much money he has? As you tell me so often, I have enough for two."

"Well, well," said my aunt, with unusual tolerance—she had just taken her first cup of chocolate. "We need not decide just yet. The year has barely begun. I have great hopes for the ball this week. Your gown . . ."

The conversation passed on to matters pertaining to the ball. I knew my music lesson was lost for that day; I knew, also, that it caused me a pang quite incommensurate with my love of music.

The drive was pleasant, after all. I wore my new pelisse trimmed with ermine, and Mr. Pomeroy was moved by it to a flight of poetic fancy that quite amazed both of us. He informed me that I looked like a flower in the snow. The compliment pleased him so much he repeated it every half hour. But however, despite my aunt's disdain for fresh air, the cold bright weather refreshed me. I had not realized how tired I was of stale air and late nights.

In one of the narrow back streets we passed a dancing bear being led along on a chain by a swarthy man in ragged clothing. Mr. Pomeroy ordered the chaise stopped at once, and commanded the man to make the bear perform. The dark, dirty rascal was all flashing white teeth; he expected, and received, a sizable tip. The bear was a great shabby brown beast, and it was comical to watch it lumber about in a poor imitation of dancing. Its owner kept jerking at its collar, which would set it off balance, and my aunt burst into laughter to see its clumsy attempts to keep its feet.

For some reason I did not enjoy the performance as I should have done. I had seen the brute's eyes as it stumbled. I knew it was only a dumb beast, without feelings; as Mr. Pomeroy said, it probably quite enjoyed being made to perform. But something in that look, from eyes as dull as unpolished pebbles, made me uncomfortable.

I dreamed of the bear that night, and woke feeling quite low. I could not recall exactly what I had dreamed. The chain, and certain rough, bare patches in the bear's dry fur were part of it, though, and then there was something about a chain on *my* neck. I made myself forget it; the ball was only a day away. So it was a surprise to me when, in the course of my music lesson that afternoon, I suddenly burst into tears.

Ferdinand went pale. His long white hands fluttered like birds, not daring to touch, but hovering all about me. Misunderstanding my distress, he thought he had said something to offend me; and as my tears subsided a trifle, I recalled enough of my feeble Italian to realize that his attempts at consolation were too warm for propriety.

"Cara . . . mio tesoro . . . bellissima . . . "

I straightened. I had flung myself picturesquely across the harp, and although it was a pretty pose, the frame made an uncomfortable dent in my body.

"Don't distress yourself," I said, sniffing. "You did nothing. I don't know why—I think it was seeing that nasty animal."

I told him about the bear. I didn't think it was the cause of my tears, but I had to say something to relieve his anxieties. As he listened, his blue eyes flooded with tears. He was a very emotional man.

"You are all heart," he exclaimed, "all tenderness. To subject you to such a sight! Ah, these cold calloused Englishmen, they do not understand such a heart as yours. Do not weep"—for his sympathy had brought me a fresh flood of tears—"ah, do not weep, *carissima*. I cannot bear your tears. . . ."

We were both weeping, copiously, so his admonition went disregarded. Our overflowing eyes met; I saw him through a watery blur, and something very strange happened inside me. Slowly I rose to my feet; slowly his slim white hands reached out. In the next moment we were in each other's arms.

It was the first time a man had held me close. My knees grew weak. I had never imagined it would be so pleasurable. I clung to him. . . .

In the hallway beyond the closed doors of the drawing room, a servant dropped a tray. We sprang apart as though pushed by unseen hands. Shaken now by a storm of vastly different emotion, I stared wildly. My handsome Ferdinand dropped to his knees.

"Oh get up, I beg you," I exclaimed, in an agony of apprehension. "What if someone should come!"

Ferdinand got to his feet. Giving me a look of wild despair, he flung himself across the piano-forte, his face hidden in his arms. From between the black coat sleeves a voice, muffled by emotion and broadcloth, exclaimed,

"Ah, what have I done? To dare to touch . . ." He stood upright, a frozen statue of despair. "I will destroy myself!"

His tears made his eyes look bigger and bluer; he was one of those fortunate people who can weep without leaving any disfiguring swelling or redness. I knew from past experience that I was not so fortunate, and I was suddenly conscious of my swollen eyes. That awareness, and another sound from the hall, destroyed every emotion except consternation.

"Please," I stuttered. "Don't talk so. Think of me!"

"Ah!" Ferdinand drew himself up to his full height and clutched his bosom. He looked so handsome. "I think of nothing else! That is my tragedy, my despair. . . . But I must be strong. I must live and endure this agony. And you—you would grieve, just a little, for the poor music master, you who shed your lovely tears for a poor dumb beast?"

"Oh," I breathed rapturously. It was just like a scene in a novel, I thought—one of those books from the lending library my aunt had forbidden me to read, but into which I had, of course, dipped, since she left them lying all about the house.

Ferdinand struck another pose, more graceful than the last.

"I go," he said deeply. "There are limits to my strength. I can endure no more. My adored one—farewell!"

He strode to the door. His hand on the knob, he turned. He gave me one long, burning look, a sob shook his frame, and he was gone.

I sank into the nearest chair.

We had no company that day. My aunt had decreed an early night, in anticipation of the ball next day. This was fortunate, for I doubt if I could have framed an intelligible sentence. I was dreaming of Fernando. (I had decided to call him Fernando; it sounded so much more romantic.) My aunt was too preoccupied to notice my state, except for a testy "Drat the girl," when I handed her her fan instead of the newspaper she had requested, and when I dreamily offered her a bowl of potpourri at tea. I was reliving that heavenly moment when his arms enfolded me; when his lips touched my cheek and moved slowly toward my mouth. . . . At that point a long, delicious shiver ran through me, and my aunt inquired suspiciously whether I was catching a chill.

Alone at last in my bed, I did not find my thoughts so pleasant. I needed no one to tell me that Our Love—for so I called it, in capital letters—was hopeless. Indeed, it required no imaginative effort to picture my aunt's face as it would look if she ever discovered what had happened; popeyed and purple-cheeked, she would probably have a seizure. "A penniless music master and—ten thousand a year!" That hateful phrase!

Wealth meant nothing to me; with the inaccurate enthusiasm of youth, I saw myself cooking (I had never boiled a pot of water in my life) and ironing my husband's shirts—though I would not have recognized a flatiron if I had seen one. I had never seen poverty either, not with my eyes open and observing; but I was unaware of the ironies in my pretty picture of vine-covered cottages and dainty suppers. No, I told myself, I could endure poverty for *him*; but I could not condemn my darling to a life of poverty for my sake. I was under age. My guardian could pursue us and tear us apart, with the help of that Law to which Mr. Beam was such a loyal servant.

I began to see some point in Mr. Jonathan's suggestion that I find out about my financial affairs. Not that it would do any good if I wished to find out, I thought despairingly; Mr. Beam would tolerate no such request. He was as cruel and worldly as my aunt; my love was doomed to die an untimely death.

With melancholy pleasure I decided to cry myself to sleep, but dropped off before I had done more than dampen the pillow. I was disgusted next morning to find there was no trace upon it of my tragic love. But my tears of the previous afternoon had left me looking as wan and languid as I felt, and my aunt's disapproval was openly expressed.

It was only noon, but she and Mary, my maid, were hard at work. The ball was an important affair; she had great hopes of it and was determined to spare no effort to make me look my best. I sat at my dressing table with the two of them hovering over me like vultures, patting and brushing and pushing me.

"Your eyes look like a pig's," said my aunt, with her usual tact. "Mary, get that little bottle of belladonna. And the box—you know the one—I keep in the locked drawer of my cupboard."

I knew the box, too; it was an open secret in the house. Any observer of my aunt's suspiciously blooming cheeks would have known they did not come from nature.

"I don't want paint on my face," I said sullenly. "Nor the drops. Mrs. Brown says belladonna is bad for the eyes."

"You must soak them first, to reduce the puffiness," said my aunt, ignoring my complaint. "What is wrong with you? If I didn't know better, I would swear you had been bawling."

Mary appeared with the required items, and my aunt turned to take them from her. As people will, they forgot I had a mirror before me, and I saw the glance they exchanged. My aunt raised an eyebrow inquiringly, nodding at me; Mary shrugged. For a moment they looked like sisters, their faces distorted by identical expressions of sly suspicion.

I had realized that though Mary was supposed to be my maid, she was more devoted to my aunt. But it had never occurred to me, until that moment, that she might be my aunt's spy. I had never, until then, had anything to hide.

That discovery put me into a state of sulky rage, and I did not cooperate at all as they buttoned me into my gown and painted me like a puppet. I must have looked well enough, for my aunt went off to her own toilette, admonishing me not to sit, lie down, eat, or otherwise disturb a single fold. I was still sulking when we set off; in the darkness of the coach I rubbed off all the paint my aunt had put on my cheeks and mouth.

Though my heart was broken I felt it stir with excitement at the sight of S—— House, all aglow with lights in the darkening evening. Thousands of wax tapers illumined the house, giving the soft light that is of all things most becoming a lady's looks. Eagerly I stepped out of the carriage—and stopped, paralyzed by the sight before me.

Held back by liveried servants, a crowd of humble folk had come to watch the great ones arrive. I could understand their desire to catch a glimpse of the festivities within, to gape at the lovely gowns and jewels and carriages. What I did not understand, or expect, was the way they looked.

The faces were like empty circles of paper, with black holes for eyes, staring, staring. Not a one of them smiled or called out; but there was a low, sullen, muttering sound, like the rumble of a distant storm. I had to force myself to pass along the narrow aisle between those dark waves of humanity; I had the queer fancy that they would swallow me up as the waves of the sea drowned the Egyptians who pursued Moses.

Once inside, I forgot the mob. The entrance hallway was larger than our drawing room at home, a vast expanse of marble floors, lit by glittering chandeliers. Hothouse flowers were everywhere, filling the air with perfume; in alcoves along the walls, life-sized statues posed—but with propriety for Lady S——, following the new fashion of modesty, had had her Greek goddesses *draped.*

The stairs, their balustrades twined with vines and roses, swept up toward the ballroom. We mounted them slowly; I was so dazzled by the lights and sweet odors, by the flash of diamonds on white throats and wrists that I felt very small and insignificant. I was painfully conscious of my weak limb; the more I tried to control my limp, the worse it got.

An attendant at the top of the stairs bawled out our names; then we were within, in the ballroom. It was such a big room that it did not look crowded, though a vast number of people were already present. We made our way to the side of the room, where there were entire trees in huge pots. Panting from the stairs and fanning herself vigorously, my aunt looked around the room, exclaiming as she recognized acquaintances and famous faces.

My eye was caught by a gentleman standing by the far wall. He was unusually tall and erect of bearing, with broad shoulders tapering down to a narrow waist. He was all in black save for the snowy expanse of his shirt front, and his own coloring echoed the somber shades of his dress. He was a striking figure; but it was not his appearance that caught my attention so much as his air. Even in the crowd he seemed apart, isolated.

As if he felt my rude stare, he turned his head, and our eyes met. An odd thrill ran through me.

Without doubt he was the handsomest man I had ever seen. His looks were not to my immediate taste, obsessed as I was by mild blue eyes and fair curls; but they were certainly remarkable. His eyes were as dark as his hair, and his features were coldly perfect: a straight Grecian nose and a beautifully shaped mouth, unmarred by moustaches or beard, and a broad white brow with one lock of black hair waving across to break its severity. His brows were perfect half-circles, his lashes as long and thick as a girl's.

One might wonder how I could make out these details at such a distance. I had, of course, later opportunity to learn his features well. But even at that first meeting I was aware of his slightest feature. I saw him as if through a glass that magnified face and figure. When, after a long interval, he turned his head, I felt as though I had been released from a physical grasp.

At the same moment my aunt's fingers grasped my arm, so hard that I winced.

"He saw you," she hissed into my ear. "He looked at you for a full half minute. Lud, who could have imagined such a thing, the very moment we arrived!"

"He looked, but did not seem to like what he saw," I retorted, still shaken. "He did not smile."

"He seldom smiles; that is his nature. But you're a greater ninny than I take you for if you misunderstood his look."

"You know him? Who is he?"

"I've not met him. But everyone knows him, he is one of the catches of the season. Edward, Baron

Clare. He is not Irish, as you might suppose, but has vast estates in the north. His father died recently, and it is rumored that he is looking for a wife."

The word made me shrink, somehow; it was as if that long, unsmiling look had awakened me to thoughts I had never before wished to contemplate. I must be someone's wife; and this man would be some woman's husband. . . . Mine? The thought was not wholly repulsive. I could only dream of Fernando, I could not be his; since I must belong to some man, this one . . . It could be worse. I knew that, from the candidates who had been paraded before me. He was handsome, titled, older, but not too old. . . .

"Rich?"

I spoke the word aloud, and my aunt, pulling me across the floor, gave me a quick approving look.

"I don't know," she admitted, with uncharacteristic candor. "His estates are large, as I said, but there are rumors. . . . You'd best hope he is not well off. The Clares are too highborn for the likes of us, but ten thousand—"

I pulled my arm away from her grasp; as always, that phrase infuriated me.

My aunt's frantic search for a mutual acquaintance who would present us to Baron Clare did not immediately bear fruit. When the dancing began I was claimed by a willowy young twig of the nobility whom I had met before ("Three elder brothers—you can do better"), and my aunt grudgingly let me go. The dance was a quadrille, which I could manage well enough; the quick country dances, naturally, were beyond my abilities, but for some reason my limp never bothered me a great deal when I danced.

During the quadrille I caught glimpses of my aunt and noted, with sour amusement, that she was accosting one lady after another, still in search of an introduction. I also noticed the Baron. He was not dancing. The arrogant tilt of his head, as he surveyed the passing couples, suggested a sultan inspecting the latest consignment of slaves; and the curl of his handsome mouth implied that he thought poorly of the lot.

After all, it was I who provided the desired introduction. A turn in the measure of the dance brought me face to face with someone I had never expected to see—a figure from out of the past. It was my old foe and later chum Margaret Montgomery, who had left Miss Plum's the year before I did. The exuberant nature which had prompted her to fling her cake at me had been subdued by time and Miss Plum, but it had not been obliterated; at the sight of me she stopped, with a cry of delight and her arms outflung. I foresaw a deplorable disruption of the dance, but Margaret's partner, a chubby young man with a beaming face, seemed to know her well. He caught her wrist and twirled her back into step, with an apologetic smile at me. Laughing, she went with him; but as soon as the dance was over she rushed up to me.

"Who would have imagined meeting you?" she shrieked, flinging her arms around me. "We must have a good long gossip. Frank—my cousin Francis, Lucy—do go and get us some punch, or smoke a cigar on the terrace—and take this gentleman with you—I must talk to Lucy, I have not seen her this age!"

Frank complied with an alacrity that told me much about Margaret's future. When I teased her about him she shrugged extravagantly, her fat brown curls bouncing.

"Yes, I expect we shall marry, in our family it is the custom for cousins to do so. We are such snobs, no one else is good enough for us! To be truthful, no one else of sufficiently good family has proposed for me! I cannot be a spinster, you know!"

We were joined then by my vigilant aunt, who demanded to be introduced to my friend. It was plain that she did not like seeing us together, and I could understand why; Margaret's pink cheeks and glossy chestnut curls always made me look insignificant. My aunt's face lengthened farther when, after a long catechism, she established Margaret's connections. She was indeed of an excellent family. Not until she discovered that Margaret was virtually engaged did my aunt begin to be civil.

"Oh, yes, Frank is well enough," Margaret said carelessly.

"He seems to be very fond of you," I said, chilled by her lack of enthusiasm.

Margaret burst into a loud, uninhibited laugh.

"But that has nothing to do with marriage," she cried. "Marriage is a practical matter. Do you remember, Lucy, our schoolgirl fancies about what husbands we would have? You wished yours to have a pretty little moustache like the Prince's, whereas I yearned for a dark, melancholy hero whose black eyes held a mysterious secret!"

Like her fancy taken bodily form, the tall dark man passed slowly through the crowd, not far from us. Seeing the direction of my gaze, Margaret turned. She laughed again, but this time there was a false note in her gaiety.

"Yes, precisely. Is he not the very image of my imaginary hero? And—if rumor be true—for once the image is not so distant from reality."

My aunt turned, nose aquiver like a dog on a scent.

"You speak of Baron Clare? What rumors, pray, do you refer to? No doubt you are acquainted with him?"

"There is a distant connection," Margaret said. "When he first came to London, my mother thought . . . But it seemed I was not to his taste. He told a friend, who repeated it, that I was like a puppy, all wriggle and bounce and health. But he really did not care for dogs in the house."

"How very rude," I said indignantly.

"Not at all," said Margaret coolly. "He did not know the words would be repeated. He had rejected several young ladies of wealth and family, so apparently his standards are high, or—or unusual. And," she added, under her breath, "I am relieved that it came about so."

My aunt looked at her contemptuously; clearly she dismissed this comment as sour grapes. But

as she turned, watching the Baron's slow, disdain-
ful progress, Margaret caught at my hand.

"She is thinking of Clare for you," she whispered. "I beg you, Lucy, do not—"

"But why not?" I whispered back. "Not that
there is any chance of such a thing, but why . . . ?"

Margaret shrugged. Her rosy cheeks had lost
some of their bloom.

"Think me fanciful, if you like; but there are
tales, in the family . . . His mother . . ."

My aunt turned. The interruption was dreadful
to me; I had heard just enough to terrify me. And
it was apparent that Margaret's suggestion was
not so unlikely as I had thought. The Baron was
returning in his circuit of the ballroom, and this
time his eyes were fixed on our little group.

He came straight to us and greeted Margaret as
a friend and family connection. It was necessary
for her to present him, and if her manner lacked
enthusiasm, neither my aunt nor his Lordship appeared to care.

"I have heard of Lady Russell from numerous
friends," he said, bowing over her hand in a manner which would have fascinated any woman
who was not already in love with his title. "I hope
I may presume upon that fact to improve our
acquaintance."

My aunt made some flattering response, and
then Clare turned to me. I scarcely heard what he
said; his glowing dark eyes mesmerized me. He
claimed me for the next dance; but, as we moved
off across the floor, he asked if I would not rather
rest on one of the seats under the potted plants. It

was gracefully done; yet I was suddenly conscious of my wretched limp, which had not troubled me for some time. Holding his arm, I glanced back over my shoulder. My aunt fairly glowed with satisfied pride; but Margaret's face was grave with a wordless foreboding.

Chapter

3

THAT EVENING CLARE OBTAINED PERMISSION TO call. He did so frequently; but his behavior bewildered me. Overly conscious, thanks to Lady Russell, of that omnipotent ten thousand a year, I did not expect Clare to be madly in love with me. Yet it was an open secret that he had rejected other girls almost as well endowed as I. So he must like me, a little. . . . As I say, I did not expect ardent passion. What I missed were the little things—the meaningful glance, the subtle pressure of the hand, a word charged with hidden meaning. . . . Any woman will know what I mean. He was gravely, exquisitely attentive; but no more.

And my feelings for him? By all rights, I should have been deeply in love. His looks alone were lovable, and his mind was as well formed as his face. We read poetry together; his deep, intelligent voice gave the verses a profound meaning.

His views on natural beauty, on painting and books and music were unexceptional. His sense of humor was deficient; but no reasonable girl expects a melancholy hero to be a wit. Two things kept me from falling in love. One was Margaret's warning.

To my fury, I found it impossible to get from Margaret any elaboration of her strange words. No doubt she would have been willing to gossip, and we saw each other several times after the ball; my aunt was eager to improve the acquaintance with her distinguished family. But my aunt and Margaret's mother, together, made confidences impossible. My aunt never left us alone, and Lady Montgomery was not anxious to improve *her* acquaintance with *us*. When, at Christmas, Margaret went off to the family seat in Derbyshire, I had not exchanged a single private word with her.

And by then I was in love, but not with Clare.

I was still taking lessons on the harp. There, as my aunt later owned, she erred; but she was slow to see what was transpiring. What girl in her senses, she declaimed, would have eyes for a feeble nincompoop of a music master when the handsome Baron Clare was at her feet?

I was such a girl. My adored Fernando and I had little time for dalliance, but many a sigh and sob and—yes, kiss—were exchanged behind the closed doors of the drawing room. I had to play the harp; prolonged silence would have roused my aunt's suspicions. But as I plucked the strings at random, Fernando bent over me, touching my cheek and breathing tempestuously into my hair.

I made little progress in music, but I progressed greatly in love. And, like all green girls who fancy themselves unhappily in love, I pined and grew pale.

My aunt's annoyance at my pallor and feeble appetite was mitigated by Clare's admiration. He did not care for bouncing, healthy girls; he had said so. He spoke of lilies and graceful, drooping nymphs; he recited verses about languid maidens.

During these weeks I improved my acquaintance with Mr. Beam, and came grudgingly to appreciate his better qualities. My aunt was constantly in need of money; she used our flourishing acquaintance with Clare as an excuse for greater extravagance. I was not included in the conferences between my two guardians concerning financial matters. I did not expect to be included; indeed, I would have been greatly indignant if anyone had proposed that I give up hours with Fernando, or dreaming over some romantic novel, to dreary discussions of money. But I saw a good deal of Mr. Beam, in his office and at the house.

An old bachelor, he lived a solitary life. In his dreary ancient chambers he was attended only by an equally ancient manservant. To my surprise, I found that among his few pleasures was a shyly concealed but passionate love of music. My exercises on the harp made him wince, but he liked to have me sing to him. He said I had a sweet little voice, and once, in a mellow mood, he told me of the operatic performances he had attended in Vienna and Germany.

Yet he was not really at ease with me, and I began to suspect that his interviews with my aunt were as painful for him as she claimed they were for her. Actually she enjoyed the battles; she was a combative old lady, and flourished on disagreements. But Mr. Beam was moved only by duty. I developed a reluctant admiration for his sense of responsibility, which forced him into continual uncongenial encounters. He was my guardian, and he had a poor opinion of my aunt's good sense. In his own way he was determined to see that I was not cheated. Altogether, his was an admirable character; its only flaws were coldness and lack of imagination. Yet, in the end, his icy rectitude was as fatal for me as was the villainy of those who brought about my ruin.

My aunt mentioned that Mr. Beam owed his bachelor state to a disappointment in love. Years and years ago he had been in love with a lady, who had chosen another man. Like a knight of old he had dedicated himself to his lost love; now that she was widowed and in difficult circumstances, he pleased himself by helping her in the only way her delicacy would allow—through her son.

I had seen something of Mr. Jonathan too, though not by choice. He was occasionally delegated to entertain me while the older couple held their business meetings. Further acquaintance only confirmed my initial impressions. He was a very strange young man. At times I thought he admired me; he would sit and stare fixedly when he thought I was not looking at him. Then, again, he would say the rudest things. He made insulting comments about my intelligence, or lack thereof; but he seemed determined to improve it, with his own radical notions. His conversation was usually gloomy and invariably dull. Tedious statistics about rural unemployment, long extracts from economics books, criticisms of his own profession of the law—of such did his talk consist, and it bored me unutterably.

On one occasion, however, Mr. Jonathan's remarks did impress me. They were gloomy, but not dull. It was in early December, I believe, that this encounter took place. It was memorable for more reasons than one.

Snow was falling outside, although it little resembled the delicate white flakes that had adorned the winter sky of Canterbury. Soot and smoke so fogged the air of the great metropolis that even the snowflakes were black. The day was dreary and dark, and we had candles lit early. Baron Clare was coming to call.

Dreaming of Fernando, I was some time in realizing that my aunt's preparations were more elaborate than usual; and when at last she urged me to change my gown, I asked her why I should.

"Mr. Beam is coming," she explained. "He wishes to meet Clare."

Already we were on such intimate terms that she could refer to him without his title. I knew then what the meeting portended. Languidly I went up and changed my dress.

During those days it seemed to me that I always had a headache. It was generally admitted that the air of London was unhealthy. The House of Commons sat with the windows closed, because the stench from the river, outside the walls of St. Stephens, was enough to gag even a strong-stomached member. Most of the streets were mired with filth; open sewers ran down the pavements. It had not been five years since the cholera had swept the city, and typhoid we had as a yearly visitor.

I knew nothing of such matters. I only knew that to my aunt an open window was anathema, and that there were days when I was so limp and fatigued I could hardly stir.

Clare arrived early that day, with an enormous bunch of flowers for me and a box of French bonbons for my aunt. His normally pale cheeks were slightly flushed. No other trace of emotion was visible in his manner; his slow, beautiful voice spoke of impersonal matters.

We were sitting in the parlor after dinner, and my aunt was preparing tea, when the butler announced Mr. Beam and his associate.

My aunt grunted. She had little use for Mr. Jonathan, but she needed Mr. Beam, and when she rose to greet them she was sweetly gracious to both.

A breath of air from the chilly hall came in with the newcomers. It roused me a trifle, as I lounged on the sofa, and I saw with some amusement that the two younger men had taken an immediate dislike to one another. With magnificent condescension Clare shook hands with Jonathan; his expression suggested that he was smelling something nasty.

Jonathan was groomed very smartly. His rampant lock of hair had been forcibly suppressed, and his cravat was tied with such smartness that he appeared about to choke. Next to Clare's poise and immaculate attire he was at a disadvantage. He looked not ten but twenty years younger, and as if he did not quite know what to do with his hands and feet.

Clare's frigid handclasp disconcerted him so that he sat down too abruptly and almost missed the edge of the sofa. The resultant jumble of his long limbs did not improve his temper, and he sat glaring at Clare as if blaming him for his awkwardness.

I disremember how the argument began, but I am sure it was Jonathan's fault. He would have taken exception to anything Clare said, and the subject was near to his heart.

We were discussing the weather—a safe social topic, one would have thought—and Mr. Beam, coughing, grumbled about the foul air and hoped there would be no outbreak of disease.

"Cholera in thirty-two, typhus in thirty-nine," said Jonathan with grim relish. "It is only a matter of time until the next epidemic."

Clare raised an eyebrow.

"Surely that is an unnecessarily pessimistic view," he drawled. "One must not alarm the ladies, you know."

"The ladies are as susceptible to cholera as you and I," Jonathan retorted hotly. "If womanly kindness does not lead them to abhor the unspeakable conditions that produce disease, self-interest may induce them to prevent it. The conditions leading to the last epidemic are unchanged."

"Ah, I understand." Both Clare's eyebrows soared. "You are one of those young—er—enthusiasts who weep over the poor oppressed working classes."

"You see no cause for concern?"

"I do not concern myself with politics," Clare said, with the most exquisite contempt.

Jonathan was really trying to control himself. He kept passing his teacup from hand to hand, as if it were too hot to hold; but except for that, and the ruddy color of his face, he showed no sign of temper.

"It is not a question of politics," he said, "but of simple human decency. Have you not read the 'Report on the Sanitary Conditions of the Labouring Classes'?"

Clare laughed. It was an unforgivable thing to do, but my echoing laugh was worse. I really could not help myself, the contrast between the solemn title and Jonathan's comical appearance was so funny. His efforts to restrain his hair had been in vain; it stood upright from the crown of his head and made him look like an indignant young cockerel.

He looked at me, and then I did not feel like laughing.

"I beg your pardon," Clare said, with apparent sincerity. "It was only that such a title, as potential reading material for the present company . . . No, I have not read your 'Report.' I do not need to read it. I am only too familiar with the sort of assumed grievances it contains. The poorer classes have always complained; they will continue to complain, no matter what is done for them."

"Nothing is being done," Jonathan said quickly. "That is their complaint."

Clare sighed.

"My dear fellow," he said, with perfect good humor, "what they—and you earnest young reformers—refuse to realize is that the condition of the poor can only be improved by themselves. The consumption of gin—if the ladies will pardon me—in the London slums . . ."

"People seek drunkenness in order to forget their misery."

"If they did not drink, they would not be so miserable."

"At least gin is an untainted beverage," Jonathan retorted angrily. "The same cannot be said of London's water supply."

"I drink the same water."

"If you ever stopped to look closely at the river from which it comes, you would not! The very color of the Thames is dark brown. The sewers empty into it; dead rats, dogs, human bodies—"

"No more, if you please," Mr. Beam barked. "There are ladies present."

My aunt looked so prim and smug, I wanted to laugh. The previous afternoon I had heard her complaining about the kitchen drains with a wealth of vocabulary that made Jonathan's references seem restrained.

Jonathan turned on his employer.

"There are some ladies who do not find suffering too delicate a topic for their ears."

I did not understand his reference then, but Mr. Beam did; his gruff face softened a trifle. Jonathan went on,

"With all respect to the ladies, I feel we cannot go on behaving like ostriches, hiding our heads to avoid seeing ugly sights. You laugh, sir, at my reference to reports; no doubt you found the report on conditions in the coal mines equally amusing? Children of seven and eight years crawling on all fours like dogs, through dank, dark tunnels, dragging coal trucks . . . Harnessed like animals—girls as well as boys—beaten, hungry, half-naked—"

There was a roar from Mr. Beam and a gentler, deprecating sound from Clare. I was glad of their intervention. I felt sick.

"I don't believe it," I said. "It cannot be true."

"The Commission saw these conditions," Jonathan said. "There was one case of a three-year-old working the pumps, standing ankle-deep in water for twelve hours—"

"Enough, sir," Clare exclaimed. "You are distressing Miss Cartwright. My dear—you are quite pale! A glass of wine . . ."

He bent over me, holding my hand, his fine features drawn with concern. I own I felt closer to loving him than I had ever felt, his tenderness was so welcome. My aunt sputtered and exclaimed; Mr. Beam made gruff noises; and I, the center of their attention, sat upright and waved away the glass of wine Clare brought me.

"No, no, I am not at all faint. I am merely incredulous. It is a lie, it must be a lie. Such things cannot happen in a Christian land."

Jonathan stood stricken on the hearth rug, still holding his forgotten cup. His eyes met mine. I saw no trace of regret or embarrassment in his face.

"I am, as they say, *de trap*," he said coolly. "If you will excuse me, ladies . . . my lord . . . Mr. Beam . . ."

With a dignified bow he walked steadily to the door. It would have been a grand exit; but he forgot the teacup, and had to come back to put it on the table. His face was red as fire.

When he had gone, everyone relaxed. My aunt's amusement could not be contained; in her efforts to conceal it behind a handkerchief, she almost burst. Mr. Beam was not amused.

"I must apologize," he said, in his stateliest tone.

"A regular young Leveler," Clare remarked. "He must be an excellent worker, sir, for you to tolerate such firebrand opinions."

"He is," Mr. Beam said briefly. He was ready to apologize for behavior he considered crude; but he would not justify his choice of employees to any man alive.

For a while Jonathan's remarks haunted me. I told myself I did not believe the dreadful picture he had painted; and, such is human nature, I found the horror of it fading as the days went on. I had other problems to engage my attention.

Clare's intentions were becoming unmistakable. He was on the verge of making a declaration; and the idea threw me into a panic. I avoided being alone with him. The touch of his hand sent a strange thrill through me; and the thrill was not wholly unpleasant. Yet I could not forget Margaret's warning.

Slyly, as I thought, I questioned Clare about his parents. Concerning his father, who had died the year before, he spoke quite freely.

"I fear he was something of a Bad Baron," he said, with one of his rare smiles. "A good man, in his fashion, do not mistake me; but he was a product of another, more profligate age, one which, thank heaven, is now passing into history. His sense of family and property was very strong."

"And your mother?" I asked casually.

"She died when I was born."

"So long ago? How touching, that your father should not have remarried."

"I can see why you might have that impression," Clare said slowly. "But it is not accurate. Sentiment was not one of my father's qualities. He did remarry, not once but twice. Both ladies died young, unfortunately, and Greygallows has lacked a mistress for many years."

"What!" I exclaimed involuntarily. "What name did you say?"

"I am so accustomed to it I had not thought how it would sound to you," Clare said. "Greygallows is the name my ancestor gave his home; but the local peasants, who resented a newcomer, twisted it into another meaning."

"How very unpleasant. Yet you use their name."

"We have, perhaps, a perverse kind of pride. . . . But you could not understand that, it is quite alien to your open, innocent nature. What does the name matter, after all? It is a stately old place and will, I hope, be even more attractive to me in the future."

If Clare's intentions were becoming plainer, so were those of another man. Fernando's adoration had ceased to be remote.

One morning he seemed more subdued than usual, and while I plucked the strings he wandered about the room instead of bending over me. Innocently I asked him what was wrong. His timid caresses had become very pleasant to me.

"I have come to say good-bye," Fernando said quietly. "I shall not see you again."

My hands wrung a painfully discordant note from the strings.

"What do you mean? Are you leaving London?"

"Yes, I am leaving."

"Oh," I said wanly. "You have, perhaps, a position in Europe?"

Fernando laughed harshly.

"I do not go to Europe. No, I seek a more distant clime, more distant by far."

He brushed his falling hair from his brow and turned away; but not before I had seen his hand go to the pocket of his coat. Moved by a sudden premonition, I sprang to my feet.

"What do you mean? What do you have there?"

"Ah, you have discovered my secret," Fernando cried, somewhat prematurely. He drew a small bottle from his pocket and held it up before his eyes. "Yes, it is here; my ticket to eternal rest. No"—as I uttered a cry of horror—"shall I live to see you the bride of another? I know the dark man means to have you for his own! And you will accept him, will you not? Wealth and title will crush true love! What they say is true—faithlessness, thy name is woman!"

By this time I was in floods of tears and could hardly speak. Fernando's wildly glittering eye softened as he watched me.

"So you do feel," he said tenderly. "You feel a little for the poor music master? One day you will think kindly of me. You will say, 'He loved me best. He alone loved me well enough to die for me!'"

The illogic of this struck me even through my distress. With difficulty I exclaimed,

"You do me no favor, Fernando, to die for me. What possible advantage could there be for me in that?"

"Oh," said Fernando, slightly taken aback. "I meant . . . that is to say . . ."

"You must live," I went on, more tenderly. "To live with the memory of a beautiful love—is that not more romantic than dying?"

"It is all very well for you," said Fernando, with a sudden descent into sulkiness. "You may cherish *your* beautiful memories in the midst of luxury—an adoring husband, a family of—no, no, I cannot bear it! I must, I will, destroy myself!"

He wrenched the top from the bottle and raised it to his lips.

I flung myself upon him; he let the bottle fall to his side and clasped me in a passionate embrace.

"Marry me," he murmured. "You alone can save me! We will run away—elope."

The words sobered me like a dash of cold water. I struggled feebly; but Fernando's passion had given strength to his slight frame. His arm tightened and his voice dropped to a hoarse whisper.

"Come away with me. I love you—adore you!"

"I don't know," I gasped, quite overcome by his burning eyes. "I can't think—"

"Think! This is not the time for thinking! Tell me you will be mine! Tell me, or . . ."

Again the small bottle went to his lips.

"No, not that," I cried. "Very well. I agree. Anything but that!"

"Ah."

Fernando released me. I staggered back, covering my face with my hands. Through my fingers I saw Fernando carefully cork the bottle and return it to his pocket. He reached for me and gently pulled my hands from my face.

It was a kiss quite unlike the other, tentative touches of lips we had exchanged; it was long and intense and—but I really cannot remember it, even now, without blushing. Even more embarrassing to recall is the response it roused in me. I found myself kissing him back. My arms held him tightly; my body pressed against his.

When his mouth released mine, I was limp. Clinging to him, I heard his whisper in my ear.

"I will return. We will make our plans. It must

be soon, before that gentleman of title carries you off. My treasure! You will not regret, I promise."

He kissed me again, completing the process the first kiss had begun; when he was finished, I would have fallen if he had not placed me tenderly in a chair. Through hazed eyes I saw him walk to the door—pause, to kiss his hand to me—and then disappear. He walked like a conqueror, and the slam of the door had a distinctly triumphant sound.

I was not quite the young fool I ought to have been, considering my lack of worldly experience. My aunt's caustic comments about fortune hunters and my wretched ten thousand a year had awakened suspicions. But—those kisses! And those mild blue eyes and waving golden locks! And my mistrust of Clare, my dislike of my aunt. . . . It was all too confusing. I didn't know what I wanted to do; I only knew that, whatever I did, someone was going to be dreadfully angry with me.

Next day a package was delivered to the house. It was mad of Fernando to risk it, though the contents were anonymous—a small gold ring, obviously antique, with the scarcely distinguishable crest of a noble house. (Fernando had told me he was descended from Tuscan aristocrats.)

I had the fiend's own time with that ring. Obviously I could not wear it, even if it had not been far too large for my finger, nor could I hang it about my neck on a chain, not with Mary watching me dress and disrobe. In the end I tossed it into a trinket case among other minor pieces of jewelry and prayed it would escape the inquisitive eyes of my maid. It did what Fernando no doubt hoped it would do—it gave me a sense of being bound, by obligation if not by love.

Matters became even more complex when, later that week, I received my second proposal.

I was in a terrible state of mind by then. My aunt had suddenly decided I needed no more lessons on the harp. It was one of those situations that are so comical on the stage and so agonizing in real life. Lady Russell had no actual suspicion of what was going on, but years of cynical experience had given her a kind of sixth sense. So she acted by instinct rather than knowledge and I, of course, assumed she knew the truth and chose not to speak of it in order to torment me with uncertainty.

Guilty and confused, unable to communicate with Fernando; visualizing him lying pale and cold on his bed with the little bottle clutched in his stiffening hand; missing his passionate kisses—and at the same time resenting his peremptory wooing—my state of mind can be imagined. When Clare finally did declare himself, I only stared at him dumbly.

The parlor was dark, lit by the flickering flames of the fire and by a few candles which had been tactfully set at the far end of the room. Clare had never looked more handsome. He was paler than usual, and his fine eyes glowed with a steady light. His declaration was couched in the most poetic language; it might have come from a book.

My response, when I finally made it, was not at all poetic. Staring at his bowed black head—for he had actually knelt to await my answer—I croaked out,

"No—no indeed. I—I really can't."

Luckily he did not inquire into my reasons. I could hardly have explained that I was already betrothed. But his response told me that instead of freeing myself I had only become more deeply involved.

He lifted his head. He really was very handsome. I felt that I was weakening.

"I understand," he murmured. "I expected no other response, at first. Believe me, my dear, your delicacy will receive no rude shocks from me. I admire your modesty more than I can say."

While I gaped unbecomingly, he took my limp hand in his and pressed his lips against my palm.

I snatched it away. The tingle that ran through my body, from that single focal point, shocked me. Was I becoming immodest, to respond so quickly to the slightest caress—from any man? Clare misinterpreted my gesture. He overflowed with apologies. As I sat struggling with shock and chagrin, he made his excuses, arranged a later meeting, expressed undying devotion and eternal hope—and pressed into my reluctant hand a small, hard object.

"The time will come when I will be permitted to place it where it should be," he said. "Until then, keep it, for it is yours."

After he had gone I looked at the object I held in my hand. It was a ring, of course; now I had two. From its appearance, this latest circlet should have been described, in capital letters, as the Betrothal Ring of the Clares. Huge and massive, it bore a singularly unattractive device—that of a snarling dog tearing at some small animal. A shiver ran through me as I looked. I did not altogether believe in omens, but this seemed a forbidding token to offer a bride.

Chapter
4

IT IS NO WONDER THAT IN THE FOLLOWING DAYS I became pale and thin. My aunt scolded, and tried to stuff me with rich foods, the very sight of which turned my nervous stomach.

My situation was bad enough, but the fact I was reluctant to face was even worse. Not only was I betrothed to two men, but I did not want to marry either! I fancied myself in love with Fernando, it is true, but marriage . . . ? As for Clare, my feelings were just as confused. I was fascinated by him, and I was afraid of him—for no valid reason. His dark, sinister good looks and the darker hints of a family mystery were surely insufficient cause for the shudder that ran through me at the thought of becoming his wife.

A sense of helplessness increased my distress. I began to feel like a pale little ghost, mouthing words no one heard. No one listened to me. Clare,

Fernando, my aunt, Mr. Beam—all of them proceeded with their own plans, ignoring me, as if I
were a doll, or an ornament to be placed where I
would appear to the best advantage. No one asks
a vase of flowers, or a china statuette, where it
would like to stand.

Clare was on the footing of an accepted suitor.
Finally, in desperation, I informed my aunt that I
had rejected him.

"So he said," she answered briskly. "Fortu-
nately, he is a man who knows his own mind. . . .
Now what shall we have for your traveling dress?
This French velvet is beautiful, but the color . . ."

Sometimes I felt like rushing out of the house,
shouting, and pounding with my fists on some
object or other. But that was impossible.

From time to time I caught glimpses of Fernando. He haunted our street, lurking in doorways. There was no chance of communicating
with him; whenever I went out it was with my
aunt, or with Clare. I began to relax. If I could not
speak with Fernando, we could not arrange an
elopement. That would be one less pressure upon
me.

Then, one morning, as I sat in the drawing
room, he was announced.

My aunt had just gone out to call on a friend—a
fact Fernando must have known. As he entered
the room, I sprang to my feet, dropping the embroidery I had been holding.

"Good morning, Miss Cartwright," Fernando
said, with a significant glance. "I have come for
the music I left with you, since Lady Russell in-

forms me you are no longer to study the harp. Her
ladyship is not here? What a pity. I had hoped to
give her my compliments. But then . . . Ah, I believe the book is there, among those others on the
table. . . ."

"Certainly," I said foolishly. "Yes . . ." And then,
as the butler went out, closing the door behind
him, I exclaimed, "You should not have come! My
aunt—"

"What is wrong with coming for my music?"

Fernando rushed toward me; I moved aside,
avoiding his outstretched arms. He let them fall
to his side and stood regarding me sorrowfully.

"Faithless, like all the rest?" he asked quietly.

"Not faithless! No, but . . ."

"You love him, this dark lord? This man of
blood?"

"What? Man of—what are you saying?"

"You are betrothed to him?"

"Yes . . . no . . . I don't know what I am," I said
pathetically, dropping into a chair and pressing
my hands to my head.

"Then you know less than the entire city. It is
spoken of everywhere, your engagement." Fernando sat down opposite me and watched me. "If
I could give you up, Lucy, I could not give you up
to him. Do you know what he is?"

"What do you mean?"

"His father had three wives. How did they die?"

I stared, speechless. Fernando leaned forward,
holding my eyes with his.

"There is a curse on their house," he said, in a
hissing whisper. "On the house and on the line. It

is not only the wind that cries across those dreary moorlands! For ten generations"—he paused for effect—"for ten generations, no bride of that accursed line has survived the birth of the heir!"

"Oh, come," I said coldly. "Now that is really— Where did you hear this nonsense?"

"They are arrogant men," Fernando went on, as if he had not heard. "Arrogant and cruel. Treachery has been their key to fortune. The first Baron betrayed his sworn liege lord to win land and title. Even in those bloody days they were known for their cruelty to the miserable serfs who served them. And the women . . ."

"Even if this were true," I said, "it would have nothing to do with Edward—with the present Baron. He is a kind, sensitive—"

"You have not heard of his escapades in his youth? Of the village girls, the missing children . . ."

I started to my feet.

"You go too far!"

With one bound Fernando reached my side. His face close to mine, he hissed at me.

"The first Baron Clare swore a pact with the devil! A pact sealed in blood, repeated by each baron as he comes of age! And the price is—the life of his bride! Ask if you doubt me! Ask anyone— ask your aunt!—about the curse of the Clares! Do you think I will see you sacrificed?" He caught me in his arms. "Tomorrow night, Lucy, I will come. You must steal out of the house and meet me; at midnight I will be here, in the street, with a carriage. I will wait for you."

I shook my head, trying feebly to escape, but his clasp tightened.

"I will do anything to prevent this marriage," he muttered. "Anything! If you don't come, Lucy, I will be here all the same; you will find me on the doorstep when you come out next day. Perhaps the sight of me dead will prevent what I, living, could not accomplish."

I started to cry out. He covered my lips, not with his hand, but with his mouth.

When he left I had not said Yes—but I had not said No, either. I was still sitting in the parlor with my neglected embroidery on my lap when my aunt returned. She stood before the fire warming her back and regarding me steadily.

"I understand that young what's-his-name— the music fellow—was here."

"He came for his music," I said listlessly.

"Indeed? Well, that is the end of him. Clare comes for dinner today. You had best go up and tidy yourself. And put some paint on your face, you look like a ghost."

I started nervously and pricked myself with my needle. Staring at the small crimson drop that formed on my thumb, I said,

"Aunt, what is the curse of the Clares?"

My aunt exclaimed violently.

"So that is it! I wondered what ailed you. You have been listening to—who told you?"

"Then it is true?"

"True, pagh!" My aunt snorted vulgarly. "Surely you are not ninny enough to believe such nonsense."

"But there are stories," I persisted. I felt as if my last hope had failed. I wanted to believe that Fernando had made up the whole thing.

"There are always stories about old families," my aunt replied irritably. "Family curses, family ghosts—you may be sure the Clares have their share of such legends."

"I know so little about him. What is he, Aunt? Who is he?"

My aunt sat down in the chair across from me. She watched me uneasily.

"You want me to marry him," I went on. "I will have to go with him, to that remote place in the north. All my life I must be with him. Surely it is not too much to ask—what sort of man is he? You are my only relative, Aunt, I have no one else. Help me."

It was a gray, lowering day; the air was heavy with fog and the threat of snow. In the gloomy room, my aunt's face looked less florid than usual. Her eyes, meeting mine, were veiled and apprehensive.

Then a log fell in the fireplace, sending up a shower of sparks. My aunt twitched and turned her head away.

"I am trying to help you. This is a splendid marriage, you foolish girl; the best you could hope for. He is a good enough man; all young men sow a few wild oats and are the better for it. Now"—she rose to her feet—"let's hear no more of these fancies. You are a lucky girl, and you should appreciate your good fortune."

"I have not said I will marry him."

"But you will. Good heavens, girl, you will be Lady Clare!"

"And what if I will not?"

Rotating slowly before the fire, my aunt did not reply at once. I expected an outburst, but her reply was, in its way, even more terrifying.

"Then you must consider the alternatives," she said in a slow, soft voice. "Do you fancy any of your other suitors? Sir Richard is a trifle elderly, Mr. Swann has that rather conspicuous wen, but if you prefer. . . . No, I thought you did not. Will you be a spinster, then? We could go on, you and I, as we are—if you can persuade Mr. Beam to be more generous with your allowance. I may tell you, he is anxious to get you off his hands; he will not be forthcoming with money if you flagrantly disobey his advice. I, of course, have not enough of my own to keep you. I daresay we could persuade Mr. Beam to let us set up housekeeping together—nothing on this scale, of course, and not in London, it is too expensive. A cottage in the country. But I think you would not find the life much to your taste."

I had no doubt she was right. She would personally see to it that I did not enjoy that life.

I seized on the one sentence in her speech that seemed to offer any hope.

"How can I ignore Mr. Beam's advice when he has never given me any? He has never said I should marry Clare."

"Stupid girl! Why should he say so when it is inconceivable to him that you should not? He assumes you feel as any normal girl would feel about such a splendid offer."

"But . . ." One by one the doors were closing; there was no way out for me but along the narrow corridor they were forcing me into. "Why should you care, Aunt? Oh, I know it is what the world calls an excellent match, a credit to the family; but you don't care for that, or for me. . . ."

My voice caught in my throat as I saw the sudden spark of emotion in her narrowed eyes, the tightening of her fat mouth; and I remembered some of the things I had overheard other, more experienced girls whisper.

"He has offered you money," I said. "It is often done, I have heard . . . How much, Aunt? How much did you take to sell me? Not a great deal, I think; you don't care much for me, do you? You hate me. I don't know why. . . ."

She slapped me across the face. Her pudgy hand was harder than it looked. Silent with shock rather than with pain I nursed my stinging lip and stared into the black eyes that were so close to me as she bent over me.

"You look so much like her," she said softly. "My sweet little sister, with her helpless ways. I caught the man of title—and she the man I wanted. Now you whimper and whine just as she did when a man too good for her did her the honor of asking for her hand. . . . I could have turned you over to Carter; he offered more. You'll do as you're told, my fine miss, and be silent. I've had enough of your vapors and your pudding face; I want you out of my life and my house."

She stormed across the room, her stiff skirts

slapping together like hard hands. At the door she turned.

"We are discussing the marriage contract tomorrow," she said, in a soft, malevolent voice. "I want no whining from you then. If you think I have been harsh, try your complaints on Beam, and see what he says to you!"

II

The sun was shining next day as we drove to Mr. Beam's office, but it would have taken more than a few watery rays of sunlight to improve my spirits. I felt wretchedly ill, in fact; my head ached dully and my stomach was queasy. I knew better than to complain to my aunt, and indeed I was sure my feeling of ill health was solely a result of troubled spirits. In one way I was less depressed than I had been; it was beginning to seem as if marriage to Clare were the lesser of several evils. If only I had not heard those frightful stories! I might have disregarded Fernando's wild tales, but Margaret's hints and even my aunt's vagueness seemed to confirm them.

It was hard for me to think, with my head aching so; but I had determined not to give in without one last effort. I would not take my aunt's word for anything; I would appeal to Mr. Beam myself. He was gruff and formidable, but he had not seemed actively unkind. Perhaps he would listen to me.

When we reached the office I found my plan frustrated by the simplest of facts. Not once did I have the opportunity of speaking to Mr. Beam alone, or even asking if I might do so. It had never entered his head that I should have anything to do with the discussion of the marriage settlement; bad enough that my aunt should insist on being present. He had made other arrangements for me.

"His lordship will be here in a quarter of an hour," he said, consulting his big gold watch. "Be off with you, Jonathan, and have Miss Cartwright back at five. And—my best regards, of course, to your mother."

It seemed that I was to take tea with Mr. Beam's old sweetheart. I had no particular objection to the plan, save for the fact that I had never been consulted about it; I assumed it was a means of getting me out of the way while my future was being decided.

"Mr. Beam," I said, in desperation.

"Yes, my dear?" He did not even look at me; his eyes were fixed on the hands of his watch, as if he begrudged every lost second.

I glanced around the room and felt my small courage seep away. There were so many people watching. All the clerks—even those hypocrites who pretended to be writing had an ear cocked— my aunt, her eyes narrowed watchfully, and Jonathan, straight as a ramrod and scowling with open disapproval of me and all my affairs.

Mr. Beam did not give me an opportunity to gather my wits.

"Off with you," he repeated. "Come, Jonathan, why are you standing there?"

"The proprieties," my aunt said suddenly. "My niece is betrothed—"

"Nonsense," said Mr. Beam robustly. "It is only the ride to and from the house, with your own coachman. Of course, madam, if you think you should accompany them . . ."

The hopeful gleam in his eye did not escape my aunt; she thought, as I did, that he had arranged the scheme in the hope that she would be forced to chaperone me.

"Not at all," she said, with seeming meekness, and a gleam as wicked as Mr. Beam's. "Whatever you say, my good sir."

Jonathan handed me into the coach in silence. After he had given the coachman directions, he sat down across from me, and it struck me that he was looking rather ill. I noted the fact, but was unmoved by it. I only thought how ugly he looked, with shadows under his deep-set eyes and his nose standing out sharply in the new thinness of his face. The drive was a short one and we passed the first part of it in silence; apparently he was no more inclined toward idle conversation than I.

The streets were in dreadful condition, with the sun melting the accumulated snow and frozen mud; the curses of pedestrians splashed by our wheels followed us like a chorus. The crossing sweepers were busy with their brooms; I saw one ragged urchin spring aside just in time as the coachman urged the horses forward. His bare black feet slipped in the mud and he went sprawling. At the sight of his mud-smeared face, I burst out laughing.

"It is too bad of James," I said. "I think he does it on purpose."

"No doubt Lady Russell encourages the sport," Jonathan said, "and gives James a tip if he succeeds in crippling one of them."

His critical tone and words were not meant only for my aunt; his steady eyes reproached me as well, and an obscure sense of shame made me all the more ready to resent his attitude.

"Your words are not tactful, sir, in view of my infirmity."

Jonathan looked blank.

"My limp," I said, between set teeth.

"Oh, that. I observe it troubles you only when you wish it to."

"If I were poor, and a servant," I said, "they would call me 'Limping Lucy,' and none of the menservants would walk out with me, not even the stableboys."

I had expressed this sentiment at Miss Plum's, to great effect; everyone rushed to pet me and deny my words.

Jonathan turned to look at me.

"That is quite probable," he said coolly, after an appraisal that was insulting in itself. "Your ethereal, delicate style of beauty flourishes only in sunshine; without care and affection, which you assuredly would not receive as a servant in today's England, you would become sickly and whining, riddled with self-pity and—"

An exclamation of anger burst from me. Jonathan subsided. I watched him out of the corner of my eyes. He was smiling, but his eyes were sad.

"You are teasing me," I said. "Do you think that kind or courteous?"

He started.

"No," he said earnestly. "It was most unkind, and unjust as well. You don't know ... you can have no idea.... Kindness is so rare, and I seem to be so deficient in it...."

"Only to people like myself," I said. "Your tenderness, perhaps, is all expended on scullery maids and pickpockets, so that you have none left for honest, law-abiding—"

"Honesty is no virtue when you have all you need or want," he interrupted, with a flash of his dark eyes. "Is the mother who steals a loaf of bread for her starving child less virtuous than a pampered lady who spends hundreds a year on hothouse flowers?"

The argument would have waxed hotter—with me on the losing side—so I was glad to see we had arrived. It was a pretty little house near the river, a doll's house, sparkling with fresh paint and polished windows. I was well disposed toward the owner before we entered the house, and the first sight of her dispelled the last remnants of the prejudice I had built up from hearing her mentioned so reverently by Mr. Beam.

Mrs. Scott wore a black gown, but its somber color was relieved by a white apron, ruffled demurely, and by crisp white frills around the cap that framed a face as rosy and cheerful as a child's. I could see no resemblance between mother and

son, but there was much affection. She ran to him
with a little cry of pleasure, and he swept her clean
off the floor till her little feet dangled and gave her
a great smacking kiss that made her round cheeks
glow even redder.

"Shameful!" she exclaimed, as soon as she
could catch her breath. "Put me down at once, sir!
Miss Cartwright will think us both quite mad."

It was impossible not to smile back at her; the
pretty pink face beaming at me over Jonathan's
broad shoulder—for he had not obeyed her com-
mand to set her down—seemed to light up the
little cubbyhole of a hallway.

We had tea in a parlor as diminutive and dainty
as its owner; the whole house was doll-sized, and
the servant was a child who carried heavy trays
and whisked chairs about with a cheerful goodwill that belied her size. Obviously she adored
her mistress and found Jonathan the most amusing creature in the world; his slightest comment,
even a casual remark about the weather, produced
a subdued tinkle of laughter.

I was completely at ease with my hostess after
five minutes, though I found it hard to recon-
cile this cheerful woman with the heroine of Mr.
Beam's tragic love story. After the little maid had
left I commented on her willingness and on the
excellent care she gave the house.

"My aunt is always complaining about her servants," I added, with a world-weary sigh. "It is
difficult to get good ones, they are so often dishonest and lazy."

A slight shadow crossed Mrs. Scott's face, but

she only smiled and said nothing. Jonathan answered me.

"Servants are usually dishonest and lazy when they are treated as if they were. Little Lisa has good cause to laugh and be grateful. If you had seen her when she came here—"

"Jonathan—" his mother began.

"Mother! I know you do not like to have your kindness mentioned, but I will give you your due." Jonathan turned to me. "Lisa's brother was one of those muddy sweeps you saw today. He was twelve when he was killed by a carelessly driven coach, and he was supporting three younger sisters on his pitiful pay. 'Support' is perhaps too broad a term; when Lisa came here she looked like a skeleton with skin stretched tightly over it."

"She is a workhouse child?" I exclaimed. "That pretty, bright—"

"She was not pretty and bright when I found her. She and the two younger ones were curled up like starving kittens in a box under some stairs. They were naked except for the mud that coated them. They had sores—"

"Jonathan!" I saw then why Mrs. Scott had her son's respect as well as his love; her tone would have stopped a howling mob. "You are upsetting Miss Cartwright," she went on, more gently. "And, so long as we are complimenting one another, you must have *your* due. It was Jonathan who saw the boy struck, Miss Cartwright, and who tried to save him. He lived long enough to tell Jonathan of the girls; and my son carried them here. Like so many good acts, it brought its own reward. Lisa is my faithful little helper, I do not know how I would manage without her, and her younger sister is doing well with a friend of mine."

"You said—you said three sisters," I muttered.

"We were not able to save the youngest," Jonathan said expressionlessly. "She was only four years old."

The biscuit I was nibbling tasted sour. I put it down on my plate; and Mrs. Scott, who had been watching me, leaned forward and patted my hand. After all, there was a resemblance between mother and son; they had the same eyes, deep and dark and full of feeling.

"It is too bad of Jonathan to distress you," she said gently. "But if there are more of us who feel as you feel about the miseries of this unhappy nation, perhaps one day we can cure its ills."

"We? What can a woman do to cure a nation's ills?" I said bitterly, remembering my troubles. "We cannot even rule our own lives."

"That, too, will change one day, if we work for it." Mrs. Scott leaned back in her chair. Her face had lost its childlike charm; it was the face of a prophetess, quietly inspired. "Change does not come of itself; it must be earned, and fought for."

"Are you—forgive me—one of the reformers I hear about?" I asked.

Mrs. Scott's sternness dissolved in a sputter of laughter.

"I don't look like a crusader, do I? Women had nothing to do with the Crusades, my dear; we are far too sensible for such wasteful extravagance! If you remember your history—"

"But I don't," I said meekly. "We only read little excerpts from history books, the parts that were morally improving. How did you learn so much?"

Mrs. Scott flushed prettily.

"I read a great deal," she said. "We women may not go to universities, or study with well-educated tutors, but books are open to all. After Jonathan's father died—really, there was nothing else for me to do to fill my time. I could not busy myself with embroidery and visits, they bored me so. Now you will think me a bluestocking!"

"I think you are a darling," I said impulsively. "But you are clever, and I am not."

"When I first began to study for myself, I thought I was very stupid! The mind must be trained by exercise, like the body. But even the great Socrates maintained that women should be educated as men are, since they have the same capacities."

I glanced at Jonathan and saw that he was beaming proudly. He caught my eye and flushed—I knew now where he had inherited that easily roused blood—and drew his watch from his pocket.

"We must go. I promised Mr. Beam to return his ward by five."

The sun was still shining when we came out of the house, but the air seemed very cold. When the door closed I felt the strangest pang; it was as if I were being shut out—no, not out, shut *in*, into a cold, dreary prison.

"She likes you," Jonathan said, settling down opposite me. "I could tell."

My headache was back, worse than ever. I felt oddly desolate and cold, and my whole body ached. . . . I snapped back at him like a virago.

"I am so glad she approves. I see now where you derive your radical ideas!"

Jonathan's face whitened as if I had struck him.

"And that is all you can say, after hearing her?"

I shrugged, and winced; the slightest movement hurt, and the pain only increased my insane anger.

"Your dreadful tales of poverty are very moving, but you can hardly expect me to take them seriously."

Jonathan's lips tightened. Throwing open the window, he put his head out and shouted at James, who was waiting for orders. The coach started off.

"Do close the window," I said angrily. "It is freezing cold."

"The day is mild, in fact," Jonathan retorted. "I have directed your coachman to take a different route back to the office. You may find the sights more interesting than those you saw when we came."

I leaned back in the corner and pulled my cloak about me. I huddled down inside it, shivering, and Jonathan's angry face relaxed a little as he watched me.

"How can you?" he burst out suddenly.

"How can I do what? Resist your mother's charm?"

"No. You cannot hurt me there. I know her worth too well; and so do you, despite your rudeness. Don't you know what they have been doing, in Mr. Beam's office, while we were sent away to amuse ourselves like children? Will you let them pack you away and deliver you, in a tidy box, as if you were a doll? Or—or do you *want* to marry him?"

I was so surprised I almost forgot my aching head and limbs that felt as if weighted with lead.

"It is no concern of yours whom I marry."

"No," Jonathan said bitterly. "I am a poor clerk; I have no title and no beauty. Whereas he . . . don't you know the sort of man he is? Has no one told you of his past?"

Now I felt ill in earnest. I had no need to question him; my widened eyes and increased pallor did that for me, and he was only too willing to talk.

"He killed a man," Jonathan said. "He was sent down from the university for that, in his youth. Oh, it was a duel, of course—one of our brutal, acceptable customs. But the other man had never fought, never been trained in the use of arms, and Clare knew it when he challenged him. He could have wounded the boy, or disarmed him. He is a first-rate swordsman. But it seems that the boy's sister—"

"Stop it," I cried. "Stop, I will not listen!"

All at once the stench from the open window

struck me like a blow in the face. I turned my
head. I thought for a moment that I had fallen
asleep and was in the grip of a nightmare.

Jonathan's hand closed over mine with bruis-
ing force. His face was transformed, his eyes were
glittering feverishly.

"Look well," he said. "You laughed, once, when
I spoke of this. Perhaps the reality will not seem
so amusing."

The street was so narrow there was scarcely
room for the coach to pass. It was unpaved; the
wheels squelched through mud and slush and the
accumulated refuse of centuries, releasing mias-
mic gases that made the head swim. The blackened, ancient houses leaned crazily on their rotting
foundations, their upper stories almost meeting.
The rays of the setting sun, which shone with a
lurid red light through the narrow gap above, had
brought the dreadful inhabitants of these hovels
out into the air.

They clustered in the dark slits of doorways like
maggots. Swathed in tattered rags like bundles
of refuse, they watched us pass, and their faces
might have been stamped out of a single mold—
pasty white, except where they were disfigured
by scars and sores.

One woman, sprawled on a stoop, held a half-
empty bottle. Her face, at least, was cheerful, but
her idiot grin was even uglier than the hatred
transfiguring the other faces. Her bodice was open
to the waist; a naked infant hung at one breast.
As we passed by, the child lost its hold and fell,
rolling in the foul gutter; the mother laughed and

raised the bottle high, so that the liquid spilled from her gaping mouth and dribbled down into her bosom.

Then a face was thrust up against mine, obscuring the woman's terrible laughter. It was a man's face, bearded and filthy, the mouth open in a shout that showed rotten stumps of teeth. His voice was hoarse and broken; it shouted words I did not know, but which needed no translation; the tone carried the meaning enough.

I have a dim recollection of Jonathan's hand thrusting the screaming face away, and closing the window, and that is all I recall, until I came to my senses to find that the coach had stopped and Jonathan was holding me in his arms. My face lay against his breast, and his hand was on my cheek.

"Burning hot" I heard him mutter. "My poor little love . . . I didn't know. . . ."

"Where are we?" I mumbled.

"At Mr. Beam's. Lucy, why didn't you tell me you were ill? I would never . . . Only a moment, my darling, I will find your aunt . . . a doctor . . ."

I was too dizzy and spent to remonstrate; and he was too distraught to be sensible. If he had stopped to think he would have left me in the coach while he went to fetch my aunt. Instead, he scooped me up into his arms and ran up the stairs with me, bursting into Mr. Beam's office like a wild bull. I heard a great explosion of voices and then saw my aunt's face bending over me. Her concern appeared genuine, but I was not deceived; a dying girl is worth nothing in the marriage market.

"In heaven's name, you young blackguard," she exclaimed. "What have you done to her?"

It was typical of my aunt that she should blame my illness on the person closest at hand, and poor Jonathan was so overcome by remorse that he had not sense enough to deny the ridiculous charge. Still squeezed in my arms, I heard his agitated voice babbling about Seven Dials and his efforts to arouse my social conscience. I muttered fretfully, but no one heard me. Then I cried out in earnest as hard hands grasped me and tore me away from Jonathan's arms. The rough handling shook me awake; huddled in an armchair I saw more clearly.

My aunt was kneeling at my side and Mr. Beam, like an animated thundercloud, glowered impartially on all. The center of the stage was held by Jonathan and Clare. It was Clare who had taken me from Jonathan, and now he confronted the younger man in an icy rage that quite transformed his handsome face. He looked like a devil. Jonathan, shriveling in the consciousness of his own guilt, cowered before him.

I had doubted Jonathan's story of the duel, but I could not do so any longer. Clare's expression was all the proof I needed. I knew what was going to happen; I knew I must prevent it, somehow, but I could not seem to move.

Clare struck Jonathan across the face. Jonathan staggered back. There was blood on his mouth, but he did not lift a hand to defend himself. I heard Clare's voice, quiet and deadly.

"Your seconds will call upon me?"

"I will not fight," Jonathan said. The blood dripped down onto his cravat.

"A coward as well as a bully," Clare said.

"Call me what you like. I will not fight you."

Clare's hand lifted, to strike again. I had to do something; I could not see Jonathan murdered, as that other unfortunate boy had been. Mr. Beam stood like a statue; why did he not intervene? My aunt would not; she would like to see Jonathan hurt. Their faces looked so strange, as if I saw them for the first time, with the masks of convention stripped away and their true characters exposed—the solicitor's essential coldness, my aunt's malice, Clare's murderous violence.

"Stop it," I croaked, and tried to rise. My limbs would not obey me; but the ugly, naked faces all turned toward me. Then blackness swallowed them up.

III

When I awoke the room was dark except for the feeble glow of a rushlight. It shone on the face of my maid, who was slumped in a chair by the bed. She was fast asleep, her mouth hanging open and her cap askew.

I was in my own room, then. I felt quite well, except for an odd feeling that "I" was located a little outside of my body.

"What day is it?" I asked.

Mary started violently.

"What . . . what?" she mumbled, and then came

wide awake. "Oh, miss! How do you feel? You fainted; they brought you home in—"

"I know that," I said impatiently. "What day is it—what hour?"

She answered; and my heart sank down into my toes.

It was ten o'clock on the evening of the same day. At midnight Fernando would be waiting with a carriage, so we could elope.

If I had been unconscious for a few more hours, I thought irritably, then I would not have this choice still before me. I had to decide what to do, and I had to decide quickly.

There were only three courses open to me—life with my aunt, with Clare, or with Fernando. Existence with Lady Russell would be one of petty tortures, penury, and monotony. Clare was more to be dreaded; today I had seen him without his mask, and the face he had kept hidden from me was as frightening as the rumors had implied. They were cruel people, all of them, even Jonathan, who babbled love and tormented me with hideous sights. Fernando was gentle and kind; he would take me away from the hard, cruel people, away from the city that bred such horrors as I had seen. If I did not go with him, I would have his death on my conscience.

So really, there was no choice.

Feeling quite sensible and collected, I made my plans. It was necessary to lull Mary back to sleep. That would be easy; I knew her weakness. I suggested that a sip of brandy might help me sleep. She fetched me the bottle my aunt kept, ostensi-

bly, for gentlemen visitors; after I had sipped a
little I pretended to fall asleep, and my eyes were
hardly closed before Mary had the bottle to her
mouth. An hour later she was snoring.

As soon as I got out of bed I discovered that my
feeling of well-being was illusory. I had to creep
about the room, supporting myself by the furniture as I gathered together a few garments and
trinkets. My cloak was so heavy, I thought I would
never get it around me. Mary had left a little of
the brandy; I drank it, and felt stronger, but even
more peculiar than before; "I" seemed to be hanging somewhere in midair, watching curiously as a
pale girl in a blue cloak stumbled toward the door
like a crippled animal.

It took hours to negotiate the stairs, or so it
seemed to me. I crept down backward, on all
fours. The hall was dark; my aunt had a great fear
of fire and would not allow a candle or a lamp to
be left burning. I had to undo the bolts and chains
of the door by feel, like a blind creature.

When the last bolt was drawn, I sat down by
the door. I was feeling very strange by then; I
think I had forgotten why I was there. After a time
a sound roused me from my half-doze; it was a
sly, scratching sound, such as a dog might have
made. I remembered the wild stray dogs that infested some of the streets and came awake with a
start of terror. Then I remembered. Fernando. He
must be waiting.

I pulled myself to my feet by means of the door
handle and then found, to my disgust, that I could
not make it turn. Fernando must have heard me;

the handle turned in my hands, and the door opened—a bare inch, before it caught, held by the topmost chain, which I had forgotten to unfasten.

"Lucy?" It was Fernando's voice. "Lucy. It is you?"

"Yes."

"My heart! Undo the chain, my dearest love."

"Yes."

I stood on tiptoe, stretching as high as I could reach, and wondering whether my head was really going to roll off my neck, as it felt. I could not reach the chain. Fernando was hissing and sputtering outside; icy air poured in through the open crack.

"I must get something to stand on," I said clearly.

"Hush—not so loud!"

I took hold of a heavy carved chair and dragged it to the door, ignoring Fernando's croaks of protest. The problem was to open the door. I really could not be bothered with lesser details, when it took all my energy to concentrate on the main issue. Standing on the chair I undid the chain and let it fall.

The door opened in a soft rush, and Fernando was at my side.

"We must hurry! They may have heard you, you made enough noise for—"

He broke off with a little shriek. I turned.

In the door to the parlor stood my aunt, wearing her frilled nightcap and crimson wrapper. In one hand she held a lamp; in the other, my late uncle's pistol. It was pointed straight at us.

"Stand back, Lucy, away from him. And you, sir, do not move. I was brought up in the country and have a number of skills a lady is not expected to learn."

I don't suppose the sense of her threat ever reached Fernando; he was simply paralyzed with terror. I sat down on the chair, not because I wished to obey my aunt but because my knees would no longer hold me up. I was shivering violently. The door was wide open and the air was cold enough to freeze one's bones.

My aunt inspected us in a leisurely fashion. She had not recognized Fernando at first; as she did so, a particularly unpleasant smile narrowed her eyes.

"I should have known," she said softly. "This is a nice return for my care and devotion! If I had not been awake, worrying about my poor sick niece, I would not have heard your clumsy preparations to leave. You stupid young jackanapes, did you think you could make off with the girl and her money? I would have had her back, in whatever condition you chose to leave her, before you had gone twenty miles. You have saved me a short journey, but you'll find yourself in Newgate all the same. There are laws to deal with villains like you. As for you, my girl . . ."

"No," I said faintly. "It wasn't his fault. He—"

". . . is the son of a petty tradesman from Liverpool," my aunt said coldly. "His real name is Frank Goodbody, and he repaid his doting mother, who impoverished herself to have him trained as a musician, by running away with what was left of her scanty savings as soon as he came of age. Do you think I would have any man in this house unless I knew all there is to know about his background?"

Unbelievingly, I stared at Fernando.

It was like a transformation in a fairy tale; only now the prince had turned back into the beast. His pallid face and trembling lip tacitly confessed the truth of my aunt's accusation. I wondered how I could have thought him handsome; his face was weak, not delicate.

My aunt waved the pistol back and forth, and laughed as Fernando whimpered.

"I ought to have suspected," she said, with an evil good humor that frightened me more than anger would have done. "But who would think you had such bad taste, Lucy? I thought at first it was the other. At least he is a *man*, not a sniveling peasant. He would have taken the pistol away from me instead of whining . . . Down on your knees, you little wretch! I'll see you grovel, like the dog you are, and then we'll call the constables."

I couldn't think whom she meant. But it didn't matter. My love was dead, but a kind of sick pity remained. I couldn't stand by and see—what was that awful name? I couldn't see him condemned to prison, whatever his name was. He had done nothing criminal. My weakness, my cowardice had brought me to this pass.

"No," I mumbled. "Let him go. He can do no more harm; I never want to see him again. But it would be too cruel to send him to that place . . . Please, Aunt."

"Hmmph," said my aunt, studying me thoughtfully. "Well, it is up to you. No more whining, no more complaints? You will do as you are told?"

"Yes, anything. I am so tired . . . and cold. . . ."

"Very well." My aunt turned to Fernando—I still could not think of him by that other name. "Get out. Get out of London, if you know what is good for you. You may be grateful that I don't have you arrested. I may do so yet."

He didn't even look at me. One moment he was there; the next moment the empty doorway gaped coldly. My aunt's eye turned with slow relish toward me.

"And now," she said, "now for you."

I could no longer speak, my teeth were chattering so hard. I knew then what my illness was; there had been several cases of typhoid the previous year in Canterbury. I was glad. Now all the doors were closed, and there was no way out for me, no way except one. I could die. And as my aunt's face, swollen by malevolent pleasure, hovered over me like a fat pink moon, I released the last frail thread of will, felt myself falling, and lost consciousness before my body struck the hard, cold floor.

Chapter
5

THREE MONTHS LATER I MARRIED CLARE.

I was still thin and pale. Worst of all, my hair was gone. It had been cut off, since long hair drains the body during illness, and I had a cap of short, clustering curls, ugly as a boy's hair. No matter, said Clare; it will be hidden by the wedding veil.

He swept everything before him during that time, including me; but I was no barrier to anyone's will, the slightest breath could have blown me anywhere. It could be said, quite accurately, that I married Clare because he told me to, just as I drank and ate and moved like an obedient puppet, following any suggestion.

I was no longer afraid of Clare. My fear of him had gone during my illness; and with it had vanished all the other emotions I had felt—love and concern and anger. It was as if those things had belonged to some other girl, who had died long ago.

Clare's behavior during my illness would have conquered the heart of any woman who had a heart capable of feeling. As soon as I could receive visitors, he came every day, sometimes sitting in silence, sometimes reading aloud, sometimes playing the soft, gentle melodies that soothed my weary nerves. He was a fine musician, a fact he had never mentioned during my inept performances on the harp and pianoforte.

I heard him talking with my aunt one day after I was able to get about, and that conversation had its effect. My aunt was demurring about the date of the wedding; I was still tired and frail, it was too soon after my illness, another month or so—

"Not another day," Clare broke in, with quiet force. "I cannot wait to get her out of this pestilential place, to the peace and clean air of my native moors. There at least she can enjoy peace of mind, if not a renewal of physical strength. The city is hateful to her; and with all due respect to your devoted care, Lady Russell—"

"Do me the honor, my lord, of being candid," said my aunt, with a sneer in her voice. "I detest the chit, and she hates me. Nothing will please me better than to rid myself of her. As soon as our arrangements are completed . . ."

"We have settled those arrangements," Clare said frigidly. "There is no more to discuss. You do not doubt my word, I hope?"

"Doubt so honorable a gentleman?"

I crept back up the stairs before they could see

me. The tone of my aunt's voice told me something I had never suspected. She detested Clare as much as she did me. That was a testimonial in his favor; the only emotion I did feel in those days was a sullen distaste for Lady Russell and everything that had to do with her. If Clare would take me away from her and her hateful house and the hideous city . . .

So I stood at his side in St. Margaret's, with the organ echoing among the high rafters, and heard the words that made me Lady Clare. When he took my hand, his fingers closed over it gently, as if he were afraid it would crumble in his grasp. The ring had been made to fit my finger, but its blazing cluster of diamonds and opals felt like a lead weight. I wore white satin with an overskirt of Honiton lace, and the coronet of pearls in which my mother had been married. Her jewels, long locked in Mr. Beam's safe, had been delivered into my hands the day before, and Mr. Beam, for once living up to his name, had offered me stately and sincere good wishes.

Afterward there was a great crush at the house. I stood stiff and proper in my lace and pearls, smiling obediently at the guests. Most of them were friends of Clare's, with a few of my aunt's less raffish acquaintances. As I made my mechanical smiles and stiff bows, I realized I had not a single friend in the crowd. It seemed to me rather sad that a girl should not have one friend present on the most important day of her life.

From across the room Mr. Beam was watching me. He thought himself my friend, no doubt; but the expression that softened his hard old face was relief and self-satisfaction. Naturally Jonathan was not present. However, I thought I had caught a glimpse of him at the church, half concealed behind one of the pillars.

Clare took my hand.

"It is time to change now. We must be out of the city before dark."

Obediently I turned to go; but a small cold frisson penetrated the shell of indifference that had protected me so long. My aunt hurried to my side. As we mounted the stairs together, accompanied by the toothy young maiden who, as a distant cousin of Clare's, had served as my attendant, there was laughter from below.

My trunks were packed and waiting. One stood with its top ajar, waiting for the wedding gown. My aunt and the Honorable Miss Allen took it off and helped me into the soft cashmere gown which was to be my traveling dress.

Despite my aunt's halfhearted objections, Clare was determined not to spend a single night in London. He was anxious to be home, after so long an absence; he disliked London, as did I, and there was no appropriate place for us to stay in town. The Clare mansion in Belgravia had been unoccupied for some years and was not in fit condition for a lady, so we were to spend our wedding night in a charming inn he knew of, on the road north.

At Miss Plum's establishment, even the old cat was bundled out of the way at certain times of the year, to reappear, after a judicious interval, with a litter of charming kittens. Of course we girls knew more than Miss Plum thought we did. Amid much giggling and speculation we pieced together certain theories. It was amazing how wildly wrong we were! The majority of us rejected, with horrified shock, a particularly accurate description by one little miss whose father let her play unsupervised in the stableyard, among hounds and horses. Horses and dogs, perhaps; but people—!

I knew that a woman's wedding night was something to be dreaded, and that "that part" of marriage had to be borne with spartan fortitude, as part of the price paid for a good establishment. But that was all I did know; and I often wished, despairingly, that my information were more exact. A known fact, however dreadful, is easier to face than the unhindered flight of imagination. My aunt was not the person from whom I would have sought such information; yet if we had been alone that day, I think I would have questioned her, risking her jeers and love of cruelty, so frightened was I. But there was no opportunity. The Honorable Miss Allen fluttered and giggled and patronized me. I would rather have died than display fear and ignorance before her; and indeed, I felt as if I might do just that.

Clare waited for me at the foot of the stairs, amid a group of his friends. Several of them were the worse for wine, and their laughter and rude jests brought the color to my cheeks. Clare was equally annoyed; he took my arm and had me out of the house and into the coach before I could catch my breath. He turned back to supervise the loading of my trunks and to exchange a few words with his friends.

The weather was bright and cold and gusty, a typical April day; but it was not the cold that made me shiver as I huddled into the corner where he had placed me. As I reached up to adjust my bonnet, I saw a face at the window of the coach, the one that faced the street.

It took me a moment to recognize Jonathan. His hair was windblown into a ruffled cockade, and his cheeks and nose were a vivid pink. But his eyes . . .

"What—" I began.

"Hush. I wouldn't want him—Clare—to see me and mar your wedding day with bloodshed. I would not be here but that—but that I promised my mother to give you her love."

"Thank you," I said. "My best love to her, of course."

Instead of leaving, he stood staring foolishly at me. I had not forgotten his incoherent words on the day my illness began, and I assumed that, like a storybook hero, he was feasting his eyes for the last time on his lost love; but he certainly did not look the part, all ruffled and red-nosed as he was.

"You haven't forgiven me, have you?" he said.

"There is nothing to forgive. Your boorish behavior had nothing to do with my illness."

"And that is all it seems to you—boorish behavior? Well, perhaps it is best so. But don't deceive yourself into thinking you are escaping such boorishness by fleeing London. You will see a few things to shock you in the north, I think; Clare's arrogance cannot shield you from life altogether."

"You are speaking of my husband," I said coldly. "If this is your notion of appropriate congratulations for a bride—"

"No," Jonathan burst out. "I didn't mean to say any of these things. I am too distraught to be sensible . . . Lucy." He reached in through the open window and took my hand. "My mother's good wishes were only an excuse. I came for one purpose—to tell you you are not so alone as you may think. If you are ever in distress, or afraid—if you ever need help—"

I pulled my hand away.

"Go, go, he is coming!"

Jonathan's face vanished precipitately; and as my husband got into the coach I leaned back into my corner and tried to conceal my agitation. Jonathan's reference to my being alone had shaken me; it was so like an echo of my private terrors. But I was not touched by his expressed concern. First he had berated me; then he had run away. Could he be "the other" to whom my aunt had referred on the terrible night of my attempted elopement? If so, she had a higher opinion of him than he deserved. Cruelty and cowardice, he had displayed both. With the illogic of youth, I abhorred violence, and yet I condemned the man who avoided it.

The coach started. We were pursued, for a time, by some of the more inebriated guests, but the coachman whipped the horses to a smart pace and we soon lost them. Clare, who had been looking out of the window, closed it and turned to me with a smile.

"What a relief, to rid ourselves of old friends! And what did your ill-bred admirer from the solicitor's office have to say to you?"

I was too astounded to answer; the tone of amused contempt with which he mentioned Jonathan surprised me as much as the fact that he had seen him.

"Oh, yes," Clare said gently, watching my face. "I saw him. You need not have feared a scene, Lucy; it would have been excessive bad taste, on my wedding day, even if I cared to stoop to chastise a clerk. Which reminds me that I never apologized to you for my behavior the day you were taken ill. I was so distressed by your state that I forgot myself. I was also laboring under a false impression; from Beam's attitude, I thought the fellow was a gentleman."

"Then you did not fight with him?"

Clare's eyes flashed fire, and I said hastily, "No, I understand. You could not meet with a . . . But I thought dueling was forbidden by law."

Clare relaxed. He gave me an indulgent smile.

"The code of honor is more ancient than any law. But it is natural that a lady would dislike violence. Let us talk of something more pleasant. I know you have had admirers; that is all in the past now, and I have no intention of mentioning the subject again."

I had wondered whether he knew about Fernando. Now I was sure that he did; and I could only appreciate the delicacy with which he told me of his knowledge, and of his indifference to it. There was something very gallant in the way he spared me even the mention of unpleasantness; quite a contrast to my ill-bred admirer, as Clare called him.

From under lowered lashes I studied my husband. Perhaps, I thought, if I repeat the word often enough I will begin to believe it. He had fallen silent; there was a slight smile on his well-cut mouth, and the profile he had turned toward me was as perfect as that on an antique coin. His slender hands, in gloves of the finest leather, rested lightly on his knees. They were as white and well tended as a woman's hands, but I knew they were not weak. I had heard of Clare's reputation as a swordsman. They could be gentle, too. I thought of the touch that had caressed my hands and, on one occasion, my cheek; and I thought of the fast-approaching night; and a shiver ran through me.

Instantly Clare turned toward me, full of apologies. He adjusted the fur-lined robe around me, and as he did so my reticule fell to the floor, spilling out some of its contents. He restored bag and objects to me. Among them was a letter.

"From Master Jonathan?" he asked. He was smiling, but his expression did not deceive me. I said quickly,

"No, of course not. It is, I think, a note of congratulation from an old school friend—but you know her, Margaret Montgomery. My aunt handed it to me as we left. I had not time before . . ."

I started to open it. Before I could remove the

enclosure, Clare's hand came across and whisked the envelope neatly out of my hand.

He proceeded to read the note, while I sat staring at him in mingled alarm and indignation. As he read, a frown gathered on his imperious brow. Calmly he tore the note into tiny pieces and flung them out the window. Then he turned to me.

"As I thought. Ill-natured gossip of the worst kind."

"It was my letter," I said. "It was addressed to me."

"It was addressed to a person who no longer exists. You are Lady Clare now, and your husband has not only the right, but the duty to stand between you and the malice of those who wish you ill."

"Margaret does not wish me ill," I exclaimed. "She is my friend, she—"

"She is a relative of mine," Clare reminded me. "I know her superstitious, hysterical disposition only too well."

If he had been hectoring or loud, I might have screwed up my courage to remonstrate. But he was not, he was smiling at me in the kindest way, and his voice was gentle. Not only his sex and his position, but his greater age made complaint from me seem an impertinence. My anger was overruled by these considerations—and by simple curiosity.

"What did she say?" I asked.

Clare laughed aloud and patted my hand.

"You are too pretty a child to worry your head with such nonsense," he said indulgently. "We must take good care of you; you are so fragile I think a breath could blow you away. They say the air of the moors is good for lung complaints; that is why I rushed you away."

"Lung complaints? I have no—"

Clare went on, as if I had not interrupted.

"I have ordered heavy draperies for your apartments; the house is inclined to be drafty. It has fallen into disrepair over the past years, but that will soon be remedied. I selected the new furniture for your room and had it sent last week. I trust you will be pleased with it."

Involuntarily my hand went to my throat, where Clare's wedding gift hung—a lovely pendant of gold twisted into a monogram of both our initials and set with tiny sapphires. His taste was flawless, no one could question that, and yet . . . A spark of rebellion flared within me.

"I would have liked to select my own furniture," I said.

Clare looked at me in surprise.

"It is not customary for ladies to select furnishings for a home," he said, with perfect truth. "And you were unfamiliar with the very shape of the rooms; how could you possibly have made a choice?"

"You are right," I said meekly.

"If there is anything you dislike we will have it replaced," Clare said.

Then his fastidious nostrils curled and he made haste to close the window. Our route led by the river; the milder air of spring had warmed the refuse and foul mud and the stench, unpleasant even during the winter, had become truly noxious.

Once we had left the city behind, the country-side was lovely, with the new green of crops and grass, and patches of primroses in the hollows. The quiet country houses crouched cozily among the trees, and Clare pointed out pretty vistas. As the day waned he fell silent; and I sat in my corner like a mouse, watching the sun set.

It was quite dark before we arrived at the inn where we were to spend the night. With excitement and fatigue and hunger—for I had eaten nothing to speak of all day—I was shaking from head to foot when we drew up in the cobbled courtyard, with its enclosing galleries. When I put my foot on the step my weakness was so great I almost fell. Clare took me up in his arms, and in that posture I was borne into the inn. He carried me as he might have carried a child toward whom he felt some kindness; and once again, as I had done so often in recent days, I told myself how lucky I was to have such a considerate husband. Even when he reproved me, his manner was perfectly kind.

I had no maid. Mary was really my aunt's servant, and Clare had a low opinion of her; I had learned to read his feelings, not in his words, which were normally restrained, but in a glance or a slight curl of his lip. When we came to Yorkshire I would have a north country maid; London servants were always discontented and surly away from home; according to Clare.

The landlord's young wife, a pretty, fresh-faced girl, helped me out of my cloak and traveling gear, and after I had warmed myself by the fire and taken a glass of wine I felt better. We dined in private; the camaraderie of the inn parlor was not for Clare. I was too nervous to eat much. The tall, mature man across the table from me was a stranger; it seemed impossible that I could be dining alone with him, much less . . . But at that point my very thoughts stopped.

We had a suite of rooms, but I did not wonder what they consisted of, beyond my own handsomely furnished chamber with its fireplace and huge four-poster bed. Clare vanished discreetly when the young woman came to help me prepare for bed. I tried to preserve an air of aloof dignity, but it was impossible; my heart was pounding with such violence that it shook my entire body and was visible in my throat and wrists. The landlord's wife must have been about my own age, but she would have made two of me. As she bustled about the room, poking the fire to a blaze and tidying away my clothes, she kept glancing at me with a mixture of compassion and merriment. A practical country girl, she was, nevertheless, accustomed to meeting the gentry, and she knew her place; but just before she left, her kind heart overcame her sense of propriety. Tentatively she put one plump brown hand on my shoulder and, smiling, whispered:

"He's a fine, handsome man, his Lordship. Don't be afraid, my lady; you'll like it fine. . . ."

Blushing at her own temerity, she ran out of the room.

Stiffly I climbed the steps into the big bed and sat there, bolt upright, waiting. I had some handsome frilled nightcaps, but my little friend had not wanted me to wear them. Knots and knotted things were bad luck for a bride. Vaguely I wondered why. Then the glimmer of an answer came to me, and I felt myself blushing, clear up from under the collar of my lace-trimmed nightgown. I felt a little warmer when it receded—or perhaps it was the memory of the girl's blunt, kind words that warmed me. I was still nervous, so much so that the lace frills on the bosom of my gown fluttered with the beating of my heart, as if in a high wind. But a new worry had partly replaced the old. Would he find me pleasing?

When the door finally opened, an absurd little yelp burst out of my throat. I must have presented a laughable sight as I perched there, with the coverlet drawn up to my chin and my pale face and enormous eyes peeping out over the top of it. Clare looked so very large standing in the doorway. He was fully dressed.

With slow, measured steps he approached the bed. My head turned to follow his approach. He had no need of the steps to reach me, he was so tall.

"You have all you wish?" he asked. "They have made you comfortable?"

I nodded mutely.

His eyes dropped to my throat, where the telltale pulse beat madly; and then, at last, a ghost of expression softened the set pallor of his face.

"You must be very tired, after the fatigue of the day," he said gently. "Rest well."

Leaning over, he kissed me on the forehead.

His lips were cold as ice. He left the room without looking at me again. The door closed softly.

I cried myself to sleep, alone in the big bed, with the eerie shadows of the firelight darting around the room; but I would have found it difficult to say what it was I wept for.

PART TWO

YORKSHIRE

Chapter
6

THE WEATHER BECAME INCREASINGLY CHILL AND gloomy as we traveled northward. I was genuinely fatigued by the time we stopped each night, so it was not hard for me to accept Clare's continued avoidance of his bride as a sign of his delicate consideration. The journey was tiring and the scenery depressing. The hills were still brown and stark with winter; the animals seemed to shiver as they stood in the barren fields. When Clare told me we had crossed into Yorkshire, I wondered whether it was all so dreary.

Owing to a breakdown on the road, we were late by half a day from the schedule Clare had laid out for us. He had planned to reach Greygallows early in the afternoon. Instead we were still some ten miles away when darkness began to fall. It had rained heavily that morning, and the roads were boggy with mud. Clare's normally equable temper showed signs of fraying under the delay and discomfort. I found his exasperation comforting; it was such a normal human reaction. Hitherto he had been too perfect, too coldly controlled to suit me.

He was courteous enough to consult my feelings as to whether we should proceed, or seek temporary accommodations for that night, but I knew what his choice would be. Up to this time our rooms had been arranged for in advance; they were select inns, where his Lordship was known and where he could expect the best. A humdrum hostelry, overcrowded by reason of bad weather, would be offensive. So I said I did not mind being late in arriving, and saw his face lighten. "You will find comfort at the end of the ride," he promised. "We were expected today, and when I give an order, it is obeyed. No one will retire until we arrive, or until I send a message that we will not be coming."

The skies began to clear around sundown, and we were treated to the spectacle of an angry crimson sun, setting in a sea of livid clouds. Wrapped in fur rugs, I started to drop off to sleep. A sudden jolt wakened me; then I heard Clare's voice raised in angry remonstrance.

"I canna help it, your Lordship," the coachman's voice floated back. "A bridge is out ahead, because of the rains. We mun go through the town, or go back."

With a muttered word Clare closed the window. He thought me still asleep and in his present mood I chose not to disabuse him. From my corner I could see out of the nearest window, but the view held nothing to attract me.

The smells should have told me we were passing through a considerable town; they were as strong as anything I had encountered in London. The houses lining the narrow street were as crowded as the dreadful dwellings of Seven Dials, but they were not as old. Small, square boxes, their drab color and dilapidated condition were visible even in the thickening dusk. Then I saw movement near the farther end of the street, movement and the flicker of a light. Forms took shape; and I watched them approach with dilating eyes.

They were shapes that might have been spawned by darkness and vile, stinking streets. Twisted, dwarfish, deformed, not a single one of that silent, stumbling procession walked upright. The weaker ones leaned on, and were supported by, the stronger. The rags that clothed them did not conceal their wasted limbs. Dark legend walked the face of the earth, and it was fitting that it should walk by night; the troglodyte demons who dwelled underground must have looked like this.

Then one of the walkers strayed near the coach, and the lamps shone on its face. I let out a sound that brought Clare spinning around.

"They are children," I gasped. "Human children . . ."

His hands on my shoulders, Clare pulled me forcibly from the window.

"I avoid the town when I can. Unfortunate, that we should be passing through at the hour when the day shift at the mill is ending."

"Children," I repeated in horror. "The one I saw could not have been more than—"

"It must have been at least nine years old," Clare interrupted. "The law prohibits the employment of persons under that age."

By its size the child had looked to be about five years old. Either the law was being evaded, or the conditions of employment were such as to produce this deformity. I could not decide which was worse.

"But there was a law," I chattered. "A law about young children working. Just this past year—"

Clare interrupted me a second time, which should have warned me; normally he was punctilious about such things.

"You refer, I presume, to the Mines Act, which did indeed prohibit the use of women and children underground. Though how you know of such unfeminine matters . . . Your radical admirer, I presume."

I did not reply to this comment, and after a moment Clare released my shoulders and settled back into his seat. I could tell he was annoyed.

It *had* been the mines to which Jonathan referred; I remembered only too vividly the words in which he described the terrible state of the children. His description had distressed me, but I was beginning to see that mere words could not possibly convey the true horror of the situation. And those pitiful infants were not even miners, they were millworkers. Mills produced cloth—cotton, wool, silk. What could they be like, to produce as well such frightful human wrecks? For the first time, but not the last, I wished I had listened to Jonathan instead of trying to close my ears. He had been right. I could not escape from misery and suffering by fleeing London.

Once again a journey marking a transition in my life had been shadowed by a grim portent. In London I had forgotten the beggars and the stinking streets when they were succeeded by the glitter of Regent Street. This time the ugly reality was not to be dismissed so easily.

II

Midnight.

The word has sepulchral connotations; it is the hour when graves traditionally yawn and the powers of evil are let loose. For me, on my first night at Greygallows, the sound of the clock striking the hour brought thoughts both dark and depressing.

I had reached that point of nervous and physical exhaustion in which the body cannot take the sleep it craves. After the encounter in the mill town we had a drive of almost an hour over bad roads, soggy with rain and dark as a windowless room. My first view of the house was not reassuring; despite the welcome glow of lighted windows it looked forbidding, its outlines muffled by the tall dark trees that hemmed it in.

Then there was the business of meeting all the servants. Clare had not exaggerated when he said his orders were obeyed; despite the hour, and our delay, the household staff was drawn up to greet us. The housekeeper, a stout little woman with a head of exquisite snowy hair, was named Mrs. Andrews. She was a distant connection of the family. Her manner toward Clare verged on the obsequious; it was unpleasant, in a woman of her age and obvious refinement. Several times, as she supervised the details of our arrival, I caught her studying me with a sidelong, rather cunning look. It was natural enough; I was an unknown factor, whose attitude toward a dependent had yet to be learned.

After the damp cold of the journey the warm rooms, with their extravagant roaring fires, made me rather sleepy. Still I was curious, and desirous of seeing more of the house; it was a disappointment to hear Clare say, in his incisive fashion,

"Mrs. Andrews, her Ladyship will take a bowl of soup in her room and retire straightaway. Her state of health is not what one could wish; we must take precautions."

"Yes, my lord." Mrs. Andrews curtsied. "Just as you say. And you—"

"Will dine at once. Send Barton in to me first. I have some orders regarding the estate." He bent formally over my hand. "Good night, Lady Clare. Sleep well."

With Mrs. Andrews puffing beside me, I went disconsolately up the stairs. Her efforts to assist me made me impatient as well as embarrassed; she needed my support, stout as she was, far more than I needed hers.

The first sight of my room brought an exclamation of admiration from me. Mrs. Andrews, who stood back to see my reaction, relaxed visibly, and the extent of her relief told me more about my husband, as master, than a long lecture might have done.

"I hope your Ladyship is pleased. I obeyed his Lordship's orders as closely as possible, but . . ."

"It is lovely," I said.

The room was vast in size, with a great stone fireplace taking up half of one wall. Over this ancient foundation Clare had designed a surprisingly dainty chamber. The colors were all light, cream and pale primrose and delicate blue and rose. The carpets were Chinese and the draperies hand embroidered. The furniture was also Chinese, carved into fantastical patterns.

After handing me over to my maid, Mrs. Andrews retired to wait upon his Lordship. I looked at Anna rather shyly; she was a big, strapping girl, and she was as near being ugly as any servant of Clare's could be. He did not tolerate clumsiness or infirmity. Anna's broad, weather-roughened face was plain rather than positively homely, and I deduced that she must be a skilled lady's maid, an assumption which was to prove correct. She also spoke proper English when called upon to do so; most of the local people communicated in a barbarous dialect that was as unintelligible to me as Greek.

That was all I learned about Anna the first night; with silent, efficient speed she performed her services and bade me good-night, retiring with the tray on which my supper had been served. Lying in the warm bed, with the softness of silk and swansdown over me and the warm glow of firelight reddening the room, I should have fallen off to sleep at once. Instead I lay wide awake as the minutes passed. I heard the clock strike twice before it finally tolled the midnight hour.

It is not hard to imagine the thoughts that kept me wakeful. After I had seen Clare's patrimony, my peculiar position came home to me with even greater force. The heir of a proud ancient family must be anxious to see his line continue. Yet each night of our journey he had kissed my hand and retired to his own chamber. My initial doubts about *that* side of marriage had not been relieved by the delay. Quite the contrary; if a man like Clare, kindly and well-bred, hesitated to approach his bride, it must be because the procedure was even more unpleasant than I had supposed!

I thought perhaps that Clare might be waiting to consummate our marriage until we reached his ancestral home. It was a sentimental notion, and Clare was not a sentimental man, but still . . . However, he had not come to me. Before midnight I heard his footsteps pass my door and then had heard another door, not far distant, open and close. There was a door in the wall beside the fireplace, which no doubt served my chamber and the one adjoining. The next room must be Clare's.

Ignorant as I was of the relations between man and wife, I found his behavior inexplicable. Was he waiting for me to indicate that I awaited his embraces? Such behavior was surely improper; but I did not know. I was groping desperately for an explanation that did not reflect on me, but it was hard to find one—unless I admitted an idea so mad that even vanity could not accept it. If Fernando's version of the family curse was based on fact; and if Clare believed in it . . . Both were so unlikely as to be virtually impossible. No, the fault must be in myself. He did not find me lovable. Or else—a more hopeful idea—was it possible he still thought me in delicate health?

My thoughts went around and around in a dismal circle. They wearied me, yet I could not sleep. I don't know how I had the courage to do what I did; it was loneliness, as much as anything, that made me get out of bed and tiptoe across the shadowy room toward the connecting door.

Tentatively I tried the handle. The door was not locked. Slowly it opened under the pressure of my hand.

The fire in this room had been built up not long before. It still flared high, and I saw clearly—well enough to see that the room was unoccupied.

Unlike mine, it was a corner room, and cross-gusts made the windows rattle. The furniture was old, heavy dark pieces that must have belonged originally to an ancestor more remote than Clare's father. It was an austere room, with only dark, plum-colored hangings to soften its paneled walls and bare floor. There was no sign of its occupant.

I wondered whether I had been mistaken. Perhaps this was not Clare's room. But the fire, the night clothes laid out on a chair by the hearth, the general air of occupation which an unused guest chamber does not have—told me I had been right.

Then where was Clare? I had heard him enter; surely I would have heard him leave the room, if he had gone out by the normal exit. . . .

A chill, which was partially pure superstition, partially the breezy atmosphere, made me shiver. Then common sense returned and with it embarrassment. What if Clare were here, in one of the corners where the firelight did not reach—behind the big armoire in the far part of the room, for instance? It would be terrible to be caught prying, like an inquisitive child. . . .

Yet there was no sense of anyone being present and my curiosity had grown stronger. If he had not left by the door into the hall, there must be another way out. It was as simple as that; yet I knew I would not sleep that night unless I saw with my own eyes a commonplace door leading into a farther room—a study, perhaps, where Clare beguiled his own sleeplessness.

I found the door easily; it was not a secret door, in the true sense. But I could not have found it if it had been properly closed. A draft from without moved the velvet hangings and betrayed the existence of something beyond. When I lifted the hangings the door was there. Over the years it had sagged on its hinges, so that it dragged across the floor. One would have to give it a hard shove to close it all the way.

I pushed the door farther open, but by then I knew what was obvious from the plan of the room. This was an outside wall. The door led, not into study or library, but onto a landing and a flight of stone stairs draped with dead vines and ivy. It was raining, a slow but penetrating drizzle. There was nothing to be seen except darkness. Not a star, nor a single point of light, broke the blackness surrounding the house.

I stood there for some time looking out into the night. Clare was out there somewhere, in the wet and the dark.

A man does not leave his warm bed after a tiring day to take a stroll in the rain at midnight. A normal man does not leave his bride of less than a week. . . . But that idea I did not pursue. Clare had some pressing errand, or he would not have gone so late—some secret errand, or he would have left by the front door.

Slowly, shivering, I made my way back to my own room. I was careful to leave everything exactly as I had found it, including the ivy-hung door. I had not stood far enough over the threshold to be wet; my feet left no marks on the floor. As I crept back to my luxurious bed I heard the clock strike one.

Chapter

7

IT CONTINUED TO RAIN FOR THE WHOLE NEXT WEEK.
I was glad to keep to my room, as Clare insisted
I should. I had suffered what he called a relapse
of health; but I knew the real cause of my attack
was nerves. It was not a subject I could very well
discuss with him.

After the first few days I suffered greatly from
boredom. Clare could not spend much time with
me, he had business about the estate. The weather
did not seem to daunt him; he would come to
see me in the evening, ruddy-faced and smiling.
Clearly his native air agreed with him. He was a
different man from the haughty lord of London;
he looked ten years younger.

One evening, when he was in a particularly
affable mood, he condescended to tell me something of his domain. I was awestruck. Thinking
in terms of parks and a meadow or two, I had not

realized that his possessions included thousands of acres and an entire village.

"But what do they all do?" I asked eagerly. "The people, those in the village, and the rest. Do they farm your lands?"

Clare smiled. He was holding my hand, stroking it as he might have stroked a kitten.

"I am not a farmer," he said amiably. "Neither the soil nor the climate here is conducive to agriculture, and I have neither time nor inclination to delve in the dirt, even by proxy. The majority of the villagers are employed elsewhere."

"The mills?"

I spoke before I thought. Clare's face darkened.

"In many places and occupations. You must learn to regulate your mind, Lucy, and not let it dwell on matters that distress you. I don't concern myself with my tenants' affairs either; what a medieval view you have of me. Did you picture me as a grand seigneur, wielding my whip and trampling down the crops? I assure you, so long as the rents are promptly paid I do not interfere with my tenants. I expect them to do the same for me."

His words came back to me later that night as I lay awake watching the firelight. I spent so much time resting that I was not sleepy at night, and in the wakeful hours, ideas I had never consciously considered worked their way into my head. "Ignorant" was one of the words that kept recurring to me. Jonathan had called me ignorant, and his mother had suggested, more courteously, that ignorance was curable. At Miss Plum's I had not thought of myself as ignorant. I had been considered a star pupil. Now I began to realize how little I knew. No wonder Clare talked to me as he might talk to a child. How could I expect him to take my opinions seriously when they were the product of unregulated emotion instead of study? Perhaps I could inform myself; if I could learn the facts, I could persuade Clare to share my feelings—and think better of me.

It was the children who haunted me. I might have made myself forget the other things—the polluted river, the contaminated air, the uncontrolled spread of disease. But the children's faces came between me and my sleep.

These things worked in my mind like yeast working in bread. They were working, fermenting, even when I was not consciously thinking of them. A year ago I would have paid no attention to Anna's words, when I overheard her one morning talking to one of the other servants about her brother. I could understand a little of the local dialect now, and the words I understood made me curious to hear more.

"How many brothers and sisters do you have?" I asked, when she came into my room.

"Six, my lady," she said, after a moment. I had never asked her a personal question before, and I suppose she was surprised.

"You are the oldest?"

"I've one brother older."

"It was not of him you spoke a moment ago," I said carelessly. "Was it not a younger brother who was ill?"

The girl's cheek reddened.

"It—it was Dickie I meant. The youngest."

"How old is he?"

"Three, my lady."

Three years old. One of the children in the mines had been three years old.

"What is wrong with him? What does the physician say?"

She gave me a look that brought the color to my cheeks. I should have known better; people of her class did not call in a physician when they were ill.

"It was the typhoid, my mother said. She's nursed enough in her time to know. But he doesn't get better as he should."

"He needs nourishing food," I said, remembering my own convalescence. "Thick broth and meat and wine. . . . Oh. Oh, perhaps you don't have . . . Tell Mrs. Andrews that she must send—no, better still, ask her to come here. I will tell her myself."

Her face turned such an odd color I thought she was angry. She ran out without replying and then I realized she was not angry, she was on the verge of tears, and did not want me to see her cry.

By the time the housekeeper arrived I had had time to think, and it was with diffidence that I explained I wanted to send some food and simple remedies to Anna's little brother. The housekeeper was too well trained to display her reaction; but I thought I saw a gleam in her eye, so I said,

"Mrs. Andrews, I am—I am not accustomed to directing a household, so I must rely on you. Is this a—a good thing to do? Will his Lordship be angry?"

"His Lordship will be pleased, no doubt. There hasn't been an act of Christian charity in this house since his Lordship's mother died, God rest her soul. It is only—" She broke off, her eyes widening. "I meant no criticism of his Lordship, my lady. A gentleman does not concern himself with—that is, I mean to say—"

"I understand."

"Thank you, my lady. I will see that your orders are carried out."

Despite her reassurance I was a little uneasy about Clare's reaction. No one could call him cruel—certainly not I, who had enjoyed so much kindness from his hands. But his comments about his tenants did not suggest a high degree of interest in their welfare.

I did not expect Mrs. Andrews to be silent on the subject, nor was she. She must have spoken to him as soon as he came in that evening, for it was the first thing he mentioned.

"So you have taken to good works," he said, smiling.

"You don't mind?"

"Why should I mind? Benevolence is a harmless occupation for a lady—up to a point."

"What point?"

He hesitated.

"There is some risk of infection. In your state of health . . ."

"I had not thought of actually nursing the sick," I said. "But I have had the typhoid, you know."

"That will not prevent you from catching other kinds of sickness. Well, well, you will please yourself, I suppose. Ladies always do. I confess I had pictured you with your little basket of medicines and your face all alight with conscious virtue, ministering to the sick and soothing fevered brows. It makes a pretty picture."

Certainly it was a pleasure that appealed to my conceit of myself. In reflecting pleasurably on the idea, I scarcely heeded the good-natured contempt in his voice.

However, my visit to the village had to be delayed. I was not foolish enough to venture out in such rain as we continued to have. I had to amuse myself indoors; so, one afternoon when Clare was off on an errand, I sent for Mrs. Andrews and asked her to show me the house. The success of my first attempt at giving orders had made me bold.

The tour was something of a disappointment. Like all schoolgirls taught by dear old ladies of Miss Plum's sort, I considered antique ruins the height of romantic loveliness. Handsome rooms filled with modern furniture held no interest; I yearned for moldering crypts, broken pillars draped with ivy, suits of armor, and a dungeon or two. When we had inspected the rooms on the ground floor and a series of guest chambers above, I said innocently to my guide,

"I thought the manor house was old."

"But it is, my lady. The central portion of the house is of the fifteenth century. This wing is modern; it was constructed less than a century ago. The other wing is even older than the central portion, but I'm afraid it is not fit to be seen. His

Lordship's grandfather closed it up as uninhabit-
able. It is one of his Lordship's ambitions to re-
store it, but as yet no work has been done."

"The central portion, then. May we see that?"

Mrs. Andrews looked at me doubtfully.

"It is drafty and cold, my lady. Your
health . . ."

"I am far stronger than I look," I said. I was
beginning to be vexed by this harping on my
health. My tone was querulous; Mrs. Andrews
said quickly,

"Of course, my lady."

The central portion amply repaid the trouble
we had in reaching it. It *was* drafty and cold, but
here was the dark antiquity I had yearned for. I
drew a long breath of delight as we stood at the
end of the chamber Mrs. Andrews called the Long
Gallery. It was like a long, high-ceilinged hall,
with windows high in the walls. These had been
paneled, but not in modern times; the wood was
dark with age and roughly finished. Along each
wall were the portraits of the Clares.

Though she had seemed reluctant to come, Mrs.
Andrews was in her element once we reached the
gallery. She knew the history of the house better
than its owner, and could identify every portrait.
It was eerie to see the painted faces materialize
out of darkness as the old lady moved her cande-
labrum from one to the next.

One of the least handsome portraits was that of
the first Baron. I did not like his looks at all. Oddly
enough, his face was like a brutal caricature of
Clare's fastidious features. The old ruffian—for,

by Mrs. Andrews' account, his deeds matched his face—had been depicted in the armor he wore at Bosworth, on which bloody field he had won his baronetcy. It was not hard to deduce that he had been on the winning side, so, remembering one of Miss Plum's little history stories, I made what I thought an appropriately flattering comment.

"He fought for King Henry the Seventh, then, against the usurper. How we used to shudder, we girls, over the poor little nephews whom Richard the Third smothered in the Tower!"

Mrs. Andrews opened her mouth as if to speak. She closed it; and then, looking amused, decided to speak out.

"That is not how they talk of him here, my lady."

"Him?"

"King Richard. He was governor of the north for many years, you know, and these wild Yorkshire-men speak of him as though he had died only yesterday! Murdered, they say he was; it was written so, in the city records of York. 'Our good king Richard, piteously slain, to the great sorrow of this city.' Would you believe, my lady, that there are old men in the village who still spit at the mention of the Tudors and who call King Henry 'that Welshman'? His Lordship's ancestor had a most difficult time establishing himself here; he was much resented by the inhabitants, who dubbed him traitor to the true king. In their eyes, the Tudors were the usurpers."

I looked up at the slitted windows and noted the thickness of the old walls.

"That is why this place is like a fortress?"

"Yes." Mrs. Andrews nodded. "The first Baron lived in fear all his life, it is said; once he was set upon from ambush and nearly killed. After that, he withdrew inside these walls and never went out again. It is said that he became a miser, and that he walked the halls each night, inspecting the locks on windows and doors, and guarding his buried gold."

"He must be one of the family ghosts; I cannot imagine a more fitting person to become a ghost."

"Oh, yes," Mrs. Andrews agreed cheerfully. "As you see, my lady, it is the sort of tale upon which these superstitious people dote. They say he walks still, and that the light of the torch he carries can be seen from without, flickering behind the window slits. At least he does not trouble our part of the house!"

She chuckled comfortably; and I said, trying to match her ease—for really, on such a dull afternoon, the shadowed hall and the horrid portrait were suggestive of apparitions—

"You have never seen him, I take it."

"No," said Mrs. Andrews, chuckling again. "Now this painting is supposed to be of his wife, Lady Elizabeth Mortimer, that was. He treated her badly, poor lady; or perhaps that is only part of the legend. Her father was slain in that same Battle of Bosworth, fighting for King Richard, so perhaps . . ."

"She was the heiress," I said slowly, looking at the painted face. It was badly done; there was no emotion in that flat, doughy mask. "He married her, I suppose, to make good his title to this estate. How did she die?"

I suppose the question sounded abrupt. Mrs. Andrews gave me a startled glance.

"Here is her son," she went on, as if she had not heard me. "The second Baron, Henry by name. His first wife . . ."

Very well, I thought to myself; you may not answer, my good Mrs. Andrews, but I think I know how the first Lady Clare died; and it should be reassuring to me, for it explains the genesis of the ugly legend Fernando had mentioned. An unwilling bride and a soldier husband who acquired her as the prize of war—partisans of two rival houses, the Red Rose and the White—so if the lady had wept away her brief married life and died giving her lord a son—no, it would not be surprising if the sullen peasants murmured of unholy pacts. Yet the thought did not console me. As we moved slowly down the line of portraits, one thing became plain, though Mrs. Andrews did not stress the point. The ladies of the house of Clare had been a sickly lot. An unusual number of them had died young.

The last portrait in line was that of Clare's father. Elegant in court costume of black satin that set off the stark coloring so like his son's, his features were rock-hard and his mouth wore a sneering smile. I looked with pity on the rather vapid face of Clare's mother, and wondered why all the women looked so—so flat. Were their faces weak only by contrast with the strong features of the men they had married, or did the Clares select wives of feeble character?

The idea was unsettling. I dismissed it.

At Mrs. Andrews' suggestion we made our way back toward the left wing; I was beginning to be a little tired. As we paced down the hall, with shadows darting out as the candles flickered in the draft, my attention was caught by a portrait hanging in an alcove, which I had not noticed before.

It was an arresting painting, particularly after my critical appraisal of the Clare brides; for this was a woman's portrait, and it was neither weak nor flat. The deep-set eyes were blue, but so dark a blue that they looked black until one examined them closely; they had an air of wildness that was strengthened by the haggard cheeks and half-parted lips. Nor was the lady's garb prosaic; she wore long floating white robes, with a veil that concealed her hair and wrapped her face around. It might have been a nun's robe and wimple, save for the texture; the draperies were gauzy. They lifted out away from the body, as if the wearer had been caught in violent, abruptly arrested movement.

"Good heavens," I said, with more emphasis than tact. "Who, or what, is this creature?"

"I don't know," said Mrs. Andrews.

"You mean she is truly unknown? What is she doing here, then, if her connection with the family is not proven?"

"She must be a relation," Mrs. Andrews admitted, "or she would not be here. As to her identity—that is a question. You observe her dress. It is of the late fifteenth century, when veils and wimples were popular. Hence it may be, as one visiting expert claimed, that this portrait, and not the one I showed you, represents the wife of the first Baron."

"Lady Elizabeth?" I said. I was disconcerted by the idea; I could not have said why. Perhaps it was because this face showed such evident emotion. I did not want to waste my sympathies on such an ancient tragedy, but no one could look on this face of incipient madness without pity. In a misguided attempt to divert myself and Mrs. Andrews from the tragic look of the face, I said flippantly,

"I suppose she walks, too."

Mrs. Andrews looked uneasy.

"Come now," I said impatiently. "Come, Mrs. Andrews, don't insult me by treating me like a superstitious fool. Of course I have heard of the family curse; I had much rather learn the true facts—if legend can ever be called true, or factual—from you than hear garbled accounts from outsiders."

"Of course, my lady. You are quite right. I feel foolish, repeating such stuff. . . . Well, this, then, is the famous White Lady of Greygallows. White Ladies are not uncommon in the lore of the supernatural; but ours, we think, is the oldest and best documented. She was first seen by the sister of the bishop of Ripon in fifteen hundred twenty-five. . . ."

I listened with growing amusement to the long list of distinguished visitors who had testified to the existence of the White Lady of Greygallows. We were moving off down the hall by then; it was easier to be amused when that painted face was not before one's eyes. As we neared the doorway, I stopped my lectress in midsentence.

"They were all women. Only women, who saw her."

"That is true, my lady." Candle-lit, Mrs. Andrews' face looked quite gruesome; her cheeks shone fatly as she nodded with grisly satisfaction. "No man has ever seen the White Lady. Only women can see her, only women who—"

Here she broke off, her eyes round as saucers, realizing she had said too much. Too much, and not enough; for all her boasted superiority she had a streak of superstition too. Urge her as I might, she would say no more.

Chapter
8

TOWARD THE END OF THE WEEK MY BOREDOM
reached fever pitch. Clare had gone off to York—
some question of furnishings that had been ordered, and found unsuitable. I had always been
an indifferent musician; my needlework was not
much better; and what else was there for a lady to
do? I enjoyed chatting with Anna about her family; she talked in a free and friendly manner now
that the ice had been broken by my interest in her
brother; but she had no time for idle gossip. Under
Mrs. Andrews the household ran so smoothly that
I had no need, nor wish, to interfere.

The house seemed strangely relaxed the morning after Clare rode off; I heard one of the housemaids laughing in the hall and reflected, with a
start of surprise, that it was the first laughter I had
heard in that great echoing house.

When Clare was away I dined at midday, in

the old-fashioned way, and had a bowl of soup in my room for supper. The lofty dining room was somber enough by day; at night, with the candles making little lost islands of light amid the gloom and the footsteps of the servants echoing in the silence, it was too much for me. I did not tell Mrs. Andrews this when I gave her my orders; I said, with some truth, that the new arrangements would be easier for the servants. That excuse astounded her even more than the truth would have done; the convenience of the servants was not one of Clare's constant worries. I don't think Mrs. Andrews approved, but there was nothing she could do about it.

One afternoon I decided to do some exploring on my own. Though it was still early when I left my room, the day was dark as twilight and the rain fell with monotonous persistence. The servants were still at their dinner; the house was very silent, and I found myself tiptoeing. I had to remind myself that I was the mistress of the place, and that no one within its walls had any right to question what I did.

I came upon the library quite by accident. Like all the other rooms, it was kept ready for its master's use at any moment. A good fire burned on the hearth. As I had expected, Clare had a splendid collection of books. Many looked new. The rows of handsome bindings, the gleaming carved paneling, the deep chairs scattered about were inviting on such a dreary afternoon.

Rather timidly I walked along the multicolored rows, my hands clasped behind my back. The soft rustle of my skirts, the beat of the rain against the curtained windows, and the crackle of the fire blended into a gentle harmony. I felt rather small in that room from the start, and as I walked on I felt myself shrinking. Some of the titles and authors I knew—but not many. The famous names were known to me only by reputation; I had not read them. The books seemed to be in all languages. My smattering of Italian, French, and German allowed me to recognize those languages; and I could identify the Latin and Greek as well. Once I thought it would be fun to learn Greek, the writing was so pretty. But Miss Plum informed me in consternation that girls did not learn Greek. Recalling one of our brief history lessons, I was pert enough to reply that the great Queen Elizabeth had been proficient in that tongue. I was told to hold mine and not introduce irrelevant facts. Of course Miss Plum knew no Greek and could not have taught the language.

I was looking for a novel of the sort the girls had smuggled into school, but I found no such title as *My Lady's Secret* or *Mysteries of the Mad Monk*. Nor were there any books on the mines or the mills. I had rather hoped to find a report such as Jonathan had mentioned, but then I realized Clare would have no such document in his collection. Finally I found a massive tome on the Middle Ages, and settled down in one of the big chairs. I had rather enjoyed our little history stories at Miss Plum's.

If I had been a proper heroine, that book would have opened new vistas to me and made me eager to study more. I am sorry to say that its only effect was to put me to sleep. Though it was called a history, its contents had little resemblance to the stories of kings and queens and saints we had studied.

When I awoke the fire was dying. I ran to the door, feeling like a truant schoolgirl. Mrs. Andrews was coming down the staircase at quite a smart pace; when she saw me her face flushed with mortification and relief.

"My lady! What a start you gave us! I had no idea where you had gone."

"I was looking for something to read," I said haughtily.

Mrs. Andrews glanced at the heavy volume I was holding, having quite forgotten to replace it. She looked impressed.

"Yes, my lady. I trust the fire in the library—"

"Quite satisfactory," I said graciously.

She stood aside as I climbed the stairs, trying not to limp. When I reached my own room I dropped the book onto a table, which rocked under its weight, and looked at it ruefully. So long as it was here, I would continue to read it. Perhaps one day it would begin to make sense.

I did read it—as a sinner performs his daily penance. I was plodding through page fifty, or thereabouts, when Clare returned the next night. He came upstairs directly; he was always punctilious about inquiring after my health. As soon as he entered I saw he was out of temper. When his eyes fell on the book—it was far too large to be readily concealed—his slight frown deepened.

"You have been in the library."

"I did not know I was not supposed to go there," I said. I meant to be dignified, but my voice ended in a squeak.

Clare took a deep breath.

"Naturally there is no room in the house where you may not go. You are its mistress. I confess, however, to a foolish fondness for my books; I dislike having them disarranged or mishandled."

"I would have put it back in the same place."

"I know." He stood in silence for a moment. Then his face relaxed. "I beg your pardon. I did not mean to sound as if I were scolding you. But what are you doing with such a tome? It is almost as heavy as you are."

"Oh," I said airily. "I thought I would just refresh my memory of the medieval period."

"Indeed? If you are interested in history, perhaps I can find you a lighter volume—lighter," he added, with one of his rare gleams of humor, "in weight as well as in content."

We talked then of his journey, which was the cause of his vexation. It had been in vain, and he feared he would have to go to Edinburgh or even London for the work he wanted. After talking for a while he took his leave with his usual courtesy.

I sat thinking after he had gone, the book heavy on my knees. I wished I had the courage to own my ignorance; he could have helped me so much if he would. Why had I not done so? He had been kind, after that first burst of vexation—and from all I had heard of husbands and male relatives, that little tantrum was unusually mild. I was forced to own the truth. I respected the man who was my husband. One day I might even come to love him. But I also feared him.

II

One of the minor vexations of my life was my inability to ride. I could sit on a horse if I had to, and a handsome riding costume was part of my trousseau. Yet I had a shuddering horror of the creatures which was wholly inexplicable to me. Mild as they might appear, I kept seeing them as wild, plunging figures with huge white teeth.

Clare took it for granted that I would ride. The first fine morning after his return from York he informed me that he had purchased a mount for me, and that I must come down and try her. My heart sank, but I was afraid to own the truth; with Anna's help I put on my riding habit.

Clare was waiting for me. I limped badly as I crossed the hall under his critical eye; and as he took my arm he said,

"Are you in pain today?"

It was the first time he had referred so directly to my infirmity. I might have seized on it as an excuse for not riding, but something prevented me from doing so. I did not want his pity.

"No," I said shortly.

As soon as I saw the mare destined for my use, I knew I would never succeed in riding her. She was a beautiful creature; a fit mount for a baroness. She seemed as large as an elephant and she was horribly spirited; how she pranced, even under the groom's restraining hand.

I knew she must have cost a great sum, and I was truly resolved not to show my fear. But as I walked resolutely toward her she flung up her head and whinnied. The sight of her teeth was the last straw. I stumbled, cried out, and felt Clare catch me. Clinging to his arm I heard him say, softly, so the groom would not hear,

"Does it give you pain? Calm yourself; I will carry you back to the house."

"No, no," I whispered, against his shoulder. "It is not my wretched foot, it is something else, something so silly. . . . Clare, I am so afraid of horses. I don't know why, but I am. I shall never be able to ride that animal. Are you very angry?"

"No . . ." I was afraid to look at his face, and kept my own hidden. His arm and shoulder felt very strong. After a moment he went on, "My dear child, don't distress yourself, you need not ride today. I must consider this carefully. . . . Now, if you are not in pain let us walk a little. I would prefer that you did not display your feelings before the servants."

I saw, to my relief, that he was smiling. He patted my head lightly and then took my arm and tucked it through his.

"Her Ladyship will not ride today," he told the groom.

The boy touched his forelock, with a shy glance at me. We walked. My foot hardly bothered me at all.

Knowing I did not have to ride them, I found the horses handsome to look at; like everything in Clare's employ, they were beautiful creatures. A pair of huge dogs sunned themselves before the stable doors and a big gray-and-white cat ignored the dogs with the loftiness of a born aristocrat. Clare explained that the cat kept fat on the mice and rats that would otherwise infest the stables. We spent a happy morning walking about the grounds, admiring the little black-faced lambs and the shaggy ponies. I liked the ponies; they were friendly little animals, more like large dogs than horses. I thought perhaps I might have the courage to ride one of them. But I did not mention it; the idea of her Ladyship, resplendent in her velvet habit and tall hat, perched atop one of the fuzzy little beasts was ludicrous. I could imagine how Clare would react to the suggestion.

Clare was to leave next morning for Edinburgh. He expected to be gone some days, perhaps as long as a week. I dreaded his absence. As yet I had not met a single neighbor, and I did not look forward to being alone for so long, with no resources and nowhere to go. His kindness and affability that morning made me even more reluctant to lose his companionship.

It continued fine all day. In the evening a warm south breeze arose. It was a restless breeze, making the tall pines sing mournfully and shaking the budded boughs. It made me restless too. Long after I should have been asleep, I rose from my bed and went to the windows, throwing them wide.

For a time I knelt by the window, letting the breeze ruffle my hair. It felt like cool fingers on my face. I was not conscious of being unhappy; it was with considerable surprise that I became aware of tears streaking down my cheeks.

A night such as this, with its seductive air and bright half-circle of moon, was meant to be shared—and I was alone. Not a creature stirred; the wide, grassy lawns lay barren under the moon. I could see one corner of the stone terrace and the steps that led down into what had been a pleasure garden before neglect had let it grow into a wilderness; the tangled shrubs looked eerie and unreal in the dim light. Half mesmerized, I turned from the window and went to the door I had opened only once before.

It was locked.

Surprise held me motionless for a moment. Then it was as if I woke from a vivid dream; the effrontery of my action came home to me with painful force. I could feel the warm blood rushing into my face. Did he think so poorly of me as that, that he must bar his door against me?

Thankful that the sound of my attempt on the door had apparently gone unheard, I went back to the window. What had come over me? At the least, I might have knocked. . . . Half turning, so that the wind might cool my heated cheeks, I glanced out the open casement—and saw a sight that froze the blood in my veins.

It might have been a statue. The pale glimmer of its form could have been marble in the moonlight, a slim draped figure ornamenting the balustraded steps. There were statues of pagan divinities in other parts of the grounds; but there had been no marble figure on the terrace when I looked before. It moved, then, and I saw the shape of the massive urn on the balustrade through its robes.

I cried out and covered my eyes to hide the vision. I might have fallen, but for the hands that caught me back from the window.

I looked into Clare's face. His features were shadowed and indistinct, but I felt his anger in the roughness of his grasp. I twisted in his hold and pointed out into the darkness, where a shaft of shadowy pallor still moved among the tangled shrubs.

"Look! Oh, look!"

"What is it?" Clare tried to turn me. "What do you see?"

"There!" For half a breath the shape stood out like a pillar of white, drifting across a cleared space with the dark pines behind it. "All in white—ah," I cried out. The form had vanished, like a light blown out.

III

It took Clare some time to calm me. He did not ring for my maid; after a while I realized why he had not.

"There was nothing there," he said, holding my eyes with his steady gaze. "I looked directly at the spot which you indicated. You were half asleep, and dreaming."

"You saw nothing?" My teeth had stopped chattering; he had brought brandy from his bed-chamber, and wrapped me in a comforter. "Truly nothing?"

"There was nothing there. Only shadows and moonlight, enough to stimulate a mind which . . . You have been told, have you not, of the White Lady?"

I could not deny it. He read my face; he nodded.

"You see? You had heard the story, you mes-merized yourself staring out into that strange light, and you saw what you expected to see. You must not give way to such nonsense. I don't want the servants to hear of this; they are an ignorant, credulous lot and will get themselves, and you, into a panic."

"But truly—"

"You saw it. Of course; you truly believe you did. But I tell you there was nothing there. You must obey me, you know; did you not promise to obey?"

He was smiling slightly.

"Yes," I said.

"Then obey me in this. Have you no laudanum, no sleeping stuff? A pity; I must get some for you if this wakefulness persists. You need to sleep."

"I am drowsy now."

"It is the brandy. You are unaccustomed to spir-its. Now I will tuck you into bed and give you another sip, and you will go straight off to sleep, will you not?"

He lifted me in his arms. My head felt very odd,

but pleasantly so. As he bent to place me on my bed, I put my arms around his neck.

"You are very kind," I said thickly. "Kind to me ... Stay with me, please. Don't leave me tonight."

His breath caught sharply. His face was so close I could see how his lashes grew, long and curving and thick. My face was mirrored in the blackness of his pupils: two miniature Lucys, pallid and small like little ghosts of myself. . . . My lips were parted, my hair curled around the high collar of my nightdress. I felt his warm breath on my lips; his arms tightened. . . .

I closed my eyes. I did not see what happened, but I felt it; it left bruises that ached for days. He wrenched himself away, so violently that my head struck the headboard of the bed. When I opened my eyes I saw him standing ten feet away. His face was barely recognizable—livid in color, transformed by passion.

"Never do such a thing again," he said softly. "Never touch me. . . . Never speak to me so. . . ."

Between the brandy and the knock on the head and the series of shocks I had experienced, I was beyond speech or movement. I lay there staring at him; and after a time the color faded from his face, leaving it calm, but pale as marble.

"Sleep," he said quietly. "I will just stand here until you do."

I slept. I had promised to obey.

Chapter
9

SINCE MY ARRIVAL IN YORKSHIRE I HAD NOT AT-
tended a church service. I began to feel the need
of spiritual consolation, particularly after the day
which had begun so hopefully and ended so di-
sastrously. I had come to doubt my mental balance; if I had imagined the figure in white—and
surely there could be no other explanation—then
I might be imagining other things. Something was
amiss; either Clare was behaving strangely, or I
was deluding myself. In either case it would not
harm me to attend church. My motives were not
wholly pious; it was an excuse for an outing, and
a chance to see new faces.

On the Saturday following Clare's departure for
Edinburgh I informed Mrs. Andrews that I would
want the carriage next day, to attend services. I was
amused, but not altogether surprised, when she
stuttered and stammered and rolled her eyes.

"You will accompany me, I hope," I said, assuming that Clare had instructed her not to let me get into mischief.

"Certainly, my lady."

Still she hovered, looking uncertain. When she finally trotted off, shaking her head, I heard her muttering to herself.

Next morning I dressed with care. I was a little nervous, for this was my first public appearance in Yorkshire. I still had doubts as to whether Clare would approve of my going out. At least I would not disgrace him by failing to look my best. My bonnet was one of my favorites, with pink plumes and cabbage roses clustering under the brim, and I wore my new pelisse, of rose velvet trimmed with fur, for the weather, though bright, was still cool.

When I came down the stairs, Mrs. Andrews was waiting. She wore maroon plush, and was heavily shawled and wrapped. She spoke scarcely a word during the drive. Such reticence was unlike her, but I decided she was thinking holy thoughts in preparation for the service.

Like many old churches, this one stood isolated on a hill half a mile away from the town, with only the manse nearby. It was a stark, forbidding structure, built of rough, dark stone. The facade was plain, and the single heavy tower thrust upward toward heaven like an accusing finger. With the tall bare trees leaning over it, and the gravestones of the cemetery in front, the church did indeed induce sober feelings.

We were early. Only a scattering of worshipers occupied the seats, and when I saw how they turned and gawked, I was glad we had avoided the worst of the crowd. Mrs. Andrews led me down the aisle to the very front of the church, where a huge boxlike structure enclosed the first row on the right side. I had not anticipated this, and was both amused and daunted when I saw the Clare device, the snarling hound, carved on the doors. I would have to occupy the family pew; and I would occupy it alone, as became my station. After Mrs. Andrews had installed me, with my footwarmer and my wraps, on one of the cushioned chairs, she retired to the servants' pew at the back of the church.

So much, I thought, for my hopes of seeing new faces. The high walls of the pew boxed me in like a cage. The wall before me was lower than the others; I could see the altar, the choir, and, by stretching my neck unbecomingly, one section of the humbler benches on the left side. There was no other pew like mine; it was evident that the Clares were the leading family in this district. No doubt the patronage was Clare's, and the minister was a protégé of his or his father's.

For want of anything better to do, I studied the stained-glass windows. They were modern windows, very bright and handsome, with vivid green and scarlet and blue glass. A plaque explained that they had been given by Clare's grandfather, to replace windows broken by the Roundheads. They were all scenes of slaughter and destruction. The central window bore a vivid depiction of the sinners writhing in Hell, with scarlet and yellow flames around them, and the figure of the Redeemer watching from above. I thought His supercilious expression quite like that of Clare's first ancestor, as He watched the sinners sizzle.

While I amused myself with these irreverent thoughts, the church was filling up. I could not see, but I could hear the shuffle of feet and the whispered comments. Then the minister came into the pulpit.

For some reason I had expected to see a genteel, white-haired old clergyman. The reality was quite different. The man's youth was almost shocking; in his robes he looked like a choirboy. Flaxen hair curled around his ears and neck; his eyes were gray, and so luminously large I could tell their color from where I sat. I will admit I stared. The face was angelic. With the sunlight shining on his silver-gilt locks, he might have stood for a statue of the young Saint John.

I did not understand the sermon, and I feel sure it was lost on the congregation; it was the most peculiar mixture of erudition and inspiration imaginable. But as the high, sweet voice went on, I ceased to worry about quotations from the early church fathers, and the Nicene council. The voice was so beautiful, it did not matter what he said. The pure, beardless face, surrounded by a nimbus of light, added to the emotional effect.

When the service ended, an unexpected wave of shyness came over me. It would have been easier if I had been visible to the congregation throughout; but to open the door of the pew and emerge,

like an actress making her entrance, seemed hard.
I wished Mrs. Andrews were with me.

Then, glancing to my left, I saw the only member of the congregation who was visible to me
from my position. She sat alone in the first pew
on the left, and I wondered who she could be, to
enjoy such a prominent place. Her garments were
modest in color and style, but in perfect taste;
from them, and from what I could see of her form,
as she knelt with her face hidden in her gloved
hands, it was clear that she was a person of refinement. I had an impression of relative youth,
though only the supple shape of her body and the
wealth of black hair, gathered into a net under her
bonnet, gave any clue to that.

She rose, and I caught my breath so audibly I
feared she must have heard it. Her face was radiantly lovely. Its beauty was so striking it took
me several seconds to realize that it was also the
image of the young clergyman's features. His
looks were delicate, almost feminine; indeed, of
the two, the girl's face had the greater strength.
Her hair was as black as his was fair, and her eyes
were a deeper gray.

The gray eyes met mine. Realizing that I was
staring rudely, I smiled and bowed. It was not
difficult to deduce that this young lady was the
clergyman's sister; such a resemblance could only
stem from a close blood relationship. As such,
she was a person I might and should notice. Her
beauty and her youth made her even more sympathetic. I was hurt, therefore, when instead of
answering my smile she stiffened and turned her

head away. Moving quickly, she passed along the bench and walked down the aisle without looking at me again.

I was so surprised at this behavior, I forgot my shyness and issued forth from my cage without further delay. The congregation was not large; most of the others seemed to be workingmen and their families, and all of them made way for me as I walked down the aisle toward the door. Mrs. Andrews was waiting. As she took my arm I saw the young lady walking rapidly down the path toward the gate of the churchyard. I could see her figure to more advantage; she was taller than I, and she moved like a young Diana.

"Who is she?" I asked. "Who is that lovely girl?"

"The vicar's sister," said Mrs. Andrews. "Miss Fleetwood."

That was almost all she would say, though I plied her with questions. She was somewhat more communicative on the subject of the vicar. Mr. Fleetwood was regarded as the "next thing to a saint," but as I discovered, his sanctity rested more in his incomprehensibility than in his acts of benevolence. No one had the faintest notion of what he was talking about most of the time. "Not of this world," was Mrs. Andrews' assessment, and remembering the glowing young face addressing its God, I could see what she meant.

With so little to occupy my mind, it is no wonder the lovely Miss Fleetwood continued to haunt my thoughts. She had looked intelligent as well as lovely, and I missed companions of my own age and breeding. I might not have ventured to introduce myself to other ladies in the neighborhood, being ignorant of Clare's relation with the local families, but surely there was no reason why I should not associate with a clergyman's sister? It did not take me long, with such specious reasoning, to decide I might call upon the Fleetwoods.

When I ordered the carriage, Mrs. Andrews fell into a bustle. She could not accompany me, she had to supervise the house cleaning. . . . I cut her short.

"Really, Mrs. Andrews, I am a married woman; I see no reason why I should not go out alone."

She did not dare ask outright where I meant to go. I saw the question in her eyes, but I did not choose to enlighten her. As I drove off, leaving her gazing helplessly after me, I could not help feeling a childish triumph at eluding her.

The coachman, Williams, was a bulky middle-aged man with a red face. Communication between us was one-sided; he understood me, but his rare remarks were all but unintelligible. I fancied that in any case Clare had not encouraged him to chatter vivaciously. He drove me, without comment, to the vicarage.

I had not seen the house before, except for those parts of its roof and chimneys which were visible through the trees around it. As we approached, along a well-tended drive, I saw that the house was charmingly pretty, and my hopes of friendship with the occupants grew. This was the sort of house I would have liked—a cottage, with low-hanging eaves and carved wooden shutters, *à la*

Suisse. It was large and commodious, however, with a garden and shrubbery to one side.

I thought I saw the edge of a window curtain quiver as I approached the door, but several minutes went by after I rang before someone answered. Finally the door was opened by the lady herself. She wore a simple morning gown of dove gray, with touches of white at throat and wrists. The dress set off her splendid figure. I felt small and insignificant and childish; my fur-trimmed cloak and second-best bonnet seemed ostentatious.

"I am Lady Clare," I said. "I hope I do not come at an inconvenient time."

"Of course." She bowed slightly. "Will you step in? My brother is in his library; I will send the servant to fetch him."

"I shall be happy to meet the vicar," I said, following her along the hall. "But to be honest, I came to see you, too. I hope—I trust I do not—"

I was vexed to hear myself stammering like a schoolgirl. Miss Fleetwood did not help me; in silence she opened a door and gestured me into the parlor. It was a charming room, as pretty and neat as the outside of the cottage. A variety of little ornaments and pictures displayed a lady's taste; the books scattered about confirmed my impression of their owner's intelligence—and made me feel even more insignificant.

I took the chair she indicated. My face felt warm. I hated myself for blushing, but could not help it; her manner was so unwelcoming. Under her direction the conversation was purely formal. I declined, with thanks, her offer of refreshment; I agreed that the mud was a great inconvenience; I said that indeed I found Yorkshire very pretty. It was a relief to both of us when Mr. Fleetwood came into the room.

Meeting him face to face, I saw that he was not as young as I had thought. He greeted me warmly; after his sister's reserved manner, his was almost embarrassingly friendly. He began to apologize for not having called. I could see Miss Fleetwood did not like this, so I cut him short, as kindly as I could.

"I have been ill," I said.

"Yes, yes," Mr. Fleetwood said eagerly, "so we were informed. Are you sure it is wise for you to come?" He stopped and blushed a fiery red as his sister made a sound of vexation. "This is—I did not mean—"

"Please don't apologize," I said, with a smile. I had quite a fellow feeling for him, since I suffered from both his handicaps—a thoughtless tongue and a fair complexion that showed every change of emotion. "I appreciate your concern, but I am quite recovered. I hope to be much abroad now that the weather is fine."

"Do you find the air of Yorkshire to your taste?"

I was really grateful for the weather; without it, conversation would have been at a loss. We talked of the weather and the beauties of Yorkshire for another ten minutes. Then I rose to leave.

Miss Fleetwood, who had spoken scarcely a word since her brother entered, had little more to say in farewell. Her brother saw me to my carriage. There was something so warm in his manner and his smile that I felt quite a little flutter, and I wondered how such a man had remained unmarried. He had the looks and the soft heart which should have made him fall prey to a determined miss already. But perhaps his sister did not fancy sharing her home with another lady.

I expected Miss Fleetwood to return my call, so I stayed home next day. She did not appear. When I returned from a short stroll the following morning, I was vexed to find that she had been, and, not finding me within, had left her card. It was almost as if she had chosen the time deliberately. I realized that was foolish. She could hardly have known I was out unless she lurked about the house watching my movements.

On the Thursday there was still no sign of Clare and no message from him. Mrs. Andrews, who knew his habits better than I, said he might be expected at any time. She did not need to say that the house would be in readiness for him whenever he chose to come. However, I saw no reason why I should sit by the fire like a faithful dog, on the chance of his coming. I decided to go for a drive.

I directed Williams to the vicarage. It was no startling coincidence that took me there; there was nowhere else to go, with my limited acquaintance in the neighborhood. As we drove up the road toward the cottage, I saw that the Fleetwoods had a visitor. A horse was tied to the front gate. I was pleased to see it; perhaps, I thought, there will be another new face to beguile my boredom.

The door of the cottage opened and a man came out. I recognized him at once, although I thought him miles away. It was my husband.

Knowledge comes in strange ways, at unexpected times. If Mrs. Andrews' unusual reticence about the lady had not made me suspicious, this single incident should not have enlightened me. There was no reason why Clare should not call on the vicar. Yet it supplied the final clue—and not because of any look of Clare's; his face expressed no guilt or shame, only an angry surprise at seeing me.

The shock left me oddly cool and clear-headed. I leaned forward and said calmly to the coachman, "Drive on, Williams."

The words were scarcely out of my mouth before the carriage jolted into movement. I did not look back, but I sensed Clare had not moved. He was still standing in the doorway of the cottage as I drove off.

Once I was out of sight of the house I could give vent to my feelings. I did—but silently. Williams could not see me, but he could certainly hear. I was determined to show no outward sign of distress. It was not pride that kept me silent, it was the same blind need of privacy that drives a hurt animal into its hole where it can lick its wounds without being seen.

It was painfully clear to me now why I was a wife in name only. How could I have imagined, after seeing that lovely face, that any man could be immune to its fascination? Clare had not needed a wife to love. He had married me for my fortune, and because of an odd paternal kindness. Even his tenderness, rarely expressed, was that of a father toward a delicate child.

But I had known this all along. I knew he would not have looked at me a second time without that hateful ten thousand pounds. So why was I hurt?

First I thought I would not mention to Mrs. Andrews that I had seen her master. Then I realized that Williams would tell the other servants, and that Mrs. Andrews would know. She would interpret my silence as the result of anger and pain— which, of course, it was. So I sent for her.

Despite my resolution I could not face her directly. I seated myself at my dressing table and spoke to her by way of the mirror.

"Lord Clare has returned," I said, busily at work among the brushes and jars on the table. "I am sure you have your usual excellent dinner planned, but just be sure his fire is lit, and—and all the rest. Thank you, Mrs. Andrews."

At least, I thought desolately, as the door closed behind her, I will keep her respect. I will not be pitied. I may not be loved, but I am the mistress of this house, the wife. This may be a small thing, compared with love, but a small spar of wood is enough to keep a drowning man afloat.

I was in the parlor, making ugly large stitches over my embroidery, when Clare entered. I found it hard to look at him. It was odd to hear his voice, sounding just the same as he inquired after my health and asked how I had been filling my time while he was away.

Under the circumstances, the last question was rather much. I looked up at him, feeling the warm blood of indignation flood my face—and met a look as inexpressive and as final as a wall without a door. If he felt shame or chagrin, there was not the slightest trace of it in his face or manner.

I heard my own voice making polite, vague replies, and inquiring after the success of his trip. When Mrs. Andrews came in to announce dinner we were chatting pleasantly, like any affectionate husband and wife.

II

During the following weeks Clare was exceedingly busy. Boxes and bundles began arriving, and as the warm weather advanced and the wintersodden ground dried, a swarm of workmen descended on the house. Scaffolding enfolded the abandoned wing like a wooden spider's web, and agile figures moved over it from early dawn until the last rays of sunset died. Clare was in and out all day long, consulting with and instructing the workers; no detail escaped his care.

We began to have callers. Not many and not often; we were in an isolated region and the few families on our social level lived a considerable distance. To them and to me, Clare gave the same excuse for not sending out formal invitations: once the house was in repair, we would entertain on a proper scale, with dinner parties and perhaps a ball to introduce the new Lady Clare to the neighborhood. At the rate the work was progressing, it seemed to me the house would not be in a state to suit him until the following winter; and then, as my visitors all explained, social activity was at a minimum because of the poor roads.

Our nearest neighbors lived five miles off, across the moor. Sir Henry Rawlinson was a bluff, hearty man, a Yorkshire-pudding-and-roast-beef sort of baronet, and his three giggling daughters were as square and red-faced as he was. They all had cherished hopes of being Lady Clare, and were not very good at concealing their disappointment. Mr. Martin and his wife, who had been the Honorable Miss Ponsonby and who took good care to inform everyone of that fact, had one child, a pasty-faced dreadful infant who whined and teased and mashed cakes into the parlor carpet. He was only one degree more disgusting than the twin terriers of Miss Bliss, the daughter of Sir William and Lady Bliss. They ate tea cakes too, and were sick on the hearth rug. Miss Bliss looked like her horse, and was vocally amused to learn I did not ride. These are a sample; it can hardly be wondered that I was not moved to form friendships, and I was forced to agree with Clare when, after one of these visits, he said dryly,

"You may understand why I am regarded hereabouts as proud and unsociable. I am happy to see that you share my opinion of our neighbors, though you conceal your feelings admirably."

"I can't blame you," I admitted.

"But it is lonely for you," Clare said. I glanced at him in some surprise. Meeting my eye squarely, he went on, "I have invited the vicar and his sister to dinner tomorrow. Jack is an old friend of mine; he tells me you called upon them."

"Yes."

"Miss Fleetwood has been unwell of late," Clare went on smoothly. "However, she has recovered now and is anxious to meet you again."

He left the room after that, which was just as well; I don't know what I might have said.

I had not seen either brother or sister since that unexpected encounter with Clare. He had suggested I was not well enough to attend church services, and I was only too glad of an excuse to stay away. Clare's religious convictions were unorthodox. We had discussed the subject once. He was a persuasive and convincing speaker—though it did not take much argument to persuade me, ignorant as I was of any serious subject. Yet I enjoyed talking with him—or rather, listening to him.

Clare called himself a rational deist, whatever that might mean. Practically, so far as I could see, it meant he attended church only as an example to the lower classes, who needed the comforts of religion, which he, of course, did not. The Bible he regarded as a collection of legends, produced by a savage people whose ethical notions were as primitive as their dietary rules, and he truly shocked me by questioning the divinity of the Saviour.

"As a teacher and moralist he was inspiring, of

course; yet one can understand why he was regarded as a dangerous revolutionary. Society has the right to rid itself of those who would destroy it; and it is always easier to destroy than build."

"But He did build," I cried. "New ideas of love and duty to one's neighbor—"

Clare laughed aloud.

"Ah," he said playfully. "You have been thinking—perhaps even reading! A dangerous occupation for a pretty child."

"I have little else to do," I said.

"Well, well," Clare said lightly. "You must not be surprised if I cling to my own opinions, or shocked when you hear me arguing with Jack. We are old acquaintances, and he enjoys our friendly debates as much as I do. But you will find an ally in him, he is quite of your persuasion."

Though I did not look forward to meeting the Fleetwoods again, the day turned out to be surprisingly enjoyable. Miss Fleetwood exerted herself to be agreeable, and I could not help but find her so. The delicacy of her mind, and her informed opinions, were in striking contrast to the other ladies who had come visiting. When Clare and Mr. Fleetwood got into a discussion of the Sermon on the Mount, she interposed little comments that showed a true understanding.

Finally the time I had been dreading arrived, when we must withdraw and leave the gentlemen to their wine. I led the way into the drawing room and took a seat. She went to the piano and stood leaning on it, looking over my music. The sunset light silhouetted her graceful form; and the half-averted face, with its fall of shining black hair, had a delicacy of line and purity of expression. . . .

No, I thought to myself all at once; no, I do not believe it. I had been misled by jealousy and malice. What I had imagined could not be true, not of this girl.

Of course Clare admired her. No one sensitive to beauty could remain indifferent to such a face; and he had known her from a child. No doubt there had been gossip among the evil-minded. But I could not believe a face so pure could hide infamy and deceit. Surely Clare would not brazenly introduce his mistress into his home. She was not unprotected; she had a brother, and he a clergyman. . . . As I considered the question impartially, all the weight of common sense was on the side of her innocence. Perhaps they had loved one another once, as children. Perhaps they still felt fondness for one another. Would that be strange, or evil? Only in evil minds.

I felt as if a great weight had been lifted from my shoulders; I had not realized, till it lightened, how it had burdened me. I did not even feel the need to converse now, I could relax and admire her. After the gentlemen came, she spent all the remainder of the time playing and singing. She was all that I was not as a performer; and when Clare's rich voice blended with her golden tones in duets, I reminded myself that this, too, they might have shared before.

Once I had convinced myself that Clare was innocent, he began behaving . . . not so much guilty as less than completely candid. He took to watch-

ing me when he believed I was not aware of it;
several times I caught him staring, with the oddest fixed glare. He would then look away, or make
a comment that had nothing to do with what we
had been saying. I began to wonder if there was
something about my looks, some change in appearance, that I was unconscious of, and I took
to examining myself surreptitiously in the glass,
without finding anything to explain the matter.
Finally, one evening as we sat over tea, I caught
the look again, and I said involuntarily,

"Why do you stare so? Am I looking more than
usually sickly?"

"Quite the contrary," Clare said slowly. "I have
been observing how your looks have improved. I
thought at first it might be only my hopeful fancy;
but there can be no doubt. You are quite recovered, are you not?"

"I have been for some time. I was never so ill as
you feared."

Unable to meet his searching eyes, I bent over
my embroidery frame. My heart was beating unevenly. If he had avoided me because of concern
for my health . . .

"My native air has done you good, as I hoped.
I am glad you have adjusted so well to life here.
You don't find it excessively tedious—the house
too lonely and gloomy?"

"Not gloomy enough," I said, laughing. "After
hearing Mrs. Andrews' tales, I had expected an
encounter with the family ghost."

"But you did have such an encounter," said Clare.
"At least you led me to believe you thought so."

Cursing my idle tongue, I began to embroider furiously. My aunt always told me I spoke without thinking, never anticipating where my thoughtless remarks would lead. During the weeks of my suspicions about Miss Fleetwood, it had not been difficult to find a rational explanation for the white-robed form in the garden. The staircase from Clare's bedchamber led down to the terrace.

Now I tried to find words that would not reveal my unjust suspicions, though I feared my flushed cheeks were betraying me.

"I was foolish. It must have been a—a woman. One of the servants, out for a breath of air."

"If you did see a human figure," Clare said, "it must have been one of the servants."

"I am not usually fanciful."

"The house is gloomy," Clare said with a reasonable air. "It would not be surprising for a lady whose nerves are delicate and high-strung—"

"You sound as though you believed in ghosts," I snapped. I had stabbed my thumb with the needle. Putting it to my mouth, I sucked it and glared at my husband. I did not like his suggestion that I was nervous and high-strung.

"I do not believe or deny. I only say that many things are possible. There are some temperaments, more spiritually inclined—since you do not care for the words 'high-strung'—that would be more receptive to such apparitions, if they do occur. One cannot deny the possibility. The weight of the evidence is rather striking."

He began to tell me legends of the supernatural. I heard of the Black Hound that pursues night-bound travelers; of poltergeists, the malicious spirits who toss objects about like naughty children; and of family curses and banshees. When the head of the house of Hastings, sitting at table, twice hears a carriage drive up to his door, and no carriage is there, he will die within the year. The Ghost's Walk at Haverholme is haunted by the ghost of a nun, whose slow steps herald disgrace or disaster for the family; and a ghostly ship passes up Loch Fune when the Chief of the Campbells lies dying.

Nothing holds more gruesome charm than a well-told ghost story. Clare's powers as a raconteur had never been more evident. I listened, in shivering fascination, as he proceeded from White Ladies to invisible spirits, from the ghostly Harpers of Scotland to the witch hare of his native heath. The shadows gathered and darkness added its spell to the magic of Clare's slow voice. When Mrs. Andrews opened the door to ask if we would not have the candles in, I gave a shriek and stabbed myself again with my neglected needle.

That night I would not have been surprised to meet the wicked first Baron, muttering and leering along the hallway.

Next day the Fleetwoods were coming again to dine. Though I had quite dismissed my wicked notions about the young lady, an odd reluctance kept me from making more than the necessary formal visits. I did not dislike her; on the contrary, I found her good company. But she seemed to have a trace of reserve with me. I thought perhaps she was shy. Yet from time to time there was a flash, a sudden burst of sympathy between us.

So on this next occasion. It was a day in June, as balmy and beautiful as only June can be. I thought Miss Fleetwood seemed pale and silent. Her brother was in a delightful mood. He had been reading Saint Augustine and had an argument, he declared gaily, which would completely demolish his skeptical friend. I was unable to follow the argument, but I enjoyed it because the participants were so delighted by it. Clare laughed, and Mr. Fleetwood kept smiling and nodding at me whenever he made a particularly killing point.

When we went to the drawing room after dinner, Miss Fleetwood wandered restlessly about the room instead of sitting down. She played a few bars on the piano and then got up; examined a book; went to the window and stood looking out into the garden. The gentlemen soon joined us, and with music and conversation the time passed until tea was brought in. Miss Fleetwood then owned she was too restless to sit still any longer, and suggested a walk. Clare agreed; he was anxious to show them the improvements he had made. He had ordered bushes and shrubs from abroad, and was in the process of having laid out a pretty little Wilderness behind the rose arbors. It seemed to me he might have left the grounds in their original state, which was wild enough, but I kept silent, knowing I would simply get a lecture, kind but firm, on my ignorance of the latest fashions in landscaping.

It was so pleasant out of doors that we walked

for some time. Clare suggested a visit to the stables. Miss Fleetwood, however, said she was too tired; she would sit on a bench under a tree near the Wilderness, and enjoy the evening air and the soft light. I said I would stay with her; she was looking rather unwell.

After a few desultory remarks she fell silent, and I did not disturb her. It was restful to sit there, watching the colors fade into gray as the sun sank below the horizon, and seeing the first bright stars pricking the sky. I felt quite kindly toward Miss Fleetwood, who seemed to share my appreciation of the mood of nature; but I own it was easier to feel kindly toward her when she was only a featureless silhouette, with that amazing face hidden by shadows. The poor lady must have suffered a great deal from the jealousy of other members of her sex; I wondered if some such difficulty had made her seek the seclusion of a country rectory.

"You are better now?" I ventured, after a long silence.

"Yes, thank you."

"Shall we go in then? The night air—"

"Not yet, please. The air is pleasant; and I like darkness. I feel as if I can hide in it."

There was a sudden energy in her voice that quite moved me.

"Why should you wish to hide? You must forgive me—perhaps I should not say it—but you are so beautiful. It must be wonderful to be so lovely."

"Wonderful?" She laughed harshly. "It is a curse. It has been so to me; my downfall, my ruin."

"If I can help you . . ." I began, and touched her hand, which rested on the seat between us.

I felt her stiffen, and when she spoke again her voice had lost its wildness.

"I do not need help. You are very kind, but my erratic manner has led you astray. I meant—I only meant that the world is a censorious place, and both men and women are more ready to think ill of a woman who is . . . well-looking. You might have found it so, if you had been poor."

The speech started well enough, but the last words were charged with venom. I did not blame her; indeed, I felt greater sympathy for her than I did before. I believed I had surprised her secret. She loved, and had been rejected because of her poverty.

"No," I said honestly. "I am considered handsome because of my fortune; without that, I assure you I would be quite plain in the eyes of the world. But I can understand how cruel and unfair it would be to have every gift of mind and body and be disregarded because of trivial worldly considerations."

She turned toward me.

"You would not say that if you knew—"

I heard no more. My eyes, looking past her toward the shadowy shape of the Wilderness, saw a sight that shut out all other sensations.

There was no chance this time of mistaking it for a shaft of moonlight or wisp of fog. The features were veiled, but they were there—the mouth, open in a wordless cry, the shadowed eyesockets and the jutting nose. It shone with its own light, a rotten, gray-green glow, which outlined the folds of the flowing skirt and long, full sleeves. A heavier veil shrouded the head and hung in ragged trails behind.

I caught blindly at the other woman. Afterward I saw the bruises my fingers had left on her white arm; I have no recollection of moving, of touching her. I remember only what she said, as she turned in response to my hoarse direction, and looked squarely at the rotting, swaying white horror in the dark.

"What is it you see? There is nothing there; only the shadows, and one white star."

Mrs. Andrews and Anna put me to bed. I was raving like a Bedlamite, and the worst of it was, they believed me. Naturally they would. Mrs. Andrews made me take some of Clare's brandy; and after a long time, when I had recovered my calm, he came to see me.

"I am sorry . . ." I began.

"You have had a frightening experience. When I heard you screaming, I thought—"

"I don't remember screaming."

"You did. We heard you as far as the stableyard."

"Has Miss—have they gone?"

"Yes."

"I must have frightened her badly."

"You did."

"She said she saw nothing."

"She would not see it. There are conditions—"

He broke off suddenly. From his coat pocket he drew out a small bottle filled with a dark liquid.

"I am glad I had the foresight to purchase this in Edinburgh. You must sleep; you are still overwrought."

Mrs. Andrews must have been lurking in the hall; no sooner had he touched the bell than she came in, carrying a tray. Drop by drop the dose was measured into a glass, and I drank it down. Clare put the stopper carefully in the bottle and returned it to his pocket.

"I will keep this in my wardrobe, and measure it out when you need it. After all, it is a dangerous drug; it would not do to leave it about where the servants might find it. Now sleep. Mrs. Andrews, you will sit with your mistress until she falls asleep?"

The dose must have been strong; already it was all I could do to keep my eyes open. Through my half-closed lids I could see Mrs. Andrews perched on the very edge of her chair, staring at me as if she were afraid to blink.

I would have been more willing to accept the existence of a ghost were it not for the implications. Like the fabled specters Clare had described, whose advent meant a warning or a threat, this apparition seemed to have a purpose. According to Mrs. Andrews, only a woman could see the White Lady. Yet Miss Fleetwood had not seen it. The spectral chariots and harpers were sometimes audible only to those whose doom they heralded. . . .

I did not believe in the supernatural; but all the

rational explanations had failed me. The thing I had seen was no truant housemaid, no fault of vision. Only one thing was certain: Whoever, or whatever, the White Lady was, she was not the vicar's sister.

Chapter
10

ONE MORNING SEVERAL WEEKS LATER I WENT TO walk in the garden. I felt the need of air. The doses from the little black bottle made me sleep only too soundly; they left me drowsy and confused for hours after I woke.

The roses were in bloom. Crimson and pearly white and pale pink, their fragrance filled the sunken garden. Through a corner of the hedge I could see the Wilderness. It was dark and gloomy even under a sunny sky, and when I saw it a shiver of memory ran through me.

The coming of the White Lady had indeed been an evil portent for me, but not in the way I fancied. Since that night, Clare's behavior had altered dramatically.

Unhappily, I wondered what our new relationship might be termed. I could hardly call it an estrangement; we had never been anything but strangers. But he had always been kind, until that night.

At first I thought it was my morbid imagination, but matters had grown steadily worse. Indifferent to begin with, he was now actively unkind. He could hardly bear the sight of me, and my touch made him shrink with repugnance. Twice he had spoken sharply to me before Mrs. Andrews. She was too well trained to comment, but I had seen in her face the extent of her surprise. His reprimands concerned my carelessness; he accused me of forgetting errands and things he had told me to do. It was true that I felt drowsy and muddleheaded all the time. I had tried to explain that I did not need, or want, the nightly dose of laudanum.

At that, he flew into a rage. It was not a violent outburst, with shouts and furious gestures; violence would have been less intimidating to me than his icy, white-faced anger. It reduced me to stammering apologies. Since then I had taken my nightly dose without complaint.

Absently I plucked a full-grown rose and turned it slowly, admiring the velvety texture and glowing red color. When I looked up, I saw him coming down the path toward me.

Instinctively I shrank back. He stopped several feet away and regarded me steadily; he had seen my fear, as he saw everything.

"I want you in the library after luncheon," he said abruptly.

"In the library?"

"Yes, the library. Must you repeat everything I say? Do I not speak intelligibly?"

Someone else had said that to me, once upon a time. My head ached dully. I rubbed it, and saw Clare frown.

"Yes, of course," I said quickly, hardly knowing what I said, but fearing by silence to annoy him further. "In the . . . I will be there. Why do you—"

"If I wished to discuss it now, I would not ask you to come to the library."

He waited, watching me. I was too clever for him this time; I said nothing. After a moment he turned away. He flung a question over his shoulder. It was true; he could hardly bear to look at me.

"You do not ride today?"

The tone was not propitious, but it was the first comment he had made for days that showed the slightest interest in my activities. I grasped at it eagerly.

"Yes, oh, yes, I will ride. Shortly; I meant to do so after I had cut these flowers—"

"If you planned to cut roses you should have brought shears and a basket," he interrupted. "If you mean only to spoil them, at least do not scatter the petals about so; they are unsightly, there on the path."

Unthinkingly, I had torn the poor flower apart; the crimson petals lay scattered all around my feet. When I looked up, Clare was walking away.

I bent to gather the fallen petals. He was right, they looked ugly on the path, as if some small thing had bled to death. But when I stooped my head spun so that I had to straighten up. Slowly I made my way toward the house, giving him time to avoid me. It was odd that he had come himself to give me the message. The appointment must be important; ordinarily he would have sent one of the servants.

So now I must ride; there was no way out of that. Too often I had been accused of making plans and then forgetting them.

He had raised the question of riding some time before; the alteration of his manner was apparent by then, and I grasped frantically at a means, as I thought, of pleasing him. When we went to the stables I limped as badly as I had that other, unsuccessful day, only this time I got no expression of sympathy from Clare. Indeed, he had all he could do to conceal his aversion for my awkward movements.

Clare left as soon as he had seen me mounted, giving brusque instructions to the groom, who was the same tousle-headed youngster I had seen before. His name was Tom; I got that much from him, but his shyness and uncouth speech made conversation difficult. However, as time went on I managed to overcome his shyness, and we communicated by means of signs and laughter. He was a cheerful lad, and he found my lack of skill highly amusing. I think it was his casual attitude that made riding less of an ordeal than I had anticipated. I could not have done as well with Clare watching.

Whenever I rode out, Tom went with me. He had been ordered to accompany me when I went out of sight of the house, for it would have been easy to lose my way on the moor; there were few landmarks. In bad weather it was the dreariest place imaginable, yet over the weeks I had begun to appreciate its peculiar beauties. The colors of bracken and heath changed with the seasons; distance, shadows, and weather produced subtle variations in color, so that the seemingly monotonous browns and greens and purples resembled a vast and delicately shaded carpet. There were no walls there. It was good to be in the open, away from the increasingly oppressive air of the house and its owner.

The moor had another advantage. The cushion of heath was thick enough so that I could fall without being badly hurt. I had taken my share of tumbles, and I preferred to take them away from Clare's coldly critical eye. Tom was no critic; when I fell, he ran up grinning and chuckling, and hoisted me back onto the horse so that I could try again.

Usually I felt more cheerful after my outing. That morning it was harder than ever to come home. The chimneys of the house rose up out of the horizon; one towering mass of clouds hovered over it, so that it was an island of shadow in the midst of a sunny sea.

The thought of the interview in the library did not raise my spirits. As I dismounted in the stable-yard I saw a strange horse and carriage standing there. It was a hired chaise. So we had a visitor, not one of the families from the neighborhood, whose equipages I would have recognized, but a stranger.

I had hoped to see the visitor at luncheon, but my curiosity was not to be satisfied so easily. I found I was to dine in my room. Clare had ordered this arrangement often of late. The ostensible reason was my poor health. It was such an absurd excuse, in view of my improved looks, that poor Mrs. Andrews actually blushed when she mentioned it the first time. Now I was accustomed to the habit. I found it easier than sitting in silence with a man whose eyes fled from mine.

I knew better than to go downstairs until I was summoned. The summons came; and I felt my heart beating unevenly as I descended the stairs. I had no idea what the interview would be about, but Clare's manner suggested that it would not be a source of enjoyment to me.

Clare was waiting for me in the library. The stranger was with him. He was a cadaverously thin man, dressed in rusty black. Slick black hair, so smooth and shiny it looked painted on, framed his sallow face. I had never seen a countenance that pleased me less, though he bowed obsequiously when I entered. Clare did not introduce him.

"I have sent for you," he told me, "because your signature is required on this document. Be good enough to write your name here, if you please."

He handed me a pen and pointed to the bottom of the sheet.

The paper was a single long sheet, filled with crabbed script. It would have been hard to read even if Clare's hand had not covered the greater portion of it.

The stranger made a small coughing sound.

"My lord, you have not forgotten—"

"What?" Clare's tone was savage. "Ah, I recollect; you said two witnesses. The housekeeper will suit, I trust?"

"Anyone, my lord, so long as he or she can write his name."

Mrs. Andrews was called. At Clare's order, she moved up to the table so she could see me write; and again Clare's long white finger stabbed at the page.

I had not wasted the interval, though I was uneasily aware that the stranger was watching me, if Clare was not. My efforts were in vain; I understood a phrase here and there, enough to understand that the paper had to do with money, with the disposal of funds; but the unfamiliar legal terms and the sly, slow smile of the stranger put my head all in a whirl. I had seen nothing to rouse any definite suspicion. I hardly know why I spoke as I did.

"What does the paper say?" I asked.

I had not dared to look at my husband. He was silent for a long moment; when he spoke, his voice was deadly.

"You question me, Lady Clare?"

"I only wish to know—"

"Sign the paper."

"But it is a question of my property—"

Clare's hand, which had been resting lightly on the table, flattened out, pressing down till the nails whitened. I felt his rage in the air like a storm building up. Then the stranger broke in.

"Your pardon, Lady Clare, if I remind you . . . A married woman has no property."

The sleek, oily voice repelled me, but it did avert the incipient outburst. Clare's hand relaxed. He gave a muffled laugh.

"Always the peacemaker, eh, Newcomb? You do well to remind her Ladyship. Now sign . . ."

He snatched the pen from my hand, dipped it into the inkwell, and proffered it once again.

My signature was barely legible. The witnesses signed after me. Clare said,

"That is all."

I knew the words were meant for me, as well as for his servant. I had not quite reached the door when he spoke again.

"Lady Clare."

"Yes?"

"I understand you have been visiting some of my tenants in the village."

I turned. He stood by the table, one white hand resting on the paper I had just signed.

"Only one," I said stumblingly, as if the paucity of the number lessened the offense. "Only Anna's family."

"I told you you were not to go there. Have you forgotten my order, as you so often do, or did you deliberately disobey me?"

"You never told me—" I saw his eyes narrow with rage, and tried to stop myself. "I know you spoke of the danger of infection, but the child is recovered, and the house is as tidy as—"

"I am not interested in the domestic virtues of my tenants. I am only interested in your behavior.

You will not go there again, or to any other house in the village. Is that clear?"

"Yes."

"You may go. Not you, Andrews, I want to speak to you."

I stumbled up the stairs, holding the banister for support; I was so dizzy with rage and humiliation I could scarcely see.

He had not forbidden me to visit the village; I could remember that conversation as if it had happened only yesterday. Was I losing my memory, or my wits? But that was not the most important thing. He had deliberately chosen to humiliate me before a servant and a stranger who was little better than a servant—a clerk or small solicitor, I would guess. I hated him for that. And I hated myself for my crawling humility, for the fear of him that left me speechless in his presence.

Collapsing at last onto my bed, I knew I had cause for fear. I was not sure what the law might say; but a law that deprived a married woman of her property could not have much concern for her happiness or self-respect. Even if I had grounds for complaint—to whom could I appeal? I was even more alone than I had been on my wedding day, removed by hundreds of miles from the few people who might have some interest in my well-being. And the worst of it was that I did not know why he hated me, or what had happened to change him so.

II

I hoped—such were the depth of my contemptible cowardice—that the signing of the documents might improve Clare's humor. I would cheerfully have given him all my fortune to win a little kindness from him.

I breakfasted in my room next day, as was my custom, and waited until I thought he had gone out before I ventured forth. Creeping down the stairs, listening for the sound of his presence and ready to retreat if I heard it, I felt like a ghost. Perhaps, I thought, if I die I will become one of the Clare legends. A small, pale ghost, seldom seen—because while living she had avoided people—but heard as a sigh and an echoing, tiptoeing footfall at twilight. . . .

No one was in the hall, so I scuttled across it and went out. I was even avoiding the servants now; I was sure they knew of my humiliation, and I could not bear looks of pity or amusement.

Clare's horse was gone from its stall, so I relaxed. I did not feel like riding—it would have meant facing Tom and the other grooms—so I stole aside into the shrubbery and walked for a while. On this morning the numbness induced by the black bottle was welcome. I was standing still, staring blankly out across the front lawns, when I saw a gentleman on horseback approaching the house.

I ducked behind a tall flowering shrub. I recognized the little brown mare; even if I had not, the rider's slender form and bright cap of hair were familiar. Mr. Fleetwood was a frequent visitor. He came to play chess, and talk, with Clare. I had not seen much of him, yet he always spoke kindly to me. . . . I wondered, then, why I had not thought of him in my distress. He was a clergyman; it was his duty, as it should be his pleasure, to advise those in trouble.

I might not have called him, however, but as he dismounted he caught sight of me. He bowed and smiled and walked toward me.

"A splendid morning, is it not? You have chosen a lovely spot in which to enjoy the air." Then, as he came nearer, his smile faded. "What is wrong? You look ill; can I help you?"

It was the first open expression of sympathy I had heard, and it broke me down completely. I began to cry; then the whole story came out.

As he listened, Mr. Fleetwood's face reddened, and he shook his head.

"Foolish—blind and foolish," he muttered. "I beg you, dear child, to compose yourself. I am distressed—truly distressed—by this latest action."

I wiped my eyes with the handkerchief he gave me.

"Perhaps I should not have told you."

"No, no." His disclaimer was prompt and eager. "You did quite right to tell me. I will speak to Edward, his hasty temper is always outrunning his good sense. You have no idea, I suppose, as to what has made him behave so badly?"

"It seemed to begin the night you were here—the evening I saw the—the thing in the garden. Perhaps my superstitious foolishness angered him."

"Ah, yes." He looked thoughtful. "I remember. I am most interested in that experience. I am something of a student of local superstition, you know."

"Do you believe I really saw it?"

"Who can say?" His gray eyes met mine. "I would not commit myself to a flat yes or no. You must remember, however, that there are family legends—family difficulties—which Clare may not wish to tell you, for your own sake. You should believe that his present anger is not directed toward you; you are only the unhappy victim of circumstances he cannot help any more than you can."

The beautiful voice was most persuasive. I could not really make out what he was saying; it was all rather vague, but it sounded so comforting. I produced a watery smile.

"Good," he said, patting my hand and smiling back at me. "You are already better. I will speak to Edward as soon as I see him."

He was off without waiting for more thanks; as I watched him stride along the path, his golden hair shining in the sunlight, I thought fancifully that he resembled a knight of old, going off to do battle for a lady. His expression of concern and indignation became him; it gave his handsome face a strength which it lacked in repose.

I wondered if I were beginning to fall in love with Mr. Fleetwood. If I did, it would only be because I had nowhere else to bestow the store of warm feelings which a young bride may be expected to feel toward the opposite sex! No,

I thought, with a feeble return of my sense of humor, it would be best if I did not fancy myself in love with Mr. Fleetwood. There were too many complications implicit in that situation.

Yet I felt very warmly toward him, and my feelings of gratitude were deepened by the results; for he did indeed speak with Clare, promptly and to great effect. When Clare returned he came directly to my room.

My nerves fluttered when I heard his heavy footsteps stop at my door. He sent Anna away before he spoke to me.

"I understand I am to apologize to you for my behavior yesterday. Apparently you misunderstood my remarks and my attitude. It is true that I was momentarily vexed by your questioning me in the presence of a servant. You will admit that was not well done? But I ought not to have retaliated; I ask your pardon."

It was not a very gracious apology, but it was far more than I had any reason to expect. My words stumbled over one another, I was so eager to reassure him.

His stiff manner relaxed; he even smiled a little.

"Let us dine, then. I understand Mrs. Andrews is giving us some of the early strawberries."

All through dinner his good humor persisted. He even asked after the rumors of sickness in the village, as if he had never forbidden me to go there.

"There is sickness," I said, watching him nervously. "I don't believe it is typhoid, but I don't

know what it can be. I thought of a doctor,
but—"

"The nearest physician is in Leeds. But it will
do you no good to suggest it; they fear doctors,
these people, and cling stubbornly to their old
home remedies."

His tone was so mild and his comment so reasonable that I ventured further.

"I have wondered whether the problem is one
of bad air and water. The houses are old and
poorly kept up; the roofs leak, and they always
seem damp, even in warm weather."

"So you think I am a poor landlord, do you?
You sound like a reformer. Has your old admirer
been sending you tracts and pamphlets?"

"My comment was the result of my own observation," I protested. "You know I have not received so much as a note from London, not even
from my aunt."

"I was joking." Clare ate strawberries with relish, but I thought he was watching me from under
his lashes as he went on. "Mr. Jonathan is abroad
this summer. I hear from your solicitor now and
again, so I know all the gossip."

"But to return to the houses in the village," I
said, not caring for this turn in the conversation.
"Could not something be done to renovate them?
And the river is so foul; they say that waste from
the mills—"

"Yes, yes, I have heard that kind of talk," Clare
interrupted. "The poor always like to blame their
misfortunes on someone else, especially the rich.
However—if you feel so strongly about it, I will

consider the matter. Perhaps next year, when my income is more stabilized . . ."

I could hardly insist, after that; I had not expected so much. In truth, I did not want to nag him with a subject that annoyed him, his friendly manner was so pleasant to me.

The servants seemed aware of the change in our relations. When Mrs. Andrews brought in the tea tray she was beaming all over her round face, and since Clare had gone out for the evening I invited her to take a cup with me, as I sometimes did. I was feeling so happy and comfortable I wanted to share it with someone.

We chatted idly for a time; and then, since his kindness was so much in my mind, I mentioned Mr. Fleetwood and said how much I had admired his sermon.

"Oh, he has the tongue of an angel," said Mrs. Andrews, with a chuckle. "He always had, even as a child."

I could see that she was in a mood for confidences, and I settled back to enjoy them. She knew me better now than she had that first week, when she had commented so stiffly on the vicar's sermon.

"You have known him a long time?" I said.

"Oh, yes. He was always here, when Master Edward was not at his home. His family was well-to-do then. They lived in that great house at the other end of the village. It is deserted now; no one has lived there for years, and it is falling to pieces. But at that time the elder Mr. Fleetwood was reputed to be one of the wealthiest men in the district, and Master Edward's father encouraged the friendship. They were a pair, those two boys, one so dark and one so fair. And mischievous! Master Jack looked like an angel, but he was not; and what one did not think to do, the other did. They kept me busy, I can tell you."

"I find it hard to picture his Lordship as a bad little boy," I said, smiling.

"Oh, but he was not bad; only high-spirited, as all boys are. And when I caught them out, in some particular prank, he would look at me with those dark eyes flashing, and say nothing. He never lied. Master Jack was the one—I cannot say that he lied, exactly. But he could talk the stars out of the sky, even then; and with that angelic face of his looking so innocent, and that sweet voice going on . . . Well, by the time he finished 'explaining,' you wanted to reward him for his splendid intentions instead of punishing him for the broken window, or muddied floor. After he ran away, I would try to think what he had said; and, do you know, I never could remember! But his excuses sounded very convincing when he made them."

She chuckled fondly. There was one omission in her description; and I decided to remedy it, to spare her embarrassment—and satisfy my own curiosity.

"I suppose Miss Fleetwood followed them about, as little sisters do," I said casually.

"Oh, yes," Mrs. Andrews said. She looked at me askance, and I went on,

"It would be natural for the three to be fond of one another; even for a boy-and-girl romance to blossom."

My tone reassured her, as it was meant to do. She had no natural slyness, poor old lady; she relaxed with a long puff of breath.

"Very natural indeed. If it had not been for Master Edward's father . . ."

"He did not approve of Miss Fleetwood? I cannot imagine why; she has every grace of mind and person."

"Well," said Mrs. Andrews, quite disarmed by my manner, "I would not gossip idly, my lady, you know that; but with you . . ."

"Of course. I have heard that his late Lordship was not a gentle man."

"He was a hard man. A very hard man . . . Only one thing mattered to him, and that was his own will; I used to think he would trample on any person or any thing that stood in his way. After my dear lady died—I was her companion, you know, she took me in after my husband passed away and left me without any money—after she died, I stayed on for the boy's sake. I felt he needed me. Though it was not easy, with his Lordship . . . But I had better not speak of that."

"The Fleetwoods," I prompted.

"Yes, yes." Mrs. Andrews folded her fat hands over her apron and settled back comfortably. "I don't know how far the affair had gone—between the two young people, I mean. There never was a formal engagement announced, but . . . Then the news came. I will never forget that day, when it was known. That Mr. Fleetwood's business had failed; he was penniless and in disgrace; he had spent money he ought not to have spent, including the dowry of his daughter. It was not only poverty he had to face, but prison. So it is no wonder that he shot himself."

"Good heavens," I exclaimed in horror. "How frightful! And those poor young people—"

"That was bad enough, but it was not the worst. In such times friendship is shown for what it is. Mr. Fleetwood had every reason to count on his Lordship. It was said that he left him a very pathetic letter, pleading for his orphaned children; but even without such a solemn appeal one would have expected . . . Instead, his Lordship forbade them the house. He called Master Edward into the library when the story became known. It was impossible not to hear what they said, they were shouting at one another so. But Master Edward had no choice; his father threatened to disinherit him if he had anything more to do with the Fleetwoods, and he would have done it, too; Master Edward knew that."

"Terrible," I murmured. "Heartless and cruel."

"And then after all there was nothing of Mr. Edward's inheritance left," said Mrs. Andrews, with morbid relish. "Only the estate and the house, which were entailed in any case. His late Lordship had not only spent everything, but was heavily in debt. Well, but you see it all turned out for the best," she said, more cheerfully. "It was only a boy-and-girl fancy, after all; and when his Lordship died, Master Edward was able to help his friends by giving them the living here, which is a very good one. They were near York at the time, where Master Jack had a curacy that paid almost nothing. He was ordained shortly after his father's death, you see. To be sure, he had no notion of being a clergyman when he thought he had a fortune coming to him; but see you, how it turned out, his splendid eloquence is given to the work of the Lord."

She nodded impressively.

"Yes, indeed, my lady, the Lord works in mysterious ways; but he has His own plans, and they come about though we poor mortals cannot see them working."

Chapter

11

AUGUST WAS HOT AND BREATHLESS; IT WAS THE warmest summer any of the oldest inhabitants could recall. The sickness in the village grew worse as the heat increased. One morning, after hearing a particularly alarming report from Anna, I determined to pay a visit of inspection.

I really had not spent much time in the village, and my visits had been limited to a few of the more prosperous families. When I explained my purpose to Anna and asked her to accompany me, she protested. She had hoped to induce my sympathy, but had no idea of my wanting to visit those who were ill; it was improper, unsafe, his Lordship would be angry, she would never forgive herself if . . . and so on. I was firm with her, having quite made up my mind. During the drive, she kept trying to dissuade me, and when I reached the outskirts of the village she suggested that I wait in the carriage while she carried in the food and simple remedies we had brought.

I own I was unpleasantly surprised when we turned off the main street into a narrow alleyway I had not seen. It might have been considered quaint at one time, with its ancient thatched roofs and whitewashed walls. Now the houses looked as if they had not been painted or repaired for centuries; weeds grew rankly in the small gardens, and gaping holes showed in roof and outer walls.

With Anna behind me, carrying the basket and muttering disapprovingly, I walked up the path to the first house. The door stood open; even at that early hour the air was hot. Peering within was like looking into a cave; a feeble fire burned on the hearth and against its glow I could see a dark hunched form, sitting so motionless I felt a thrill of fear.

As my eyes grew accustomed to the dim light, I made out the form more clearly. It was that of a man. He looked up as I entered the room, holding my skirts high above the dusty floor; and then, as he recognized me, he struggled to his feet, his eyes shining whitely.

"My lady," he exclaimed, in tones of amazement.

"You have sickness in the house," I said. "I have come to see how I can help." Then, as he said nothing, but only continued to stare, I turned helplessly to Anna. "Does he understand? Speak to him: ask him who is ill."

"He understands," Anna said. "This is Will Jenkins. He was a groom at the house, until he grew too old to work and his Lordship turned him out without so much as a twopenny bit to drink his health. It is his daughter who lies sick."

She indicated a door that seemed to lead to an inner room. I decided to take no notice of her criticism of Clare; I could hardly blame her for resenting an act so cruel, but it would have been improper for me to join in abusing him. I took a step toward the door; and then Jenkins moved. He lurched horribly; it was easy to see why he had been considered unfit for service. I recoiled; the movement had been so violent, and seemed designed to oppose my entrance.

"No, my lady," he said earnestly, "you must not go in. You will catch the sickness."

Before I could speak, the inner door opened and another man came out. He was younger, tall and broad-shouldered. He stood in the doorway, blocking it. I could not see within, the small windows of the room were so grimed with dust, but I could hear the heavy breathing of someone in pain.

"Will's son-in-law," said Anna, "Mary's husband. How does she, Frank?"

Unlike the older man's speech, that of the younger was pure dialect. Anna interpreted.

"She is better, he says. He wants us to go. We will leave these things. . . ."

She took some of the things from the basket, put them on the table, and took my arm. I resisted.

"I want to see her, Anna. Is there no woman here? These men cannot give her the care she needs. . . ."

Apparently the younger man could understand me, even if he could not speak plainly. He made a low grating sound, like an animal's growl, and moved toward me. I needed no interpreter to sense his anger; it was clear from the tone of his voice and his hulking movements.

Anna spoke sharply to him, and he stopped. He was now visible to me, in the light from the open door; and as I saw his features plainly I lost my fear. His face was rough and not very clean; he had not shaved for several days. But the eyes under the heavy brows held a look of pain and bewilderment that went to my heart.

"Don't worry," I said to Anna, who was plucking urgently at my sleeve. "He means no harm. Is he—is he simple, then? Is that why he does not work, a big husky fellow like that? With his wife ill, I would think they would need his earnings to live."

"You don't understand," Anna began; and then the man began to laugh. It was a shocking sound in that house of illness and gloom. He spoke urgently, and Anna turned to me.

"He wants me to tell you what he says."

"Go on," I said.

It was a strange monologue that ensued: the man's harsh voice, followed by Anna's softer, calmer tones. I don't think I will ever forget what he said.

"Work? I would work if I could get it, and thank God for the chance. What work can I do? It was his Lordship's father who took our land, so we cannot get a living from the fields. Now my lord brings workmen in from London and York while our people starve; he spends nothing in this poor place. They will not hire me at the mill. Why should they, when they can hire women and children for half a man's wages, and get a full day's work from them? My wife worked there till she fell ill; before five in the morning she left here, and was not back until long after dark, too tired to cook or sweep. I try to help her, I can do no less, but I don't do it right; and it takes the heart out of a man, to let his woman work for him. Simple? Yes, I am simple, and soon I will be worse, sitting here and watching her fade away, and not knowing how to help. . . . Get me work, my lady! I don't want your charity; I want my rights as a free man. Get me work, any work, and see how simple I am."

He would not let me go in to his wife. I did not insist; he meant it kindly, for all his rough words, and I sensed that whatever love could do, the woman received from this man.

I paid two more visits in that terrible little street. There were six children in one family; four of them were sick at home, sleeping all together in the single bed. Two others were at the mill. The other family . . .

But the stories were all the same; I heard the same complaints, from men and women alike. Poverty and lack of work, houses that were rotting because there was no money for repairs, polluted streams, inadequate food.

I spoke to Clare at dinner. I had to speak, though

I knew the subject would anger him. The things I had seen and heard that day would not let me be silent.

"So," he said, when I had finished my little speech, "you have been playing the grand lady. I promised not to interfere with you; but I must say I admire your courage more than I do your good sense."

"I am not brave. But these things are so terrible! Cannot we do something for the people? Only to repair the houses—they tell me the autumn rains here are hard, and every roof has holes."

Clare took a bite of cake.

"Repairs cost money," he said calmly. "At the moment I have none."

Through the window I could see the finished facade of the restored wing. The windowpanes sparkled, and the stone was as white as marble. Within, the rooms were handsome, with new furniture and mantelpieces of imported Italian stone, costly ornaments . . . Clare saw my look.

"I have none," he repeated, and took another bite.

"But I thought I had—"

I stuck there; I could not put it into words. For one thing, I did not know what I had in the way of money. I had never known the amount of my fortune, and I had no idea how much he had spent.

Surprisingly, he did not take offense.

"You had, and have, a considerable fortune," he said mildly. "But even you must realize that one cannot continue to spend capital without diminishing and eventually dissipating the income from it. Leave business matters to me. I assure you they are in good hands."

So once again the subject was dropped because I had not the courage to pursue it in the face of Clare's superior knowledge. But this time I did not drop it from my thoughts. Clare was away from home a good deal, and since he didn't seem to care how I spent my spare time, I did not enlighten him. He would have laughed heartily if I had told him I was educating myself. I would have laughed too, a few months earlier, if anyone had told me that one day I would be learning from a crowd of semiliterate peasants and a little old man crippled with rheumatism.

I often wondered what sort of man old Jenkins would have been with the advantages of wealth and good birth. Before her death, Clare's mother had supported a short-lived village school. Several of the older villagers had learned to read and write; but Jenkins had gone farther. He had never stopped learning, and he had the rare gift of seeing beyond his immediate troubles to their underlying causes. I heard tales of distress and injustice from all the villagers, but it was Jenkins who told me about enclosure and the Poor Laws, about the Anti-Corn-Law League and the mills.

We must have made a comical picture on those mornings, as we sat side by side on the bench outside Jenkins' cottage—the old man, all bent and crippled by disease, his long white hair framing his wrinkled face; and the young woman of fashion in her furs and laces and jewels. I cared noth-

ing for that, I was too busy learning. With Jenkins'
help I began to understand the reasons for the decline of this village, which was a sample of hundreds of others throughout England.

A century before, every family had farmed its
own land, with the common pastureland open to
all. Ownership of land was never questioned, for
the plots had been in the same families for centuries. When the new laws were passed, most of
the small farmers could not afford the work of
fencing and draining required by law, and those
who lacked formal titles to their land—the great
majority—had no claim at all. They had to stand
helplessly by and see the fields which had been in
their families for generations enclosed within the
lord's estate, leaving them nothing.

Jonathan had mentioned the evils of enclosure,
as this process was called; but it was one thing to
hear the dry statistics and quite another to see the
results, in the pinched faces of hungry children
and the helpless anger of their parents. The old
village crafts of knitting and weaving had failed,
replaced by the cheaper products of the mills, and
the mill-owners would not hire an able-bodied
man when they could get his ten-year-old son for
less than half the wage. It did not take a man's
strength to run the machines.

"One law for the rich and another for the poor."
Jonathan had said that, too. Now I knew what he
meant. One set of laws deprived the poor of their
land. Another law taxed imported corn, in order
to keep up the price of home-grown agricultural
products. But the agricultural land was now in

the hands of the rich, so that even the price of the poor man's bread was controlled by those who had stolen his cornfields. There was no avenue of protest open; for the law gave the landless man no vote and no representation in Parliament.

The revolution in France was not so far in the past. Miss Plum had spoken of those bloodstained years with horror; this, she implied, was how *foreigners* conducted their affairs. But as I listened to Jenkins, and saw the faces of the younger men gathered around him, I wondered how many Frenchmen had tried milder means of obtaining justice before they took up their pikes and marched out to murder and burn.

I wondered even more at my own thoughts. They were undergoing a kind of revolution too.

In his lighter moments Jenkins regaled me with local legends and history. His memories of the past were not dry excerpts from books; they were eyewitness accounts, handed down for generations. They may have been inaccurate, but they were certainly vivid. It was uncanny to hear him speak of Great Warwick and the Young Pretender as if they had lived only yesterday.

I was amused to find Mrs. Andrews' warning about King Richard confirmed. He was still a local hero, and disparaging remarks about him were not well received. Old Jenkins called him "Dickon," and described him so accurately I could almost believe it was he, and not his remote ancestor, who had been in the cheering crowd the day the young king made his triumphal entry into York.

"They called him 'Crouchback,'" said Jenkins

angrily. "He was no such thing, my lady. He was a slight man, 'tis true, and only of medium height; but as straight as a spear, and a bonny fighter. Light-brown hair, worn long to his shoulders, and a dark eye that could pierce you like an arrow if you had guilt hidden in your soul. But a very sweet smile he had, if he favored you. Then his eyes would light up and one eyebrow would lift as he laughed. . . ."

"Good heavens," I said. "You might have seen him yourself, Jenkins."

"Well, but I heard it from my granther, who had it from his, and he from his mother's mother's mother," said Jenkins. It sounded very convincing; I did not even stop to count up the generations, to see if they worked out.

Jenkins was too well bred to criticize my husband's family in my hearing, but some of the other villagers were not; it was plain that they considered the Clares to be usurpers as well as tyrants, and that they had never forgiven the first Baron for conniving in "Dickon's murder." One dear vicious old lady, the terror of her downtrodden family, informed me that the Curse of the Clares had originated with no less a personage than King Dickon himself.

"Cursed them all, he did, as he lay dying," she mumbled merrily through her toothless gums. "Root and branch, flower and stem, the traitor Clare and his last living son."

After someone had translated this for me, I couldn't help but admire the poetic ring of it. It didn't bother me a bit; like Fernando's silly story of pacts with the devil, Dickon's curse was too un-likely. I fancied Dickon had too much on his mind that day at Bosworth to spare breath to curse a single minor foe.

Thanks, in part, to my frequent trips to the village I had learned to ride reasonably well, though I never mounted Sultana without an in-ward qualm. I did not mention my fears to Clare; he was pleased at my prowess and I wanted to keep him in a good humor with me, though some of the feats of jumping and galloping to which he urged me left me secretly shaking for hours afterward.

When he was at home, we rode out daily, and he taught me the moor paths. Without such knowl-edge a rider could have been in serious danger, for there were bogs and concealed pitfalls under the seemingly smooth surface. One afternoon we rode clear across the narrower part of the moor to Rawlinson Hall. The Rawlinsons were our nearest neighbors, only a few miles away by this direct route, though by road the distance was longer. I was not very fond of the family; Mr. Rawlinson's tendency toward improper grammar and bad language was restrained only by his obsequious respect for Clare. How dull he was—and how ill-bred—compared with my old friend in the vil-lage! Yet even this visit had its pleasurable aspect, because I made it with Clare.

How often, during the days of Clare's anger, had I wished for the old relationship of friendly indifference. Now that it was restored, I real-ized that it was not enough. Yet my feelings were ambivalent; when I dreamed, as women will, of Clare's arms about me and his lips on mine, the shiver that ran through me was not wholly one of rapture. I wanted love, but I was afraid of his; and as the days went on, the ambiguity of my situation grew more intolerable.

A letter from my aunt, the sole communication I was to receive from her, brought this home to me. I puzzled my way through her sloppy, sprawling hand, and grimaced as I read her frank comments on marriage—for now that I was a married woman the reserve she had placed on her tongue was removed. She congratulated me on having gained "such a strong, hearty man" for a husband, and wondered why she had heard no announcement, as yet, of an expected heir. "It must be your fault, my dear niece, for if rumor be true Clare has already proved his capabilities in various inns and pleasure houses. . . ."

I was about to cast the ill-spelled epistle down in disgust when a phrase in the next paragraph caught my eye and made my heart flutter. "Our young musical friend" was the phrase in question; and what I went on to read did not quiet my palpitations.

Someone had called at my aunt's rooms—for she had given up the expensive house—to inquire after "our friend." The inquirer had represented himself as a solicitor, making private inquiries on behalf of a client, but my aunt questioned his bona fides. "Such an ugly fellow I have never seen," she wrote. "He would hardly inspire confidence as a solicitor, with that smirking, shifty face; even his garments were rusty, and his hair looked painted on his head."

I gathered that the "ugly fellow" had had persuasion of a successful character to offer—money, in short—because my aunt had taken pleasure in informing him what a worthless fellow "our friend" was. I did not doubt that she had told the solicitor all the horrid facts of my frustrated elopement. As for tracing Fernando, she could give no help; she understood he had gone abroad the week after "that famous event which you well remember."

This tale struck me most oddly. I could not help but connect the man who had called on Lady Russell with Clare's unattractive solicitor. Yet it seemed unlikely that Clare would stoop . . .

The more I thought about it, the more likely it became. I had no proof; the description was too vague to be definite, and my aunt gave no name. Yet in my growing need to explain Clare's indifference, I was grasping at straws. Did he still doubt my fidelity?

At any rate, Fernando had disappeared. That was a small consolation. I found the very thought of him repulsive, and wondered how I could have imagined myself in love with such a creature.

September came, and with it an abrupt change in the weather. The sultry days of August were but a memory; fog and damp and cold nights set in. The incessant rain did not help my patients in the village. Some died and some recovered, but always there were those who suffered.

One of the victims of the sweating sickness was

Miss Fleetwood. Her brother assured me she was not in danger, but of course she did not receive callers; beyond sending every few days to inquire, and dispatching the usual invalid offerings of jellies and fruit, I could do nothing. And indeed, when I thought of her in her pretty little house, waited on by servants and a devoted brother, I could not help contrasting her state with that of the villagers, and I did not care to do much.

One day, when I called on my rounds with my basket of medicines, I found all the doors barred against me.

I went home in tears, and could not stop crying. Clare saw my red eyes at dinner, and inquired as to the cause. I told him what had happened.

"They said it was not safe," I ended, fresh tears coming to my eyes as I spoke. "That I had risked myself too long for them, and they would not let me do so any longer. It is not the sweating sickness now, but something worse; I told them I had had the typhoid, but . . ."

"Cholera," Clare said, half to himself, voicing the word I was afraid to speak. His lips were tight and his brow scored with lines of anger; I could not understand its cause until he went on, "When I think of you standing outside those mean hovels and pleading for entrance . . . No, I am not angry with you. I suppose I should not be angry with them, either; I had not expected gratitude or sensitivity from churls."

"They are not churls, only unhappy, sick people. Clare, can we not—"

"We shall speak of it later." Clare rose. "I am

spending the evening at Rawlinson House; Rawlinson has a party of gentlemen down from York. I may stay the night. If I do not return home, what do you say to riding out tomorrow and meeting me? You know the path now, I think."

I appreciated his efforts to distract me, though I was scarcely in spirits for any adventures. I agreed. Later, after he had gone, it began to rain heavily, and I was not surprised when, by late evening, he had not returned.

Clare had said he would set out for home next morning after breakfast, so I got ready to leave early. The rain had stopped, but the sky was still gray and lowering, and Mrs. Andrews tried to dissuade me from going.

"You will be wet to the skin, and ruin your gown," she declared. "His Lordship will understand your not meeting him."

Her tone was unconvinced, however, and I shared her doubts; Clare's suggestions had the weight of commands, and he had been so pleasant of late I did not want to do anything to incur his disapproval. I rather looked forward to a ride. It was not actually raining, and the wind that tossed the trees about had a wild, free air that tempted me.

When I went to the stableyard I found Sultana saddled, as I had ordered; but my faithful groom was nowhere in sight.

"Where is Tom?" I asked the head groom, who stood holding my stirrup.

He looked askance and muttered something I did not understand. I gathered that Tom had absented himself without leave, but I did not stop to worry about it; it was growing late, and I expected I would meet Clare before I had gone very far. The groom called out after me as I directed my mount toward the gate; but I was impatient, and went on without listening.

At first I enjoyed the ride. This weather suited the moors; in the gray light they had an austere, diabolical grandeur. I thought of the blasted heath and the witches muttering over their fire; the branches of the wind-lashed shrubs looked like bare arms waving about, and the coils of mist in the hollows swayed eerily.

Then all at once I awoke from one of these flights of fancy to see that the mist was no longer hovering in isolated wisps. It was gathering in all about me.

I stopped Sultana with an incautious jerk that made her prance; and I realized that, dreaming, I had come quite a long way. The house was nowhere in sight, and I was still some distance from Rawlinson House.

I was not afraid. I thought I could not lose the path; it was faint and hard to see, but there were a few landmarks. Straight ahead I saw the lofty shape of one of the odd rock formations that crop up here and there upon the moor; and even as I watched, the rolling blanket of fog crept over it and swallowed it up to the very pinnacle.

Sultana began to stir uneasily as she sensed my increasing concern. Her restiveness created a new source of alarm. I had always been a little afraid of her. . . . I tried to tell myself there was nothing to be afraid of. I had to decide whether to go on, or turn back. Finally I thought that Clare must be on his way and that I might meet him sooner than I could retrace my steps all the way to the house.

I went on, slowly; I did not dare let the horse set her own pace, for fear of missing the scanty traces of the path. She did not like our creeping progress, and my arms ached from holding her in. I was wearing a cloak with a hood; I pulled the latter up over my head, but it did not prevent the damp from settling on my face and making my lashes stick together.

We went on for what seemed like hours. In the stillness—for even the birds seemed to have taken shelter—I could hear the uneven beat of my heart. Sultana's light hooves made hardly a sound on the thick bracken. And then a thrill of genuine terror went through me. The path, though narrow, was of beaten earth. I looked down and saw it had vanished. I was lost.

This time when I reined the horse in, she reared. I slapped her, and told her sharply to be still. But my voice shook so, and echoed so oddly through the muffling fog, that I knew better than to speak again. For the first time it occurred to me that a lady's sidesaddle is surely the most idiotic invention of modern times. Riding astride, a man has a good grip on the beast, and if he knows what he is about, he cannot easily be thrown; but a lady has no hold on the horse at all. Surely modesty is less important than safety.

This heretical notion astounded me so much I forgot for a moment where I was and what my peril was. I had acquired a number of peculiar ideas in the past few months, but I had not questioned the basic ideals of womanly behavior. Perched absurdly on my steed, I remembered Jonathan's mother; I could almost see her face wrinkle in a smile as I expounded my wild ideas. She would not be shocked, not even at the idea of ladies wearing trousers; for that, of course, was the only possible answer to the problem.

Fascinated by these thoughts, I forgot for a few moments to be afraid; and the horse quieted with the quieting of my alarm. I then tried to think, calmly and rationally, what I should do. It might be worthwhile to dismount and lead the horse; I could see better then, and if I did by mischance step into a boggy patch I could hold the reins and let Sultana pull me out. On the other side of the argument was the fact that she was unruly and strong. If she decided to leave, I would not be able to hold her. Yet it might be better to be on foot, if she should run away, than risk being thrown. Perhaps the best thing was to remain where I was. At least the ground here was solid, and I knew I could not be far from the path. Clearly I had missed Clare in the fog. When he reached the house and found I had set out to meet him, he would send the men to look for me.

I was, therefore, in perfect control of myself and my mount when it happened.

The sound might have been a bird's call, or the cry of a frightened animal. The muffling fog distorted it beyond recognition, and made it impossible to locate. In that white dripping stillness the effect was terrible. I started violently; and Sultana bolted.

Luckily I fell off at once. If I had been a better horsewoman—or had been riding astride, in my imaginary trousers—I might have kept my seat until she had reached a gallop; and if I had fallen then, I would have been badly injured. The fall dazed me, but the bracken was wet and soft. I lay flat for a moment, shaking my spinning head and listening to the hoofbeats fading into silence.

The shrill screaming sound came again, farther away. I thought I heard Sultana answer it. Then silence closed in again.

I started to stand, and thought better of it. I was already as wet as I could be, and my limbs were none too steady. Yet as I grew calmer I realized that my situation was still not alarming. There was nothing for me to do now but wait. If I tried to find the path I might lose myself thoroughly, since I had no idea of the direction in which it lay. Surely someone would come before long.

As the time stretched out, seeming even longer because I could not measure it, I became aware of an enemy just as dangerous, if more insidious, than the bogs I had been warned of. The damp cold penetrated my garments and seemed to settle in my very bones; my teeth clicked together and my hands went numb. I stood up and began to walk, back and forth, in a narrow path; but even that failed to warm me and finally I sank down on the soggy ground, too weary to replace the hood over my dripping head.

When I heard the voice I thought I must be

dreaming. I was in a daze of cold and fright, and when I tried to answer my voice failed, producing a feeble croak that was inaudible a few feet away. The voice called again; it was a human voice, and it called for me, but I could see nothing, not even a shadow, through fog. Then I knew that unless I could answer, I was lost. A searcher could pass within a few feet and never see me; and those fogs sometimes lasted for days.

I staggered to my feet. This time necessity came to my aid. I bellowed like a lost calf, and the answer was immediate. Something plunged toward me out of the mist, as if materializing from the spiritual world. But it was no spirit, it was Tom, my groom, his red hair shining like a flame, his face alight with joy and relief.

I have only the vaguest recollection of the journey back. Tom tried to carry me, but the poor lad was no taller than I, and could not lift my water-soaked weight. So I walked, or was dragged, and toward the end of the tramp I was only a plodding automaton.

When I came fully to my senses I was in my own bed, so packed around with heated bricks and hot bottles that I felt like a broiled fish. Anna was piling blankets over me, and Mrs. Andrews was poking the fire as if she would make it burn whether it wished to or not. Mrs. Andrews was sobbing loudly.

"Why are you crying?" I asked, sitting up. "Has someone died?"

Mrs. Andrews dropped the poker with a little shriek. Anna said nothing; but the color came back into her face with such a rush that she looked feverish. She put her hand over my forehead, then turned to the housekeeper.

"It is warm," she said.

"Of course it is warm," I said grumpily. "Anyone would be warm with all these coverings. May I not have some water? And something to eat; I am absolutely ravenous."

Mrs. Andrews would not believe it until she had seen me devour a huge pasty and a salad. Then she began to cry harder than ever.

"It's God's mercy, that is what it is. If you had seen yourself when they brought you in, looking like a little drowned kitten . . . Oh, forgive me, my lady, but I am silly with joy. His Lordship will be so relieved."

"Where is he?" I asked disinterestedly. I was looking at the tray for something more to eat.

"Gone to Leeds for a doctor; he was in such a state, he would go himself. Oh, what a relief for him when he returns! If you had seen yourself . . ."

There was a good deal more of this. I appreciated her concern, but found its expression tiresome; and the doctor, when he arrived, was even more exasperating. Having come so far, he was quite put out to find me in good health and eating like a groom; he kept shaking his head and mumbling portentously. I finally got him out of my room, together with Clare, who stood staring dumbly at me as if I had returned from the dead. Then I turned over and slept quite comfortably—

or would have done, except for Mrs. Andrews, who kept feeling my head every hour and waking me up.

The doctor stayed the night. He came in to see me in the morning and found me up and dressed. He went away in an evil humor, predicting delayed effects, but I felt so well I only laughed. How people did enjoy the disasters of others! They all seemed disappointed that I was not gasping out my last breath.

I got a hearty scolding from Clare as a reward for my prompt recovery.

"I thought you would have enough sense to stay home on such a day," he said severely. "And then to take the moor path—of all the follies—"

"But you told me to take that path," I interrupted. "At least—"

"Recall my words, and you will know I said no such thing. Do you realize that you might not have been found except by accident? We were searching the area near the road."

"But I thought . . ." I had to admit that I could not recall precisely what he had said. "How was it then that Tom found me? I must go down and thank him; I hope you will reward him generously, since it appears he saved my life."

"He is not here," Clare said, his face hardening.

"Not here?"

"I dismissed him. Wait," Clare said, raising a hand. "He found you, it is true; but you would not have been lost if he had been here, doing his duty. He went off without a word, so there was no one to accompany you; though Mark tells me he did call after you, to warn you of the fog and tell you to take the road. He assumed you had followed his advice."

"He did call out, but . . . Clare, you can't dismiss Tom! His are the only wages in his family; there are four younger children, and his father has a lung complaint. Where was he, then?"

"He tells some wild tale of being called away," Clare said angrily. "Obviously the boy was shirking. Of course he is half wild with guilt now; and well he might be. In the old days he would have been royally beaten for neglecting his duty with such dangerous results."

"But if he—"

"No doubt he is skilled at playing on your soft heart," Clare said. "The matter is finished—except for one admonition. I won't have you going down to the village to commiserate with and encourage the lout. In fact, I have decided that your visits there must end; I have been lax in letting you follow your own childish inclinations so long. Since you have no concern for your own health, I must insist that you do."

"But—"

"I said, the matter is finished!"

He strode from the room.

Evidently no one wanted me in the village. The villagers had already closed their doors against me, which rendered Clare's order somewhat superfluous. If he had not objected before, when the sickness was even worse than it was lately . . .

It was then that the first sly insinuation crept into my mind. I started to my feet as if I had seen an actual serpent. This was a thought I could not, dared not, think.

Chapter

12

MR. FLEETWOOD CAME TO CALL THE NEXT DAY.
I saw him ride up as I sat sewing in the parlor.
I was tempted to waylay him, for I was in a de-
spondent mood; but then I thought it was not fair
to constantly vex him with my complaints. And
in this case I could hardly complain of Clare's action; there was danger of infection, and he had
been more than patient in allowing me so much
freedom.

The vicar and Clare were in the library together
for a long time, but I was still sitting, staring at an
embroidered cloth into which I had put scarcely
six stitches, when Mr. Fleetwood came out. Instead of leaving, he sent the parlormaid to ask
whether I would receive him.

He was smiling when he entered the room; the
smile became a hearty laugh as he took the chair I
indicated and looked at my embroidery.

"How I pity the poor ladies of our time. You are all so accomplished, it must weary you—embroidery, drawing, music, Italian. . . . Will you think me impertinent if I suggest that this piece of work is not so neat as others I have seen you do?"

"I have been preoccupied," I admitted.

"Yes; I have been talking with Clare." His smile faded. Leaning forward, he placed a hand on my arm. "You will pardon me for interfering; you will excuse it because of my profession and my old friendship?"

"Of course."

"It is a trivial thing," he said indulgently, his smile returning. "He is a proud man, you know. You will understand that concern for a loved one sometimes appears arbitrary and arrogant."

I suppose my face must have shown some of the cynical amusement I felt at that description; Clare might love me, but if he did, he had an odd way of demonstrating it.

"My visiting in the village . . . ?"

"I have persuaded him that that must continue," Mr. Fleetwood said. An unmistakable glow of sincerity warmed his face. "It is a noble work, and may lead to untold good."

"It doesn't matter," I said dismally. "The village people refuse to let me come."

"I think they will relent. The sickness has decreased in intensity, I understand."

Again he would not wait for my thanks; he took his leave gracefully but in haste. I felt so warmly toward him I wondered once again why I did not fall in love with him.

Clare confirmed Mr. Fleetwood's statements. His mood was much improved, almost gay. When he told me I would be wanted, soon, to sign another document relating to money, I did not demur. He mentioned the document in the same breath in which he recalled my hopes of making repairs in the village. I concluded that the money would be used for that purpose, and signed, when the day came, with real pleasure. Even the smirking solicitor did not distress me that day.

So matters went for several more weeks. Though I resumed my visits to the village, I decided to be cautious about one thing; I did not visit poor young Tom and his family. Clare had made such concessions to me I felt it only fair to try to please him in minor things. But I did send, secretly, such small money as I had to help the family. I had a tiny personal allowance, and it was really no hardship to give it up for such a cause, since I had nowhere to spend it.

It was nearing the end of October when the course of my life took a decisive change.

The dire predictions of old Jenkins, who forecast an unusually severe winter after our unseasonably warm August, looked liable to be fulfilled. There was a fire in the parlor that morning, but the scene through the window was indescribably sad; the trees had lost their leaves and the bare branches waved in the cold wind. I saw the carriage drive up and leaned forward with interest; we had few visitors, and even this shabby hired chaise intrigued me. But when the visitor stepped out, I almost fell out of my chair I was so astounded.

Jonathan Scott.

It was as strange to see him there as it would have been to meet the Emir of Arabia strolling across the moor in his gold-embroidered robes. I had thought of Jonathan more than once in recent weeks. More and more often his once-disregarded speeches had recurred to me. But to see him here . . .

In his great caped traveling cloak he looked heavier and older than I remembered. He had grown moustaches, not neat ones like the Prince's, but great flapping black wings that drooped down over his mouth.

As I sat gaping he ascended the stairs and disappeared from my sight. A moment later I heard the bell, and the quick footsteps of Martin, the parlormaid, going to answer it.

I ran to the mirror to tidy my hair. By chance this brought me close to the door, so that I could overhear what was being said in the hall. His voice was as I remembered it, deep and rather rough. He asked for Lord Clare.

I waited, half concealed behind the draperies, while Martin took the message. She returned to say that his Lordship would receive the visitor shortly. Then Jonathan asked after me.

"I will see whether her Ladyship can see you," Martin said.

"No, no. I don't wish—that is, I will not disturb her Ladyship. I only wanted to know . . ."

The voice faded as Martin led him to the drawing room across the hall. I bit my lip in vexation. I could hardly rush to greet him, yet I was extremely curious and a little alarmed. The sober look with which he had studied the house, the tone in which he had answered Martin—these, and the very fact of his presence, made me uneasy. I assumed he had come as Mr. Beam's representative, but he would not be sent on such a long journey unless there were serious reasons for it. Something was wrong.

It was a reasonable conclusion; equally reasonable was my suspicion that I would not be told of the difficulty unless it suited Clare to tell me. Yet this does not explain my shocking behavior. Only someone who had lived through the months of my peculiar marriage could understand why I acted as I did, in violation of every rule of proper behavior.

Next to the library was a small room which had been fitted up as a summer parlor. There was a door between this room, which I seldom used, and the library. This door was ill-fitting. It had warped so badly that there was a distinct gap between door and frame. I doubt if Clare realized this; he never used the parlor, and the door, not being in use, was concealed behind a hanging near his desk.

I waited until Martin had escorted the visitor to the library. Then I slipped through the parlor door and went down the corridor.

I settled myself with my mistreated embroidery in a chair near the library door. I soon realized this would not do; I could hear voices, but could not make out the words. There was nothing for it but to stand with my ear up against the gap in the door—a compromising position, if one of the servants should come in. Then Clare's voice rose in a cry of anger, and I abandoned the lesser considerations of dignity.

"How dare you come to me with such a message?" Clare demanded.

"I but convey Mr. Beam's own words," Jonathan said stiffly. "I will carry your message back to him if you like; but you know, Lord Clare, the terms of the settlement. You were assiduous in making them out."

"They were subject to change by mutual consent," Clare argued, and then broke off. "Good God, why do I condescend to dispute with you? You are but a messenger. Why did not Beam come himself? It was hardly proper to send a subordinate to deal with *me*."

"Mr. Beam is an elderly man. His health is such that he ought to take a rest, but his sense of duty drives him. Strong as that sense is, it cannot cure crippled limbs. Rest assured, Lord Clare, that I speak for my employer and am empowered to do anything I can to accommodate you and—and her Ladyship."

After a moment my husband spoke again, more mildly.

"Then you speak for Mr. Beam when you tell me nothing can be done?"

"I do. There is, of course, the possibility of a note."

"I do not need you or Mr. Beam to advise me on that."

"It is for your Lordship to decide. But I repeat,

we are ready to serve you and her Ladyship in any way possible."

"So you are," Clare said musingly.

There was a long silence, without so much as a rustle of paper or a sound of movement; unashamedly straining my ears, I pictured them standing and contemplating one another in watchful silence. Finally Clare said,

"Well, well, there is nothing more to be said, then. I will consider the matter. Since this avenue is closed, I must take time to investigate others. Mr. Scott, you will be in the neighborhood for a time, I trust? Or does your own admirable sense of duty require that you return to London at once?"

"I have been instructed to wait upon your Lordship's wishes."

"I am glad to hear it. I know you will want to see her Ladyship before you return."

"I had hoped for that pleasure."

"I know it will give her equal pleasure."

It made me shiver to hear them; the smooth false words were like a coating of paint and powder over an old woman's ravaged face. I knew Clare too well to believe he would accept disappointment gracefully. Being Clare, he would blame Jonathan for bringing an unfavorable response, and dislike him even more than he already did. I assumed that the matter they were discussing had to do with my fortune. So Clare would be angry with me, too. He was angry with me whenever anything went wrong with any of his plans.

None of this disturbed me so much as Clare's sudden change of manner. Pretense was foreign to his nature. If he pretended amiability toward a man he thoroughly disliked, it must be for a reason. I would have preferred an honest fit of rage to that silken charm.

II

I met Jonathan with a fair show of surprise; to hide the fact that I had seen him come was another of those subterfuges which were becoming more and more common to me. All through dinner Clare watched both of us, and his comments carried many a hidden barb.

One example:

"I have bidden Mrs. Andrews make ready a room for our guest," he remarked. "You will forgive me, Lady Clare, for intervening in your domestic province; but since you did not know of Mr. Scott's coming, you could not tell her, could you?"

"I cannot intrude on your hospitality, my lord," Jonathan said.

"But where else would you stay? I may want to consult with you at any time; you can hardly expect me to summon you from Leeds or Ripon each time I have a question."

"I am staying in the village, my lord."

"There is no inn in the village."

"I have bespoken a room with a family there."

"Which family?" I asked with interest.

"The Millers. They have an extra room now, since the death of the mother."

"Yes, I know. It was a sad loss; Janet is only thirteen and there is a baby."

Jonathan's look of surprise made me flush. Clare, who had been genuinely stupefied, finally recovered himself.

"But you cannot be serious. There are no suitable accommodations for a *gentleman* in the village."

The slight emphasis on the word may not have been deliberate. But Jonathan's lips tightened. Clare went on good-humoredly.

"No, my dear fellow, I cannot allow such sacrifice. You will stay here. I trust we can amuse you. I am much occupied; but Lady Clare will be delighted with your company. There are interesting rides and walks hereabout, if you are fond of natural beauty; we can mount you, of course."

Jonathan looked sulky, but said no more; he could not insist without deliberate rudeness. Clare studied his flushed face with amusement. Then he turned to me, and I stiffened. I had not seen that look before.

"You have not taken Sultana out, I notice, since your adventure."

"I do not trust Sultana," I said.

"You must not allow yourself to give way to those unreasonable fears."

"My fear is not unreasonable," I protested. "If I had lost control of Sultana, or mishandled her, I could try to overcome that weakness; but I did not, she bolted quite deliberately; and if a sound such as that can startle her—"

"Sound? What sound?"

"But I must have told you. It was the strangest noise, almost like a whistle. It must have been a bird, I suppose; but if she cannot be trusted to ignore natural sounds—"

Clare broke in. He interrupted me often, and I wondered whether he knew how hard it was on the nerves, never to be allowed to complete a sentence.

"You cannot imagine I would give you a mount that had not been thoroughly trained. Sultana is the most tractable horse in my stables. She would stand if she were in the midst of a battle."

"Very well," I said. It was a meaningless remark, but agreement and docility were what he wanted. I did not look at Jonathan. It was bad enough to be scolded like a willful child, without seeing his look of pity and, I felt sure, contempt.

I got through the rest of the meal by remaining silent. After I left them to their wine I went up to my room instead of going to the parlor. But I was not to escape so easily. After a time Clare came up.

"Master Scott has gone to the village to collect his valise. I offered to send a servant, but he insisted on going himself. What a common fellow he is!"

"Why did you ask him to stay, then?"

"For your sake, of course. I thought you would enjoy having a former swain sighing at your feet once again."

I yawned with affected boredom.

"I could never understand how you got that

notion. Mr. Scott was never my admirer; he did nothing but scold me and sneer at my stupidity."

"What other expression of interest would you expect from an ill-bred boor? Credit him with fidelity, at least; he has come a long way to see you."

"He did not come to see me. He came on business."

"And why," Clare inquired gently, "should you think that?"

"Why—why, because there is no other reason why he should come."

"Triumphant feminine logic! But I fancy there is a reason."

"What, then, for heaven's sake?"

"Oh, he has an excuse; a minor business matter, as you say. But I fancy he has been concerned about you. He wishes to be sure you are well and happy; that I am not beating you."

He laughed lightly, but something in his look turned me cold.

"You would not beat me," I said. "And if you chose to—what could he do to prevent you?"

"Oh," said Clare absently, "he could do something. Not, perhaps, what he would like to do, but . . ."

The words trailed off into silence and he sat staring, not at me, but at the flames flickering in the hearth. For a startling second they were reflected in his wide eyes, so that his pupils blazed crimson.

It was only a momentary illusion. I don't know why it should have frightened me so, but it did;

and when he got stiffly to his feet and, still staring, walked out of the room without saying another word, I began to shake like a fever patient seized by a chill.

III

In the morning I was able to recall that strange conversation more calmly, but I could not help regarding it as significant. Occasionally I had wondered whether Clare doubted my fidelity, but I had dismissed the idea as absurd. Yet his sneering remarks about Jonathan sounded for all the world like those of a jealous husband.

Absurd or not, I determined to act as if it were true. I would not give Clare the slightest excuse to doubt me. I would be cool in manner and circumspect in behavior.

Like so many good resolutions, this one did not survive very long. I had made one fatal error; I failed to see where the danger lay. A silly flirtation like the affair with Fernando was what I meant to avoid. I did avoid it; there were no sidelong glances or tender sighs. But while I escaped the appearance of love, I fell into the reality, as one might tumble into a concealed pitfall. Not a very romantic simile, perhaps, but far more accurate than a poetic phrase. Nothing I had heard or read about love had taught me what it was really like; I was in it before I recognized it.

I could talk to Jonathan. It sounds so simple. But it was like taking great gulps of air after being half drowned, like being born with wings and never allowed to use them, until one day the bonds fall away, and the creature soars, and cries, "This is what I was born for; this is what I wanted!"

I remember the first morning we walked out together. I was being careful; I had directed one of the stableboys to follow us, saying I no longer trusted my sense of direction after my disastrous day in the fog. We had not gone fifty yards from the house before the bonds were off, and I was flying.

Jonathan began it by asking a single question about the village. I answered; and the words poured out of me like water through a broken dam. The waste of manpower, the suffering of the children, the fouling of the rivers—all the new ideas that had been bubbling up in my mind and boiling inside me with no outlet, no one to share them with.

He listened, nodding, his keen black eyes fixed on my face. He listened! I must have talked for a good ten minutes before I realized what I was saying. I was preaching him the same sermon he had once preached me.

I stopped speaking abruptly, feeling the blood rush into my face. There was no need to tell him what I thought, or why I blushed; he sensed it, and he began to laugh. After that, it was like walls falling. There was no restraint on our talk, we could not talk fast enough to say all we wanted to say; we interrupted one another in our eagerness, and leaped great conversational gaps as if we could read one another's thoughts. We talked. . . . But it cannot be described, it must be felt, that complete sense of sympathy with a fellow human being.

Very little of what I told him was new to him. In an hour with the Miller family Jonathan had learned as much as it had taken me six months to get out of the entire village. But, as he said, he was a man and a stranger, and they could speak more freely to him.

"They adore you," he said, giving me a quick sidelong look. "They speak of you as a cross between the Queen and an angel of mercy."

"I have done so little," I said soberly. "I can do so little."

"But you could do—" Jonathan began impetuously, and then stopped himself.

I knew what he had started to say, and why he had not said it. The disposal of my fortune was not mine; any comment of his could be interpreted as criticism of my husband. After a moment he went on, in a different voice.

"The relief of immediate misery is admirable; but we need more, much more. We must enforce existing laws and make new ones. A ten-hour day, a sixty-hour week; more rigorous safety regulations; free schools, sanitation in cities and waterways . . . The list is endless!"

I answered; and that danger point was gotten over. But it was bound to recur, for the situation worsened, subtly but steadily.

Clare's behavior was inexplicable. His moods varied so, from moment to moment, that I never knew whether an innocent comment of mine would produce a smile or a sneering retort. He watched Jonathan like a bird of prey, and yet he would not dismiss him. I knew that Jonathan had suggested leaving. He had a reasonable excuse; with Mr. Beam in poor health, it was absurd for him to hang about waiting on the wishes of a single client, however distinguished. Yet he could not leave so long as Clare demanded his assistance.

Clare developed one alarming new habit. He had been an abstemious man; now the after-dinner port hour lengthened, and twice, long after I had retired for the night, I heard his unsteady steps stumble down the hall.

One afternoon, less than a week after Jonathan's arrival, they remained at the table for a long time; and when they finally joined me in the parlor, I knew Clare had taken too much wine. His face was flushed and his hair disheveled, and as he came into the room he stumbled and would have fallen, had it not been for Jonathan's arm. He cast it off with a drunken laugh.

"What the devil—keep your hands off me, sir! You think I need help, eh? 'F I do, don't need yours. M' loving wife; loving wife'll help me. Come here, Lucy . . . lean on you."

I put my embroidery aside and rose. I had never seen him in this mood, but it was easier to obey without question.

He caught me by the shoulders as I came to him, and I staggered, bracing myself against his weight.

"Will you not sit down?" I suggested. "You are unwell; let me call Phillips."

"No." He shook his head so violently that his

hair flew all about. "Walk it off; walk, that's the thing. Lean on loving wife. Walk! Up and down, up and down—"

We took a few turns about the room. Clare was staggering and stumbling; his weight was actually painful, and I could barely keep my feet. Jonathan stood rigid by the door, where he had retreated after Clare flung him away. He was unwilling to leave me, and in a way his presence was a comfort; yet I wished he would withdraw. He could not interfere without making the situation worse.

Suddenly Clare dug his fingers into my arm with such force that I cried out. My weak foot gave way, and in a grotesque embrace we fell against the wall, with Clare's arm tight about me and his breath hot on my face. In a drunken burst of energy he spun me around, laughing, and spoke over my shoulder to Jonathan.

"Devoted wife, eh? Can't help it, poor girl, if she is a cripple. Limps. You notice? Can't stand it—deformity, ugliness. Ugly! Hate it . . ."

He tried to push me from him; since I was already flat against the wall the movement succeeded only in overturning him. He crashed to the floor at my feet and lay there breathing stentoriously through his open mouth.

Jonathan said something under his breath and came quickly toward me. I threw up both hands to ward him off. My state of mind was not at its coolest; but I could have sworn I had seen one of Clare's eyes open and look at me.

"No," I stammered. "Please—take care of him; call the servants. I must get away, I cannot . . ."

I had no doubt that the butler was in the hall, drawn by Clare's loud comments; but he had the grace to keep out of my sight when I came running out. I was able to reach my room without encountering anyone but Anna. In her usual taciturn fashion she made no comment, except for a harsh indrawn breath when she helped me off with the rumpled dress and saw the reddening marks on my arm.

Soon the servants, and the entire village, would know that poor Lady Clare had a drunkard for a husband. Some might say that her Ladyship had driven her husband to drink. Yet it was not these thoughts, nor fear of Clare's future rages, that filled me with dread. It was the memory of his eye, open and alert and watching.

Chapter
13

I COULD ONLY IMAGINE IN WHAT STATE OF MIND Jonathan spent the evening. I did not leave my room. I knew I must not see him or talk to him. It was no longer his pity I dreaded, it was something far more perilous. When I came down to breakfast next morning, I was in a considerable state of trepidation, but I had decided not to breakfast in my room; the situation had to be faced, and the longer I put it off, the more difficult it would be.

I had pictured Clare in a number of possible moods—repentant, ill, self-justifying, angry. The reality astounded me.

He greeted me with a smile and a reference to the pleasant weather.

"We are to enjoy St. Martin's summer, it appears; it is a short lull, to prepare us for the rain and snow to come. You must take advantage of it while it lasts. Of course I will not press you; but I do wish you could bring yourself to ride Sultana, for her sake as well as your own. With a groom, and Mr. Scott beside you, you would not be afraid, I hope?"

I looked at Jonathan, who was already at the table, but he looked away. Clare continued to talk in the most affable voice; either he did not remember what had happened, or he was determined to pretend it had not.

"I must make my excuses. I am off to Edinburgh for a few days. I hope to get the facts I need to settle our business, Scott. I know you are anxious to return to your duties in London, and I am grateful for your patience."

He left the room then, with the excuse that he must prepare for his trip.

My conversation with Jonathan was exceedingly stilted; he was as amazed as I at Clare's incredible performance, but we could hardly discuss it so long as the servants were in the room. It was not long before Clare returned, dressed for travel. I saw at once that something had happened to vex him, and I was almost relieved to see the familiar haughty frown.

"I understand that lout of a groom has been hanging about," he began. "You know, Lady Clare, that I forbade you to see him or speak with him?"

I knew no such thing; Clare had told me not to visit the boy's home, but he had not specifically forbidden a meeting. He gave me no time to raise this objection, even if I had thought it wise to do so.

"I have instructed Williams to thrash him if he comes here again. I won't have you sneaking off to meet him elsewhere, do you hear?"

I cast a glance at Martin, the parlormaid, who was standing paralyzed, with a dish of muffins in her hand.

"But I never did—"

"Spare me your lies," Clare interrupted. "I trust you will obey my orders without making it necessary for me to confine you to your room. Scott, I require you to see that my instructions are obeyed, and that I am told of any violation of my wishes."

With a curt nod, he left. Martin put the muffins on the table and fled; and Jonathan raised his eyes and looked directly at me.

"No," I said, as if he had spoken. "Not here. Let us go for a ride. I must follow orders. . . ."

I reached the stableyard before him, having flung on my habit any which way. Even the thought of Sultana did not daunt me. I wanted something violent to do; I wanted to rush about and strike at things with a stick. My own feelings surprised me. I could not imagine where I had got the courage to be angry, after so much weeping and fear. It was not long before the answer came to me. I had taken courage from *him*, and I would need it, for his sake.

Clare had assigned a horse for Jonathan's use, and at my order Williams saddled it, and Sultana. He then went on to saddle a third beast.

"There is no need for that," I said, as Jonathan joined me.

"Your pardon, my lady," Williams said, looking oddly. "But his Lordship has given orders . . ."

"For you to come with us?"

"Not I, my lady." Williams' eye shifted.

From one of the stalls a man slouched out into the yard. His size alone was alarming; he was a great hulking fellow with arms that hung down to his knees. His nose was a twisted lump. I had not been long in London, but I recognized his type. This was no local peasant.

He touched his cap to me with a sly insolence that wrung a low growl from Jonathan—and reminded me of the need for caution.

"Very well," I said, addressing Williams. "But tell the fellow to stay at a distance. I don't like his looks."

We were out of the stableyard and on the moor path before I allowed myself to speak.

"What can he mean by setting such a villain on me? Who is the rascal?"

"A fair description," said Jonathan, with a smile. "I have some slight acquaintance with the good old English art of wrestling, and I fancy I have seen this fellow in the ring."

"Well," I said, controlling my anger, "he is a slight annoyance. We cannot be silent any longer, Mr. Scott. The situation has gone far beyond reticence or apology, and through no action of ours. I am sorry you should be forced to witness it."

"You said no apology." Jonathan forced a smile. "Lady Clare—"

"Pray do not call me that; I wish it had never been my name!"

"There was a time when I might have called you Lucy; a time when I could, and did, say things I can no longer say to you."

"What has changed," I cried rebelliously, "except a formal name and an empty legal fiction?"

"That fiction rules our lives," Jonathan said quietly. "But if I cannot obey the dictates of—of emotion in speaking to you, my duty allows, nay, demands, that I give you the benefit of my knowledge of that legal fiction. Do you know what recourse the laws of this enlightened nation allow you against such acts as I have reluctantly witnessed?"

I shook my head. The repressed feeling under his formal words shook me, and his self-control filled me with admiration. At least I could try to control my own emotions and not make his task any more difficult than it was.

"It allows you no recourse," Jonathan said. His voice took on another note, and I sensed he was quoting. " 'By marriage, the husband and wife are one person in law; that is, the very being or legal existence of the woman is suspended during marriage, or at least is incorporated and consolidated into that of the husband. . . .' That is Blackstone, the foundation of English common law. You have no legal existence. Your husband has custody of your property and your person. Should you have children, he may determine the course of their lives, and you may not interfere. If under extreme pain and provocation you leave him, he may force you to return. Should you refuse, he may imprison you. If he does not want you back, he may divorce you, although you have no such right, whatever your provocation. If he divorces you, he retains the custody of your children and may prevent you from seeing them again. He retains your property; even the clothing you wear is not legally your own."

He fell silent; and I was silent too, from a kind of shock that had nothing to do with surprise. None of the facts he had stated surprised me; if I had not known them consciously, they had been part of my thinking for so long that I took them for granted. No; the shock lay in my reaction to hearing the facts stated so coldly and flatly. As a log may smolder sullenly upon a hearth for hours and then suddenly burst into flame . . .

"It is not fair," I said. "It is not right."

"No. And it will be changed; but not, perhaps, in your lifetime. Certainly not in time to help you in your present circumstances."

Jonathan glanced back over his shoulder at the ungainly form of the stranger.

"I did not tell you these things to anger you, or to recruit you for the secret army of females, as my mother calls it," he said, with a wry smile. "I spoke only because of my responsibility. Mr. Beam is the only male protector you have; and I am his deputy. As he would advise you, were he here, so I may advise you."

"I think he would not advise me as you do," I said, answering his smile.

"No; but he would remonstrate with Lord Clare, and that, for a number of reasons, I cannot do. In practice the situation is not so grim as

I have pictured it; but its mitigation comes from public opinion and private character, not from the law."

"Clare cares nothing for public opinion."

"That I can believe. You must depend, then, on his character—his notions of right and of honor. I have no high opinion, perhaps, of his honor; and yet I confess I find his behavior astonishing. I could picture him as cruel and brutal toward inferiors, cold and satirical toward his peers. But this drunken jealousy—this petty malice toward his wife, who bears his name—"

"I know," I said. "It is incomprehensible to me too. He was not always like this, and it is not like him."

"He has no—" Jonathan stopped, flushing.

"No," I said. "He has no cause for jealousy. Did you doubt that?"

"Lucy . . ." He turned toward me, holding out his hand. The impetuous movement and the color that flooded his face recalled the outspoken boy I had first met in Mr. Beam's office. It was a gesture full of meaning, conveying apology and a tacit reaffirmation of his belief in me—and another emotion I dared not name. Even as he made the gesture, he remembered; he did not need to glance back to remind me of the figure that followed us like a visible manifestation of Clare's suspicion. Jonathan's hand fell and we rode on in silence until, in an effort to find a less dangerous subject, I said,

"It must have been here that I lost my way the last time I rode Sultana."

"Oh, yes," Jonathan mumbled, still lost in his own thoughts. "I recall your husband mentioning it. What happened?"

I told him the story. I made light of it, but as he listened Jonathan's face lengthened, and when I mentioned the sound that had driven Sultana into flight, he looked most peculiar.

"A whistle, you say?"

"So it sounded. I suppose it was a bird."

"A bird," Jonathan muttered. "Yes . . . It must have been."

When we returned to the house we found Mrs. Andrews in hysterics. A domestic catastrophe had occurred. She was in such a state of red-faced chagrin that I was quite alarmed; but when she was finally induced to tell me what the trouble was, I burst into laughter.

There was an Aroma. That word was as close as Mrs. Andrews could bring herself to saying "smell." It had infested all the guest rooms, including the one assigned to Jonathan.

When I could stop laughing I started upstairs. Mrs. Andrews tried to hold me back, assuring me there was no need for my delicate nostrils to be affronted; they had cleaned and searched and inspected, yet the smell persisted, and nothing but time would cure it. I went on, all the same; and in the upper hall I met Jonathan, who had gone to investigate.

"No, don't go up there," he said, grinning broadly. "It is a phenomenon of a smell, I assure you; rather like all the drains gone wrong at once, or a profusion of dead bodies. Mrs. Andrews," he said, turning to her as she followed me, on the verge of tears, "I beg, don't let this distress you, it happens in the best of families. I remember visiting his Grace the Duke of Eastham, when a rat got behind the wainscoting. . . ."

As he admitted later, the story was quite apocryphal. But it served its purpose, which was to comfort Mrs. Andrews.

"Well, then," she said, sniffing a little, "it is kind of you, Mr. Scott, indeed it is. Of course your things have already been moved. His Lordship saw to that."

"His Lordship?" I asked. "I thought he had left for Edinburgh."

"Oh, he has, my lady. But he came back. . . . Oh, dear, I am so fuddled I don't know what I'm saying. . . ."

"His Lordship left before we set off on our ride," Jonathan said. He was no longer laughing. "He returned after we left. . . . He had, perhaps, forgotten something?"

"Yes, sir, that is just it. He had forgotten a paper, a business paper he said it was. He went up to see whether you had gone; that is how we discovered the—the—"

"Aroma," said Jonathan, straight-faced. "Yes, I am sorry I was unable to oblige his Lordship; he did not think it worth sending after me?"

"No, he said it was not important, whatever it was. But the—the—"

"Aroma," I said.

"Yes, my lady. Thank you. He was most vexed. He ordered Mr. Scott's things moved, and wished me to convey his apologies. . . ."

"Of course, of course," said Jonathan. "And where am I to go now?"

"The Green Room. If you will follow me, sir."

"Oh," I said. "You are next to me. You should be honored, Mr. Scott. That is the room usually reserved for visiting royalty!"

As always, with Clare gone the house relaxed, like a dignified lady who has removed her tight stays. I had never spent such a pleasant day. After dining, we went to the library. It was—how can I express it?—it was like exploring a new country with the help of a guide who knows every foot of ground. I had tried exploring alone; I had found nuggets of pleasure and improvements here and there, but had to wade through miles of incomprehensible swamp to find them. Jonathan led me straight to the gold. He found books he loved and read me excerpts that made me eager to read more; he looked at the volumes that had baffled me and suggested other, simpler texts that would unlock the mysteries of the more advanced. We did not speak of personal matters. We were in Clare's house, with Clare's servants about. Naturally the door of the library remained open while we were together in the room.

I asked Jonathan about one phrase that had intrigued me—his "secret army of women." He laughed heartily. He laughed or smiled whenever he spoke of his mother; it was not derision, but pure affection and delight. He did not agree with all she said, but he quoted her often—as he quoted Blackstone and Tacitus. That was a revelation to me, to hear a woman quoted as an authority on anything.

It was an astounding day altogether. Jonathan explained his mother's little joke, which even she found quite amusing, of a secret revolutionary army of women, ready to strike for their rights as the Greek women had done. Only instead of demanding the end of wars, they would demand a voice in making the world better in all ways.

I had never heard of Lysistrata, and Jonathan had to explain who she was and what she had done. (As I discovered later, he did a considerable amount of editing.) Then I told him how I had failed to find that quotation by Socrates to which his mother had referred. He found the book at once; it was in the original Greek, of course, so it was no wonder I had not been able to find it.

"'There is no occupation concerned with the management of social affairs which belongs either to woman or to man,'" he read. "'Every occupation is open to both, so far as their natures are concerned. We should not have one education for men and another for women, because the nature to be taken in hand is the same.'"

"How does it sound in Greek?" I asked.

Jonathan read. The great rolling sounds were like drums in the mind.

"I wanted to learn Greek," I said.

"According to Socrates, you should have been taught."

Mrs. Andrews had to call us twice when the tea tray was ready.

That night my mind felt the way my body did after I had taken much exercise. It ached, but it felt alive. I lay awake for a long time. As I was dropping off to sleep I remembered Clare's uncouth watchdog, and I smiled as I thought what an innocent evening we had spent, Jonathan and I. The most evil-minded spy could have found no harm in it.

I was wrong. There was no evil in our acts or words, but the damage had been done. Our minds had met; and for a woman, that is a temptation greater than any lure of the flesh.

I could not have slept for long when a sound woke me. I sat up in bed staring about the room. The fire had died down; a sullen red glow from the coals turned the shadows ominous colors. Then the sound came again, a weird, hollow howling. It came from outside—from the terrace.

I got out of bed and went to the window. Not once did I think of Jonathan; I had forgotten he was only the thickness of the wall away from me.

It was there, on the terrace. It moaned, and moved; it darted back and forth, with horrid sudden little movements. I found myself thinking what it would be like to have it dart at me, with groping arms; and I turned cold. But it could not get at me, it could not enter. . . . Even as the thought crossed my mind, the thing lifted its veiled head. It seemed to stare straight at my window. With an odd contorted twist of body and arms it darted to the side and passed from my sight. One last howl of menace or grief floated up to me.

Then I remembered the stair that led from the terrace to Clare's room.

If I had stopped to think I would have wondered why a supernatural creature needed steps in order to ascend. I was not thinking. I was too frightened. I ran to the hall door and threw it open, intending to summon help.

The door next to mine opened. Jonathan stepped out into the hall.

"I heard a noise," he said. "What in heaven's name—"

He was wearing a dark dressing gown. I had been too frightened to remember mine. My nightgown reached from chin to floor and was far more modest than my evening dress. But I was suddenly conscious of it, and of my flowing hair.

I don't know what it was that warned me—not, I fear, any sense of propriety or shame. I wanted him to hold me, protect me. . . . Suddenly I seemed to hear an inner voice, a wordless cry of alarm. I brushed past Jonathan and ran down the dimly lit hall to the top of the stairs. An ancient oriental ornament hung there; it was a heavy bronze disk or gong, adorned with carved figures of mythical beasts. Seizing the hammer that hung by it, I swung with all my strength; and the silence exploded. Before the echoes had died, Mrs. Andrews came running down the east corridor, her nightcap all askew; the house servants tumbled down the upper stairs, crying out in alarm. And then, from the shadows of the lower hall, came another figure, stick in hand, still wearing his traveling coat. It was Clare.

I clung to Mrs. Andrews, gasping out my wild tale.

"I was afraid," I whimpered. "I could only think of making a noise and summoning help. . . ." I raised my eyes and gave a startled cry. "Clare! It must have been you I saw, then, on the terrace. I feel so foolish! If I had known you were returning earlier than you said . . ."

"My business took less time than I expected," Clare said in an expressionless voice. "I don't believe you could have seen me, however. I came straight to the front door."

"The White Lady," Mrs. Andrews gasped.

"Don't be a superstitious fool," Clare said sharply. "There is no such thing. If her Ladyship is susceptible to hallucinations . . ."

"It was no hallucination." Jonathan came down the hall. "Or if it was, I too am subject to them. There was something on the terrace. I caught only a glimpse of it from my window, but it was certainly there."

"Indeed? As a confirmed rationalist, you ought to have gone down to investigate."

"I was about to do so when Lady Clare sounded the alarm." Jonathan gave an exaggerated shiver. "It was far more startling than any apparition; I feel shaken even yet."

"I am so sorry," I said. "I had forgotten you were in that room."

Jonathan bowed. It would have been comical if it had not been in deadly earnest; one part of my distracted brain admired the skill of our playacting while another part contemplated incredulously the reason for its necessity. It might be accidental that Clare's unexpected, unannounced arrival coincided almost to the second with the most recent appearance of an impossible apparition. But coincidence became strained beyond belief when I remembered that another inexplicable accident had caused Jonathan's removal to a room in close proximity to mine. Earlier, I had felt like someone walking a tightrope in my relations with my husband. Now I knew that the abyss below that tenuous support was deeper and darker than I had supposed.

II

The following hours were like a truce between battles. I waited, watching Clare; and he bided his time. His mood was pensive; he seemed abstracted and indifferent. To my relief—and disappointment—Jonathan made no attempt to speak with me alone. He followed Clare into the library after breakfast, remaining with him most of the morning; and he emerged from his tête-à-tête with a furrowed brow.

At dinner his conversation turned to superstition and tales of ghosts and hauntings. Inevitably, the family legends of the Clares were mentioned; and, with a satirical glance at me, Clare spoke of the White Lady.

Jonathan's reaction was skeptical.

"There are altogether too many White Ladies," he objected. "Supposing that such a thing could exist, one might suspect that the story has a single origin, and has been adopted by other families in search of sensation."

Clare was visibly annoyed at the suggestion that his ancestors had been reduced to stealing other people's ghosts. He gave a long, circumstantial account of the appearances of the White Lady to members of his family, ending with my own experience, in the garden.

"Hmm," said Jonathan, unimpressed. "Very interesting, my lord; but hardly evidence. I am afraid I have the legal habit of mind and cannot accept such accounts without substantiation. With all due respect to her Ladyship—"

"You discount the evidence of your own senses?"

"Oh, that." Jonathan waved a contemptuous hand. "A lost, bleating sheep; a housemaid, out for a breath of air—"

"What would you consider evidence, then?"

"Oh—a *raison d'être*, let us say. To remain in a state of limbo, haunting a drafty house and cold garden, a spirit must have a strong reason—a desire for revenge on the family or a strong attachment. Why does your White Lady haunt the Clares?"

His humorous tone irritated Clare, as it was no doubt meant to do. He replied haughtily, with a glance at me.

"Not a tactful question, sir, since often such apparitions presage danger to those who are unfortunate enough to see them."

"Only if one is a believer," Jonathan said. "I am sure her Ladyship is too sensible to believe in such superstitions. At any rate," he added, smiling, "I must share her danger, since I too saw the specter last night."

After I had left them to their wine I went into the parlor and took up my embroidery; but I had determined I would not remain there if they sat long at table. There was nothing to prevent Clare from coming to my room, but at least any abuse he chose to administer there would be in private.

It was a gusty windy evening; I could see the branches of the trees lashing like live things straining to break free. As I glanced out the window I saw that, despite the weather, someone had come to call. The wind seemed to seize him and fling him at the door.

Martin went to answer the bell and I expected she would show the newcomer into the dining room. He must have asked for me, for in a moment he appeared in the doorway.

He looked very fresh and healthy, his hair ruffled by the wind and his cheeks glowing. I rose to greet him with real pleasure, and sent Martin to tell her master that Mr. Fleetwood had called.

As he advanced to meet me, he caught a glimpse of himself in the mirror, and burst out laughing.

"What a figure to call on a lady! My apologies; I had not realized how windblown I was."

"It becomes you," I said, smiling. "Sit by the fire, you must be chilled."

"No, I enjoy the wind and the exhilaration it brings. The condition is purely physical, no doubt, arising from fresh air and heated blood; but I always feel as if I were engaged in a struggle of will—myself against nature—and when I defeat her, even in so slight a matter as walking in the wind, I am transfigured!"

I made some slight reply. Then he grew sober.

"Edward will come soon, I expect; before he does, may I venture to inquire how—how you are feeling these days?"

"Somewhat improved," I said, imitating his oblique manner of speech; the servants were all about. "But I fear the underlying cause is not really better."

"Indeed I am sorry to hear that. I had hoped—"

"It was better, much better, after you—after I spoke with you before." His sympathetic look and melting eye were too much for me. I burst out, "Something is wrong, Mr. Fleetwood, very wrong. I cannot fathom what it can be, that is what makes me desperate. There is no reason, nor even any consistency in his behavior—"

"Hush!" The word was firmly but gently spoken; he raised his slender hand. "I understand your distress, but we may be overheard. Shall I try again? Heaven knows I am only His unworthy servant, but—"

"I would be so grateful."

"Hush," he said again, with the same gesture; and I heard the footsteps approaching. When the two men entered, Mr. Fleetwood was chatting idly of music.

Clare performed the introductions, and the two men greeted one another in characteristic fashion. As soon as everyone was seated I remembered my manners, and asked after Miss Fleetwood.

The vicar looked grave.

"She does not improve as she ought. I have been

thinking I may be forced to try the effect of a more salubrious climate this winter. Italy, perhaps."

"By all means," Clare said. "Don't concern yourself about the parish, Jack; if there is the slightest question of her health, spend the entire winter abroad."

The idea distressed me. I had not realized to what extent I depended on the vicar. I must have looked upset, for. Jonathan gave me a puzzled glance, and Clare said sharply, "Such a face, Lucy! I know you will miss your friend; but you must not be so childish. Her health is more important than your pleasure, surely."

The irony in his voice was so heavy that Jonathan heard it too.

"Ladies are inclined to dote on friends," he said, addressing Clare, but looking intently at me. "No doubt her Ladyship and Miss Fleetwood share many confidences, as ladies do?"

"I have not been as good a friend to Miss Fleetwood as I should have liked," I said steadily. "I had hoped our acquaintance would improve in the future."

"As it would have done," the vicar remarked. "Had it not been for this unfortunate illness . . ."

"I regret that I shall be unable to make her acquaintance," Jonathan said.

"Oh, my dear sir, so do I," said Mr. Fleetwood, with an engaging smile. "She is—you will allow for a brother's prejudice, I am sure—but she really is a remarkable creature. Beauty, intelligence, and that indefinable charm of manner which only a true lady possesses.... Ah, but her Ladyship will call me partial."

"I hope you are," I said, with a smile. "I can think of no more charming quality in a brother. But indeed Miss Fleetwood cannot be praised too highly. I have never seen such a lovely face; and although I have not spoken long or often with her, the beauties of her mind are as outstanding as those of her person."

"That is quite a tribute," Jonathan said. He was not looking at me; he was watching Clare.

The next subject of conversation was not so happy. Mr. Fleetwood was the innocent cause of the unpleasantness; he mentioned casually that he had seen Tom in the village and that the boy had asked him for employment.

Clare's face darkened.

"Is that fellow still about? I told him . . ." He turned on me. "You have encouraged him, I suppose. Have you met him? Seen him? Have you dared to disobey my orders?"

The unexpectedness and injustice of the accusation left me speechless. Before I could recover myself, Mr. Fleetwood spoke.

"Your pardon, Edward," he said, with quiet dignity. "But I cannot permit such language to be used to a lady in my presence. You cannot have any reason to suppose Lady Clare disrespectful of your wishes; and if you did, you should not admonish her in public. I must request that you apologize."

I held my breath. To my amazement, Clare shriveled before the other man's steady gaze.

"Sorry," he muttered. "A mistake."

"Enough," Mr. Fleetwood said gaily. "We all have moments of choler, do we not? It is forgotten."

After a time Mr. Fleetwood took his leave and Clare offered him the carriage, which he declined with another of his infectious laughs.

"Your company, by all means," he said cheerfully. "But to huddle inside a stuffy box on such a night would be a crime. Come, gentlemen, and walk with me; the air will blow the wine out of your heads and quicken your brains for an evening of chess and conversation—if you will do me that honor."

The invitation was accepted. Clare took the vicar off to the library to get a book he had promised him, and Jonathan lingered. As soon as the others were out of earshot, he bent over me and said in a low voice,

"What is his name?"

"Name?" I was bewildered. "You mean Mr. Fleetwood?"

Jonathan's brows drew together and he made a little irritated sound, like an old lady scolding.

"Does your mind always turn to that popinjay? The boy—the groom your dainty admirer mentioned. What is his name?"

I told him. His rudeness did not annoy me; I found it rather amusing.

The vicar's remonstrance had little effect. Clare came home that night much the worse for liquor, and he continued to drink heavily all next day. I kept out of his way by pleading a headache. Toward evening, when Clare had shut himself up in the library, I ventured out of the house, feeling the need of air. I had no sooner left the shrubbery when the ill-favored Londoner appeared. He touched his cap with the same slouching insolence he had shown before, and made no attempt to move out of my way. When I turned, he followed me. With Clare inside the house and his Spy—there was no other word for him—outside, there was nowhere to hide except in my own room. And by the end of the day I was forced to recognize that even this was no refuge.

I was preparing for bed when I heard Clare come up. It would have been hard not to hear him; he was shouting at the top of his lungs.

Anna was brushing my hair. Her hands stopped moving as the voice came nearer. In the mirror our eyes met. I was moved, not only by the silent sympathy that flashed between us, but by our helplessness. She was servant and I was wife, yet so far as the man outside the door was concerned, there was little difference in our status.

When the door burst open I could not hold back a cry of alarm. I had never seen my husband in such a state of disarray. He was in his shirt sleeves, his cravat askew and his collar undone, baring his throat. He stood in the doorway for a moment, studying me with glittering eyes; then he turned his head and called out,

"Goo' night, goo' night! Sweet dreams, ol' fellow; tha's all you can do is dream, poor ol' fellow, but not me, I've better things to do tonight. . . ."

Laughing, he advanced into the room. His hand swiped at the door, but missed. The door did not close; and all through the scene that followed I suffered more from my awareness of that open door than from anything he did to me.

I stood up, backing away as he came toward me. I was aware of Anna standing by the dressing table, with the ivory-backed hairbrush dangling from her hand.

He lunged for me. I tried to move away, but my foot betrayed me and as I stumbled he caught me by the sleeve of my robe. The cloth tore but did not give way; with a twist of his arm he pulled me toward him.

If I had kept my wits about me, I would have submitted. The situation was bad enough; my struggles only made it worse. But I could not help it. I was seized by a violent revulsion, and I fought as I would have fought against touching a snake. My resistance angered him. He drew back his hand and struck me across the face.

It was not really a hard blow, but it made my lip bleed and my head spin around. I heard Clare give a start and a loud curse. He released me, and I fell in an undignified huddle onto the bed.

Clare had turned to confront Anna, who crouched before him. The hairbrush, lifted for another blow, and the hand with which Clare was rubbing his head, told what had happened. The greenish pallor of Anna's face showed that she realized, too late, to what enormity her loyalty toward me had led her. She made a whimpering sound and dropped the brush.

Her sacrifice had not been in vain. Not only had she freed me, but the blow seemed to have sobered Clare. He stood motionless for so long I thought he was paralyzed. Then he spoke, in the deadliest voice I had ever heard him use.

"Get out. If you are in this house in the morning, I will take my riding crop to you."

"My lord," Anna whispered. "I did not—"

"I will give you until tomorrow morning to leave the village," Clare went on, as if she had not spoken. "If I see your face again, I will place a complaint before the magistrates. Should you be ignorant of the penalty for a servant who strikes her master, I suggest you inquire of Mr. Scott, who is, no doubt, lurking safely there in the hallway."

I got to my feet, my hand pressed against my mouth. My lips were beginning to hurt.

"She did it to help me," I mumbled. "I will beg you, if I must; don't do this to her."

Clare turned; as soon as his eyes left her, Anna ran for the door.

Clare did not look at me. It was a terrible thing, to see how he tried to look, and could not; the very sight of me was unendurable to him. He started twice to speak, but his voice broke—with sheer fury, I think—and after a moment he walked quite steadily to the door and closed it after him. I heard the key turn in the lock.

Chapter
14

THERE WAS WATER IN THE JUG BY THE BED, BUT I wondered, as I moodily contemplated that receptacle, how long I could go without eating. Or would Clare have food brought to me? Bread and water—stale bread and water—were the customary staples for a prisoner, as I recalled.

It was morning, a dreary, blustery morning, with clouds rushing across the heavens like frightened animals. I had slept, finally, from sheer exhaustion, and I slept late. The first thing I did upon awakening was try the door. It was still locked. I was not much surprised.

My lip looked frightful, all swollen up like an abscess, but it did not pain me too much. I suspected it would, if I ever got anything to eat. The worst aches came from a set of bruises I could not even remember acquiring during the excitement of the encounter; there was a fine group of them on my shoulder and upper arm, and a welt along my jaw. I examined them in the mirror with dispassionate curiosity. I did not need Jonathan's law knowledge, or the great Mr. Blackstone, to tell me that this latest act of Clare's did not alter my situation. I did not doubt that if I should ever display such bruises to a magistrate he would simply give Clare a lecture on kindness to inferiors and me a sterner lecture on submissiveness.

Having nothing better to do, I settled down by the window with a glass of water. The morning wore on, and nothing of interest occurred, except that my neglected appetite began to make itself felt. I had had no breakfast and it was now approaching luncheon time. I took another sip of water, and then sat up. Williams was bringing Clare's horse around to the front of the house, and shortly Clare himself appeared.

He stood for a moment looking about him, drawing on his gloves in a leisurely fashion. He was impeccably groomed, in a splendid new coat and cravat; a diamond sparkled on his shirt front.

I shrank back as his eyes approached my window, and when I ventured to peek out again he was riding off down the road.

If I had not seen him ride off I would have looked for a hiding place when I heard the sound of the key turning in the lock. Knowing Clare was gone, I had only one interest—not so much *who* stood at the door but *what* he or she was bringing. I was very hungry.

The door creaked open, and there stood Mrs.

Andrews. Her face was red with emotion, and at the sight of me she began to cry.

"Oh, my lady! Oh, my lady . . ."

I found myself in the absurd position of consoling Mrs. Andrews for my bruises.

"Now, now," I said briskly, patting her shoulder. "You would serve me much better if you would get me some food. Unless his Lordship has ordered that I be starved."

The strangest look came over the housekeeper's face. She even forgot to cry.

"His Lordship left no orders with respect to you, my lady. I heard, last night, from Anna, what had happened. The girl was in such a state I thought she would fall into a fit. I have never seen—"

"Yes, yes," I said impatiently. I was concerned about Anna and had every intention of inquiring after her; but at that particular moment I did not want Mrs. Andrews' powers of concentration further distracted. "Did his Lordship say nothing to you?"

"Not a word," said Mrs. Andrews solemnly. "This morning he came down cheerful as a lark. He was in the best of spirits, planning his trip; I suppose he thought you had breakfast in your room, as you often do, for he did not mention you until he was about to leave and then he said— now let me see, what was it exactly—yes, he said: 'Her Ladyship is a slug-a-bed this morning, Mrs. Andrews; be sure she eats a hearty luncheon, if she has not breakfasted. Tell her I will return tomorrow or, at the latest, the next day.' He went off humming, my lady."

"It is incredible," I muttered, forgetting my status and speaking to her as woman to woman. "Mrs. Andrews, what do you suppose is wrong with him? You see what he has done—"

"Yes, and I stand here babbling," said Mrs. Andrews. "Sit down, my lady, and let me tend to you. I'll tell you what it is," she continued, leading me to a chair, "it is the drink. I've seen it before, to my sorrow, it is one of the troubles women must suffer from. 'Strong drink is raging,' the Scripture says, and a truer word was never spoken; it can turn a good man mad. Of course his Lordship did not mean to do it. He was such a dear little boy—"

"I am sure that is true," I said. "But it has no bearing on the present case, unfortunately. What shall I do?"

To my surprise, the old lady looked askance.

"My lady . . . if I might venture . . ."

"Say anything you like to me. When have I ever reproached you for speaking frankly?"

"But this . . . it is a delicate thing, and not my place . . . Only, you have no mother, and so I thought . . ."

"Pray go on," I said, wondering.

"It is a great trial for women, certainly," Mrs. Andrews mumbled. She was very busy with a pot of ointment, and did not meet my eyes. "Especially to so young and delicate a lady . . . But it is a cross, my lady, that must be borne, woman's punishment for the sin of Eve, you know. A man, a gentleman—even a well-bred gentleman—well, after all, my lady, he is a man, whatever else he may be, and there is nothing a woman can do to prevent it!"

She ended in a rush of words; she was purple with embarrassment and anxiety. I might have laughed, if she had not been so much in earnest— and if her words had not held such unconscious irony. She thought Clare had turned to drink because *I* rejected *him*. She had reason; no one could know that his advances the previous night, before an impartial witness, had been the sole such incident in our marriage.

"Thank you, Mrs. Andrews," I said. "I will think over your good advice."

I went down to luncheon. I was shy at seeing Jonathan after what had happened, and—I am ashamed to say—I was a little angry with him. It was illogical of me to resent his not coming to my rescue, when any interference on his part would have worsened my situation, as well as his ability to help me in the future. Yet when has emotion ever been logical? Mrs. Andrews had rubbed soothing ointment into my bruises and reduced the swelling on my mouth with cold water. I had, however, resisted her suggestion that I cover the bruise on my cheek with rice powder.

The look on Jonathan's face, when he saw me, made me ashamed of my petty trick. He went quite pale.

"We will eat at once, if you don't mind," I said quickly, to prevent an outburst. "I am so hungry."

It was fortunate that I was hungry, otherwise I would have found it impossible to carry on a casual conversation during that meal. Jonathan hardly spoke, and touched almost no food. The air between us was heavy with unspoken words. After dinner I suggested a walk. Even with Clare's hideous henchman following, we could talk more freely outside the house.

It was gray and windy; the wind tugged at the veil I had tied over my hair, and blew my cloak about. As I had expected, the lurking figure was waiting. It fell in behind us. The cold air seemed to calm Jonathan. He strode along beside me in silence until we were out of sight of the house. Then, gesturing me to remain where I was, he turned back toward our follower.

I watched the ensuing conversation with interest and some concern, but it did not end, as I half expected, in violence. Instead the man grinned evilly and took something from Jonathan's hand. He went off without a backward glance, and Jonathan returned to me.

"What did you say to him? He will tell Clare you sent him away."

"He will not dare admit he was bribed to leave his post," Jonathan said coolly. "I thought I recognized him; we met once, in the ring, and it seems I made an impression on him. No, I think we are safe from Master Sam. I had to be able to speak with you, Lucy, without fear of being overheard. I have a strange feeling that we may not have many more opportunities."

"Why do you say that? You are—you are leaving? Or do you have a presentiment, a warning—"

"No, no." Jonathan smiled, and then became serious. "You are falling into one of his traps when you say that; it would please him to see you cowering and terrified of his specters and ghosts. But that is only one of his traps, Lucy. If I could see the reason for them, I would not be so afraid."

"You, afraid?"

"I have acted a heroic part, have I not?" Jonathan said bitterly. "I have done hard tasks in my life, but I never had a harder thing to do than stand by last night, hearing him. . . . But Lucy, I know that is what he wants! Several times I have tried to take my leave, but he detains me here, for a purpose which is still obscure. So long as we are in ignorance of his motive, we are safest in resisting the roles he is trying to thrust upon us. Do you understand?"

He felt it, very deeply; in his eagerness he took me by the shoulders and turned me to face him. Gentle as he was, he touched the sore places on my arm, and I winced with pain. Jonathan saw my look; with a low exclamation he caught me in his arms. I could hear the pounding of his heart under my cheek, and the way his voice shook as he muttered,

"It is too much for me, I can't do it; no man could. If he touches you again—"

"No," I said, without moving; I felt as if all my life I had been searching for this moment and this place, in his arms. "You are right in what you say, and you have seen his most dangerous trap. He wants you to attack him. He wants to drive us both to some desperate act. Why? That is what we must think about." And then, as his arms loosed their hold, I caught at his coat front. "Only—only hold me for another moment, before we begin thinking."

With a sound that was half laugh and half groan he complied; we stood locked together, with the wind blowing my cloak about us both. The open moors stretched out all around, and anyone might have seen us; but for a few seconds I did not care if the whole world saw.

"Very well," I said, after a time. "You may begin to think now."

I put myself away from him, and he let me go. His face was drawn as though with actual physical pain.

"I can't think reasonably any longer, not where you are concerned. I want to do mad things— snatch you up and run away with you, to a place where you will be safe."

"You think I am in danger?"

"No, no." He shook his head vigorously. "You see? I am in such a state I let my wild fancies run away with me, and frighten you. . . . Let us walk; it will clear my head, and I will tell you what I think, and you will tell me when I am wrong."

He took my arm and we started off along the path.

"Your husband's anger seems to arise from jealousy," Jonathan began. "At least that is how an outsider would interpret his behavior. I know you have given him no cause—"

"No cause," I interrupted. "But there was an incident. . . . It sounds foolish, but I want you to know it."

I told him about Fernando. I had long since lost all feeling except contempt for that creature, and yet it was extraordinarily difficult to tell Jonathan about him. I could not look him in the face, but kept my eyes fixed on the rusty bracken on which we walked.

"Clare knew of this?" Jonathan asked. "Surely your aunt did not—"

"She ought not to have told him, but she may have done. I have the feeling that he does know, and has for some time."

"It is unfortunate. Foolish and trivial as it was, to a man of Clare's temperament the thought that you preferred another—and that other a lowly music teacher—"

"He married me."

"Yes, but it might prey on his mind, particularly if—"

"If what?" I inquired innocently.

"If some later incident should confirm his suspicion."

"I don't know what you mean."

Jonathan took a long breath.

"I have talked to the groom, young Tom. There is a rumor in the village that he was dismissed because your husband suspected that he—and you—"

I knew then how an innocent man might be convicted of a crime he had never committed. I must have looked the picture of guilt; the blood rushed to my face and my limbs grew weak.

"No," I said, in a voice that did not sound like my own. "No, not even Clare could think . . . He's a boy, a little—"

"He is sixteen. Only a year younger than you. No, Lucy, don't pull away from me; can you suppose for one instant that I believe this slander? I may tell you that few of your friends in the village believe it."

"There was opportunity," I said, calming myself with an effort. "That was Clare's doing—he insisted I have a groom with me when I went out. It was very natural, since I didn't know the paths. . . ."

"Good," Jonathan said approvingly. "This is what we must do—consider the dangers and not lose ourselves in righteous anger. As you say, the thing is possible; and it is possible that Clare would develop a kind of monomania on the subject. Don't you see, Lucy—if he does believe this, his treatment of you becomes explicable. It is even fairly mild. He does not mistreat you unless he is intoxicated, and any judge would consider him justified in drinking to forget his fear of his wife's infidelity."

"Judge," I repeated, horrified. "Are you thinking in such terms as that?"

"I am considering all possibilities. If he should threaten you physically—"

"He has struck me."

"I know exactly what he has done to you," Jonathan said, in a voice that made me shiver. "And if I were able to exchange ten years of my life for the chance of returning those blows . . . Well, but now I am talking like a hero in a silly novel. I must talk and think like a solicitor. And from that viewpoint I must tell you that he has done nothing which he is not entitled to do, under the circumstances which he would certainly plead."

I was silent. There was nothing to say.

"I spoke with Tom about your accident on the moor," Jonathan went on. "He tells a rather strange story. A message called him away that day, to a person to whom he feels an obligation even greater than that which he feels for you. He will not tell me who sent for him; it is a girl, I suppose, and contrary to the prejudices of our aristocrats, delicacy is not limited to the upper classes. What is important is that the message was a counterfeit. It was not dispatched by the person whose name was signed to it."

"That is strange."

"More than strange."

"Oh, I know," I burst out. "I know what you are thinking. I have had similar thoughts, when I was frightened. But they make no sense. No one has any cause to hate me; and my adventure on the moor could not have been designed to harm me: I might have been killed, it is true. There are bogs and crevices; the horse might have thrown me onto my head. But no one planning evil would have left so much to chance."

Jonathan nodded; I could see the same objections had occurred to him.

"I believe there is something I ought to tell you," he said. "I can't see how the knowledge could help you just now, but one never knows. It concerns your marriage settlement."

"You told me once I ought to understand it. If I had insisted then—"

"It would have made no difference. Mr. Beam respects one woman's good understanding, but he regards my mother as some people regard a well-trained dog; she is the exception that proves the rule of the general inferiority of the species. Yet the subject is not difficult, when it is stripped of legal quibbles. It amounts to this: On your marriage, your property was divided into three parts. One was made over to your husband. He had complete control of both income and capital. This part . . ." He hesitated, and then went on. "This part has been spent, to settle Clare's huge debts and to clear the title of the estate.

"The second portion was settled on you. This money too is gone. You signed it over to Clare several months ago. What he has done with it I do not know; but the amount spent on refurbishing the house has been enormous, and there may have been other debts.

"The third portion, by far the largest, was put in trust for—for your heirs. The income is to be enjoyed by your husband, but he cannot dispose of the property from which that income derives without the consent of Mr. Beam. I see by your face that you anticipate what I am about to say. It was indeed this question that brought me here. The second paper you signed requested Mr. Beam to release this vast property to your husband's control. Mr. Beam has absolutely refused to sanction such a step. He holds strong views on family succession and the rights to a potential male heir."

"I see." I avoided his eyes. "And if—if there should be no heir?"

"That is a possibility Mr. Beam will never admit," Jonathan said dryly, unaware of my real meaning. "The income is Clare's in any case; the agreement merely prevents him from dissipating the property until his son inherits, in the normal course of time."

I did not reply; I was thinking. I could not help but connect this news with Clare's avoidance of me; and yet I could not see what bearing it could have. Unless . . . The idea was preposterous and repulsive. But I had to ask. I found it hard to speak, my mouth was suddenly so dry.

"What if I should die without having children? What would happen to the money then?"

"Women cannot make wills," Jonathan said bitterly. "Not unless that right is specifically guaranteed them by the marriage settlement; and Mr. Beam is the last man to suggest such a radical procedure. The money would go to your husband, of course, and . . . Lucy!"

He stopped short, facing me. We had climbed a slight hill and the wind pulled the veil from my head and tore my hair loose from its pins. It had grown since my illness and was now long enough to touch my shoulders; it rose from my head in a cloud, like wings trying to lift me from the ground. A lock brushed Jonathan's face, and he caught his breath.

"I am mad with worry," he said tightly. "I am thinking thoughts I dare not utter. Lucy, is there anything I do not know—any incident, any word that might confirm my insane, groundless suspicion? For if there is—if there is a single solid fact to confirm this madness—then you must come with me, today, and escape from that house!"

"What would happen," I said quietly, "if I did come?"

"I would take you straight to London, to Mr. Beam, and we could tell him—"

"He would send me back. I don't believe the thing you fear, Jonathan. Do you think Mr. Beam would admit such an idea about a man like Clare?"

"Your aunt would not help you?"

"She would lock me in a room until Clare came to fetch me. No one will help us, Jonathan. And if we did defy them, if I hid, like a criminal escaping the law—you would suffer. Mr. Beam would dismiss you, he would have no choice. You would never find employment in your profession. It would ruin you. Even if Clare gave me up—divorced me—you would still be ruined. He is a vindictive man; he would see that you paid for interfering with his property."

"I would risk that, Lucy, if you would let me."

"I know you would." The sharp wind brought the tears to my eyes and I brushed them away, angrily; I would not have Jonathan suppose I was using this last, despicable woman's weapon. "I will not let you. There is no such proof as you ask for. It may be that your first idea is right, that Clare is jealous. If so, my duty, and my sole recourse, is to convince him he is wrong, and so win his regard."

"There is something you haven't told me," Jonathan said. "I can tell by your face."

"If so, it is not a matter that confirms your fears,"

I said, flushing. "On the contrary. His character combines delicacy and pride to a high degree. If he thought I truly disliked him, it would explain why he does not—why he has not—"

"Lucy, what are you saying? Do you mean Clare has not . . . that you are husband and wife in name only?"

Jonathan took me by the shoulders. I put my hands up to hold him off. If I let him hold me again, if I let him kiss me, there would be no more talk. I would not have the strength to resist the course I wanted so desperately to take—the course that would ruin him.

"I should not have told you. I have no right to discuss such things."

"He must be mad," Jonathan said.

Perhaps I ought to have been offended; instead his candor filled me with amused delight. He saw my look; his eyes narrowed with rueful laughter and for a moment we stood looking at one another in that perfect understanding that is so rare even between lovers.

"But it is inexplicable," Jonathan insisted. "There is something in what you say of Clare's character. But, Lucy, I am a man; and I find this incredible. Unless he has . . . that is . . ."

"I know what you mean," I said, as he paused in embarrassment. "Poor Jonathan, I fear I am destroying all your pretty ideas about the innocence of females. With such a mother as yours you cannot think we are utter fools; even the girls in school knew about mistresses and illegitimate children."

"What a world it is," Jonathan muttered; my effort to speak cheerfully had not amused him. "We preach chastity aloud, and go out by night to destroy it wherever we can. And think, in our folly, that the two worlds can be kept apart. . . . You are right, Lucy. I should be ashamed of treating you like a child. I will leave off doing so. Does Clare go frequently to York and Edinburgh? He would hardly lower himself to an alliance with one of the village girls."

"Not *that* often, no."

"I confess, then, to an increased interest in the beautiful Miss Fleetwood."

I shook my head.

"If you had met her, you would not entertain such an idea for a moment. Oh, I thought of her, all the more so because they were childhood sweethearts. But it is impossible; she would never consent to an illicit attachment."

Jonathan looked skeptical, and I laughed.

"You men! Very well; if you feel like a longish walk, we will stroll toward the vicarage. Her brother mentioned that she sometimes walks out, in the morning, near the house. Perhaps we will be fortunate enough to meet her, and then I will see your doubts destroyed."

He assented, and we walked on. The wind was chilly, but I scarcely felt it; I was filled with the oddest mixture of happiness and bitter pain. This might well be the last time we could be alone together; certainly our conversation had convinced me of the impossibility of any permanent relationship between us. The censure of the world could strike down even the innocent; I well knew the punishment it would inflict on any man who defied its rules. Jonathan's promising career, his hopes of service to the poor, would end if I went to him. His mother depended on him for support, and I would be able to bring nothing to him, for Clare would never let me go if it meant losing a penny of the fortune that was in his control. We might have children. . . . The thought made me catch my breath. Yet through the bitter knowledge, the simple fact of being with him was joy enough.

The grove of trees surrounding the vicarage came into view and Jonathan sighed deeply, as if he, like myself, were being forced to withdraw from a brief interval of peace.

"This fellow Fleetwood," he said abruptly. "Can he be trusted?"

"Why—what makes you ask that? He is a clergyman; he came to my assistance, as you saw. . . ."

"I can believe in Clare's being jealous, because I am too," Jonathan confessed, with a smile. "I hated the man because he was doing for you what I dared not do."

"Any word from you would have made Clare worse."

"I know that; it did not relieve my jealousy! I should be glad—and in my heart I am glad—that you have such a defender. Clare seems to heed his opinions."

"They have been friends for many years." I went on to relate what Mrs. Andrews had told me of the relation between the three young people. Jonathan listened attentively.

"It is a sad story," he agreed. "And only too typical of the social ills of our time. To think that worldly pride could interfere with true attachment! From what you say, the lady is as admirable in character as she is beautiful. I am quite curious to see her."

"You are in luck, then," I said, gesturing.

She was walking slowly, so preoccupied with thoughts of her own that she did not see us until we were almost upon her. That was as well, I thought, seeing the startled movement she made when she did catch sight of us. If she had been able to retreat without rudeness, I felt sure she would have done so.

She wore a heavy fur-trimmed cloak with fur around the hood; the soft dark stuff framed her face and softened its outlines. It was thinner and paler than it had been when I last saw her. Her great eyes seemed to fill most of her face.

I heard the catch of Jonathan's breath, and then it was my turn to feel jealousy. She was still beautiful; illness and suffering could not rob that face of its charm.

I introduced them and stood by as Jonathan's captivation was completed by the lady's exquisite manners. He stuttered like a schoolboy, the silly thing. I then asked about the plan of going abroad and hoped that her health had improved to such an extent that we would not be deprived of her society that winter.

"We have not quite settled our plans," she said. "I am torn; I love this bleak barren country and my snug little house."

"Italy would suit you," Jonathan said, still staring. "The art, the picture galleries, the ruins—"

"Yes," she interrupted eagerly, a faint flush coming into her face. "I yearn to see it. Art is my passion, and reproductions convey only a poor impression of the reality."

They went on to speak of paintings, and then of books, while I stood by sulking. She had always made me feel ignorant, but I had never felt the contrast so keenly, knowing Jonathan's admiration of intelligence. Yet learning had not affected the delicacy of her feelings; when Jonathan mentioned several novels written by women, she frowned slightly.

"Miss Austen's books are charming, it is true. But that unwomanly creature, who has even taken a man's name—she is no credit to our sex, Mr. Scott. It surprises me that such books are published. They are immoral."

"But very well written."

"What does that matter, when the content is so pernicious? Her demands for greater freedom for women are ridiculous. And the unregulated emotion, the almost masculine passion—"

She broke off, flushing.

"Women feel no such emotions?" Jonathan asked.

"They feel them," she said quietly. "They feel them all the more for suppressing them, as they are required to do by the rules of God and society, and their own natures."

"We are keeping you standing in the cold," I said sharply. "Mr. Scott—"

We took our leave; when we had reached the edge of the grove Jonathan stopped and looked back.

She was standing where we had left her. The wind had dropped, and the heavy folds of her cloak hung unmoving. With the muffling hood hiding her head she did not look like a woman at all, but like a pillar or a tall-standing stone, featureless and inhuman.

I jabbed Jonathan rather sharply, and he started like someone waking from a dream. He took my arm and we walked on till a slight rise in the ground hid the vicarage and the trees and the motionless figure from our sight.

"Well?" I said.

"She is too beautiful," Jonathan said slowly. "A face like that is destined for tragedy. It commands men, and leads them to extravagant follies. Perhaps that is why she hides herself here. With such a commonplace mind—"

"What?" I cried, astonished. "She is brilliant!"

"Well taught," Jonathan said coolly. "No doubt she shared her brother's tutor. Certainly she has read widely and understands what she has read. But there is no originality, no flash of imagination, no humor. Now," he added, with a sidelong glance at me, "have I regained favor, or must I abuse the lady further?"

I began to laugh, in spite of myself, and Jonathan grinned.

"What I said was true, however. You laugh at such absurd things, Lucy! You can even see the ironic humor in your present uncomfortable situation. You laugh, you smile, when you think of loving. That is how loving should be. And that is why I love you, because of your laughter and your courage and your undisciplined imagination. Now, now! How dare you cry, after I have just said I loved you for your laughter?"

"You never said it before," I said, sniffling and laughing at the same time—a deplorable combination.

"I will never say it again, probably. I had to do so once. And you? You must show that courage I credit you with. Say it!"

"I love you."

"So, then," he said, after a long silence. "We have considered the evidence—which has nothing to do with those three words—and what conclusion have we reached?"

"There is nothing we can do," I said, almost indifferently; and I added, because I could not help saying it, and because it was the only thing just then that really mattered, "Is this what it feels like, to drink too much wine? This illogical joy, this happiness that is unrelated to reality? If so, I can understand why gentlemen get drunk."

"Don't," Jonathan muttered. "Don't say such things."

"I thought it might help," I said, ". . . for you to know that whatever happens . . . if I never see you again . . . this hour makes it all worthwhile."

"I am glad it does for you," Jonathan said violently. "I wish I could feel the same. It doesn't help me to realize that the best hope for your future happiness is in an act that will drive *me* to drink when I think about it."

It was several seconds before I realized what he meant, and some of my fine rapture evaporated.

"What else can I do? I can't—I can't make overtures to him, not now. . . . But if he wants me . . ."

"I'll tell you one thing," Jonathan said. "If he doesn't, you will be in serious trouble. The situation is so abnormal it can't continue."

I stopped, pulling my arm away from his grasp.

"How can you speak so? You sound as if you didn't care!"

Jonathan took my arm again.

"I am a solicitor as well as a man and a lover. I can't help thinking like a solicitor—especially when I must think in those terms or go mad. That would not help either of us. No, Lucy, I won't rush off like Romeo and take poison, or fall into a decline, or be driven to drink. I am not so foolish, or so romantic. Does that disappoint you?"

"No. What sort of lover would I be, to want you to destroy yourself as a measure of love?"

"And that is another reason why I love you." He went on, with a faint smile. "You have persuaded me of one thing, and that is your assessment of Miss Fleetwood."

"I could see you admired her."

"My admiration has nothing to do with it. I agree with you that she is not the explanation of your husband's coolness. Under no circumstances could such a woman stoop to the disastrous folly that—"

He stopped walking; his fingers tightening on my arm jerked me to a sudden halt. I looked at him in surprise and annoyance—and then stood rigid, my protest frozen on my tongue. Every vestige of color was gone from his face. Even his lips were white.

"What is it?" I cried. "Are you hurt—in pain? Why do you look like that?"

He moved his head to look at me; it moved stiffly, as if his neck hurt.

"No," he said. "No, it is nothing. . . . I *am* going mad. Such a thing is not possible. . . . I am sorry, Lucy. Let us go in; you are shivering with cold."

I was shivering, but the cold I felt was not physical. What could he be thinking, to make him look like that?

Chapter
15

BY THE FOLLOWING MORNING IT WAS RAINING heavily; the sky was as dark as evening. It was a forecast of winter, when I would be virtually isolated at Greygallows. Like Clare I had grown accustomed to thinking of his home by that name, though not, I imagine, for the same reasons.

Jonathan had gone out the night before and had not returned by the time I went to bed. My state of depression was not improved by my new maid, whom Clare had selected to replace Anna. Apparently he harbored a universal grudge against the village; this girl was from Ripon. I did not like her. She had a cheap pink-and-white prettiness, but she was terribly stupid; I had to repeat the simplest commands twice over before she responded.

After her clumsy ministrations I went down to breakfast in an evil humor. Jonathan was not yet down; I was alone at the table when Clare returned.

The mere sound of his voice in the hall was enough to make my heart contract. A premonition of sheer disaster came over me; my hands went cold, and I dropped my cup. It was one of a set, a family heirloom that Clare cherished, and Mrs. Andrews squeaked with horror on seeing it shatter.

Clare was in the room before I had time to recover. He had not stopped to remove his greatcoat; it was black with rain, and water dripped off its hem onto the polished floor. He glanced around the room, his eye passing over me disinterestedly; he did not even notice the broken cup.

"Where is Mr. Scott?"

"In his room, your Lordship," said Mrs. Andrews. She knew his moods too; her voice was tremulous.

"Get him."

"I beg your—"

"Fetch him here!"

Mrs. Andrews retreated hastily. I sat fingering the broken bits of china and trying to match them together. Clare went to the window and stood looking out.

Jonathan came in. His eyes were sunken, and his moustaches had a weary droop.

Clare turned.

"Where were you last night?"

"Out," said Jonathan.

"Damn you, sir, I asked you where you were!"

"Here and there," said Jonathan. "My lord, it can hardly concern you—"

"You will admit that the nocturnal activities of my wife concern me."

In spite of all that had happened, I was dumbfounded to hear him speak so openly. Jonathan was not; evidently he had expected some such development. He replied, quite coolly.

"My lord, you have no evidence whatsoever of such an act as you are implying."

"I need no paltry lawyer's proof!"

Clare crossed the room and stood glaring at Jonathan. This time, for me, it was not Jonathan who appeared at a disadvantage. He was not as cool as he pretended; I saw the muscles in his cheek knot and then smooth out as he mastered his rage.

"Get hold of yourself, Lord Clare. You shall not provoke me by such an insane accusation. Strike, if you will," he added, eyeing Clare coolly as the latter raised his hand. "I will not strike back. What, are we children, to exchange slaps?"

For a moment there was no sound in the room except for Clare's heavy breathing.

"Splendid," he said finally. "You are a credit to your trade and your low breeding, Scott. Let us see how far your admirable humility will carry you." He turned to me.

"Go to your room," he said.

He might have spoken in that tone to his dog. I suppose I looked half-witted, gaping at him. He strode toward me, and reached out; I tried, with undignified haste, to move out of his way. My shoulders still ached from our last discussion. But before I could shift the chair, or he could grasp me, Jonathan stood between us.

"My humility, as you guessed, stops here," he said, in a low voice. "Be careful, my lord; you go too far."

Clare's arm moved. I could not tell which of us he was striking at, and I never found out; for quickly as he moved, Jonathan was quicker. Half hidden by the shield of his body, I did not see exactly what happened. It ended with Clare half lying, half kneeling on the floor, held in a complicated grip. Kneeling by him, Jonathan held him with seeming ease. Only his quick breathing showed the strain.

He looked up at me.

"Quickly," he said, in a low voice. "Go. Please."

I hesitated, knowing he was right, but hating to desert him; then Clare tried to move. He was caught in an even tighter grip. I saw his face; and I ran as if all the fiends in hell were after me. I did not stop running until I was in my room, with the door bolted and a chair pushed under the knob.

II

I paced the floor for a long time, torn between fear and self-reproach. I kept telling myself there was nothing I could have done. Bad enough that I had witnessed Clare's humiliation. He would never forgive me for that; and as for Jonathan . . .

At least Jonathan had left the house safely. I had seen him go; there was something magnificent about the way he strode out into the rain, coatless and bareheaded, as if even the elements must

yield to him. At the foot of the steps he paused
deliberately and looked up at my window. I don't
suppose he could see me. It was raining heavily;
he was drenched as soon as he stepped out of
shelter. I struggled with the window, but before I
could get it open he had gone, walking off down
the graveled carriageway. His soaked shirt clung
to his body, and the water streamed from his hair.
I started to cry, idiotically, because he was so wet,
and I was afraid he would take cold, and there
was nothing I could do for him, not even give him
his coat. . . .

I sank down by the door in a miserable huddle.
At least I could cry, now that no one saw me.

I must have fallen asleep. When I woke it was
still pouring, and the leaden skies had taken on a
darker hue. I pulled myself to my feet. My limbs
were so cramped I could hardly stand, and my
head was dizzy with hunger and nerves. The
house was ominously still.

As the hours wore on I would have screamed
aloud, just to break that waiting silence.

It was growing dark outside before there was
a sound at the door. I sat bolt upright in the chair
where I had fallen into an uneasy doze.

"My lady?" said a voice from outside. "Are you
awake? Let me in."

I sank back in my chair. The voice was not
Clare's. It was my new maid, Betty.

"What do you want?" I croaked.

"Your dinner, my lady. I was told to bring it. If
you don't want it—"

"Leave it. By the door. Go away."

I waited for some time before I took my barricade away. Common sense told me I must eat; it would serve no purpose to let myself get weaker. The lock, and the chair, were only a relief to my mind. If Clare wanted to come in, he would come.

After I had eaten there was nothing to do but sit and wait. Night fell; the rush of the rain was the only sound. Wrapped in a comforter, I dozed and woke again, and dozed—and dreamed, and woke shaking and crying from the vague terror of the dream. So the night passed, one of the longest I had ever known. Morning was only a lighter grayness; the rain, the interminable rain continued. When I looked out my window I saw little pools of water spreading across the drive.

I got no breakfast. It was almost noon before someone came, and by then I would even have admitted Clare. I was desperate with curiosity; I had to know what was happening if I had been struck dead the next moment. But the voice was not Clare's, nor the timid knock. I recognized Mrs. Andrews, and opened the door.

She started violently when she saw me, and I realized what a spectacle I must make. I had not taken off my clothing for twenty-four hours, nor put a comb to my hair. My eyes felt hot from so much crying.

"I have brought you tea," she said, extending the tray as if I were a wild dog who might be propitiated by a bone. "May I come in?"

"Certainly." I stood back; as she entered I put my head out the door and peered suspiciously into the hall.

"His Lordship is in the library," said Mrs. Andrews, putting the tray on a table. "He spent the
night there."

Was it possible that there was reproach in her
voice? I spun around, looking at her incredulously; she did not meet my eyes, but her mouth
was pursed in an expression of disapproval.

"I spent the night in that chair," I said, indicat-
ing the untidy nest of comforters. "How Mr. Scott
spent the night I cannot imagine—in a ditch, if my
husband had anything to say about it."

The housekeeper's mouth tightened. I had
made a mistake in expressing concern over Jonathan; but if she had not been prejudiced against
me to begin with, she would not have taken my
words as she did. She had always been kind. It
hurt me to see her looking at me as she did now.

"I came to say good-bye, my lady," she said
stiffly. "And to wish you well; and if there is anything I can do—"

"Good-bye?" The word destroyed my self-
control. She might hate me, she might take Clare's
part; but her honesty and rectitude acted as a
shield. With her in the house there were limits to
what Clare would do. With her gone . . .

I ran to her and caught at the pudgy little hands
folded primly at her waist.

"Mrs. Andrews, don't abandon me! Please—I
am afraid—"

"My lady, I am not abandoning you; I am only
going ahead of you, to London, to see to opening
up the house there. I will see you again in a few
days. If there is any errand—"

"Oh, don't speak to me of errands! You don't know what he will do to me!"

Her pink face pursed up again. She had adored her Master Edward too long to admit the slightest criticism. He was a male, and a peer of the realm, and her employer. If he came after me with a club, she might begin to doubt his good intentions; even then she would probably make excuses for him.

"Now, my lady," she said firmly, "I must be frank; I do it for your own good. You have hurt his Lordship terribly—"

I laughed. I could not help it; but it was not the wisest thing to do.

"Terribly," Mrs. Andrews went on, frowning. "And you would hurt him even more if you persist in speaking so—so—well, so madly, so wildly. Can you imagine that he would ever . . ." At that point she remembered that he had, in fact, struck me; her face reddened, but she went on, with the dogged illogic of the prejudiced. "That was nothing; a man might do such a thing, in a fit of passion; and if you will be so thoughtless with other men—"

"You can't believe that," I said; but my voice was hopeless. I knew she would rather believe ill of me than of him.

"I don't believe you are wicked," she said, more gently. "Only young and foolish; but you do not think how he feels."

"Never mind," I said. I lifted the teapot and poured some of the hot liquid into a cup. "Will you join me? Forgive me, then; I am really quite weak with hunger and thirst."

"You must forgive me," she said coldly. "I forgot my place."

"You can say anything you like." I took a bite of toast. "I will listen to you. I only wish *you* would listen to *me*. Why has he decided to go to London? Or am I to go alone, and be imprisoned there?"

"He is trying to be kind. He thinks you have been bored and lonely here, and so have made the wrong friends. Most husbands would not be so thoughtful."

"I see." I took another piece of toast; it was good. "So he is taking me into the world of gaiety and pleasure. I thought the London house was unfit for occupation."

"It is for that reason that I am being sent ahead, with the household staff. It is to spare *you* discomfort."

"I see," I said again. I finished the toast.

Mrs. Andrews stood watching me, her look openly hostile now. My forced calm was creating a bad impression. She would have preferred to see me prostrate and repentant, wiping away my tears with my hair, perhaps.

"Then if you have no instructions . . ." She moved toward the door.

"Mrs. Andrews. If I asked you to take a letter . . . No, you would give it to his Lordship, would you not?" Her face answered me. I said wearily, "You would. And no doubt Mr. Beam would also think me mad—or bad. . . . Will you carry a message to the vicar for me? You cannot object to my asking him to come to see me. Unless you think that he and I . . . No? You look shocked; I am surprised you think me incapable of corrupting him. He is a personable young man, after all."

"He is a man of God," said Mrs. Andrews, through tight lips. "I will deliver your message, my lady. You might profit from seeing a clergyman, certainly."

The cup I was holding rattled in its saucer as my hands began to shake.

"I may not see you again," I said. "If I do not— please think well of me, Mrs. Andrews, as I do of you. You can't help it. You were kind to me, once."

Tears welled into her eyes. She glanced uneasily back at the open door; it was strange and pitiful to see how she feared him, and yet stubbornly maintained her belief in his goodwill.

"Child," she said, in a voice so soft I could hardly hear it, "if you would only—"

"It's no use," I said. "But I thank you."

Automatically, like a good housewife, she picked up the tray containing the remains of my dinner. There were enough broken bits remaining to show that in that meal, at least, I had conformed to the expected picture of distress. She glanced slyly at me.

"I sent Mr. Scott's valise and coat to the village," she whispered. "He is staying with the Millers. He took no harm, my lady."

III

From my window I saw Mrs. Andrews' departure. Williams was driving the large traveling carriage. With the housekeeper went the butler and three of the housemaids, as well as Williams and a pair of grooms. I wondered how many servants were left. I had never kept count; a dozen, perhaps? It did not matter. With Anna and Mrs. Andrews gone, there was no one left who had the power or the will to come to my aid. There was no one anywhere. The villagers were helpless against Clare's wealth and power, and any gesture from Jonathan would only confirm the vile slanders about us.

Late in the afternoon Betty came with another tray. She was grinning with gratified pleasure in my disgrace, and her eyes followed me greedily, hoping for signs of grief or guilt. Her hatred was not a personal thing; she hated all of us, all those who had wealth and position and security. In a way, I could not blame her, but I would not give her the satisfaction of seeing my distress. I said "Thank you" when she brought the tray, and "You may go," and that was all.

Night fell, and my faith in Mrs. Andrews as a messenger began to dim. Mr. Fleetwood had not come, and I did not think he would now. It was still raining heavily, and the incessant pound of it was weighing on my nerves. The puddle on the driveway had spread another foot by the time it grew too dark to see out. There was a skin of ice on it, and the rain had begun to sound like sleet.

I tried to start a fire. I would not call Betty to help, but I had a frightful time with it. It had seemed so easy when I saw the servants do it, but the wood would not catch, it only smoldered. My hands were black and my back ached before I had achieved a small blaze. I crouched down before it, holding my hands to the warmth and feeling like Cinderella in my wrinkled gown and ash-smeared face.

It was then, of course, that Mr. Fleetwood arrived. I didn't care; I was past worrying about how I looked. I left a smear of soot on his cuff as I caught the hand he extended to me; his look of chagrin would have amused me if I had been less distracted.

"Thank you for coming," I babbled. "Oh, thank you! I am sorry to receive you so. . . . I look so. . . . And the room is so cold!"

"Now don't distress yourself," he said cheerfully. "The room *is* cold. You have been a careless child; you will make yourself ill."

He was very deft; before long he had picked up the fire without even dirtying his hands. He sat down across the hearth from me and smiled.

"The worst is over. There is nothing to be afraid of. You may cry, if you like."

"I don't want to cry," I said; "I want to smash something. Why am I subjected to this? Before God, I am innocent! But if Clare persists in treating me as if I were guilty . . ."

A spark flared up in the placid gray of his eyes.

"By heaven, I admire your courage!" he exclaimed.

My eyes fell.

"You would not," I muttered, "if you could read my thoughts."

"I do read them. I do not approve of what you were about to say; I can hardly do so, as a clergyman. But as a man, I understand and sympathize. I have often wondered how many unfortunates have been driven to sin by the expectation that they would."

"I thought of running away," I admitted. "But where would I run to?"

"You have no friends hereabouts? No relatives?"

"Only an aunt. And she would not receive me."

"Not even temporarily?"

"Mr. Fleetwood," I said uneasily, "you do not mean to do so, I know. . . . But you alarm me, you really do. Are you suggesting that I should leave my husband?"

"My dear Lucy—I may take that liberty? I may call you Lucy?"

"Of course," I said impatiently. "Go on."

"My dear Lucy, I will speak honestly. I make it a rule never to interfere between husband and wife. But there are advantages to—what shall I call it?— a truce, a brief separation, to give you both time to think. You need not assure me of your innocence; I believe in it as I believe in that of my own sister. But in Clare's present mood . . ."

"If I could talk to Clare . . ."

"Good heaven no! That would be the worst thing you could do. Give him time to calm down."

"I may not have time. He means to take me to London."

Mr. Fleetwood shook his head. He looked grave.

"Do you think I should not go?"

"You must go," he said heavily. "I only wish I were not going away myself. I am not worried, mind you; but . . ."

"You are going?" If he was not worried, I was. One by one, every person on whom I might depend was being taken from me. "But you—oh, yes, I forgot. Forgive me for not inquiring after your sister. How does she do?"

"Badly. I am anxious to get her away."

"And you came here, when you have so much to do. I am ashamed. Of course you must think first of her. When do you go?"

"Tomorrow, at first light."

"In such weather? Is that wise, in her state of health?"

"All the more reason why I am anxious to be away. If I dared delay I would, for your sake. But the rain is only beginning, and the weather is much colder tonight. If this continues, the roads will soon be impassable."

"Then Clare must mean to leave soon," I muttered.

"I think I heard him speak of tomorrow."

"It makes no difference."

"It means you have only tonight," said Mr. Fleetwood. Then he raised his hand to his mouth. "I did not mean to say that. Forget I said it."

"I don't know what to do. . . ."

"It will all come right in the end," said Mr.

Fleetwood, with a smile that looked like a snarl, it was so obviously forced. He rose. "I must go. Charlotte will be expecting me."

"Give her my best."

"Thank you." He hesitated, and then said, "I will take Edward to sleep tonight at the vicarage. You may rest more easily, knowing that."

I had read of people wringing their hands, but I never thought they really did, until that night. I paced the floor, twisting my hands until they hurt. Instead of bringing the reassurance I had hoped for, Mr. Fleetwood's visit had only increased my fears. His vague, indefinite habit of speech had never been so irritating. But surely he would not have left me if he really feared for my safety? He might reasonably fear for my peace of mind; but no man, much less a clergyman, would abandon a woman to real danger.

I felt more relieved when I saw Clare go. The carriage came round, and by its flickering side lamps I recognized my husband and the vicar as they got in. The carriage drove off, looking like one of those ghostly chariots Clare was so fond of describing, as it vanished into the rain, and I drew a long breath as I turned from the window. I was really very tired, not having slept well for several days. Since Mr. Fleetwood's visit I was painfully conscious of my disheveled state. I forced myself to call Betty. She answered so promptly that another half-formed suspicion was confirmed; no doubt Clare had ordered her to hide in the hall and watch me.

I ordered her to bring hot water and then sent her away; I could not have her watching me with that sly look in her eye. I washed myself and changed my clothing, and then I felt much better.

In spite of everything, I had no intention of trying to escape from the house. Aside from the fact that I had nowhere to go, I felt sure Clare had people watching me. It would be too degrading to be caught and forced back to my room. I remembered the big rough hands of the London pugilist, and his sneering smile, and I literally turned sick at the notion that those hands might touch me.

I took up a book, to try and distract myself; but it did not hold my attention, and I sat staring into the dying fire while my thoughts went over and over the same well-worn track. The firelight made me sleepy; I was drowsing when a sound at the door brought me wide awake.

It was not a knock or a rattle of the knob, but a scratching sound such as a dog might have made. I had not locked the door. It had not seemed necessary with Clare gone from the house. Now I regretted that omission, as I watched the door slowly begin to open.

It opened only a crack. Then something white appeared in the slit, and fell to the floor. Sounds and movement stopped; but I thought I detected a faint creak, as if someone tiptoeing down the hall had stepped on a squeaking board.

I went to the door and nerved myself to open it. There was no one in sight; the lamps shone steadily on emptiness. At my feet lay a folded piece of paper.

This time, before I opened the note, I locked

the door. I can still remember every word it contained.

"My love: Come to me. I wait for you without, at the foot of the stone staircase. Do not fail me; my very life depends on your actions now."

It was signed "Jonathan."

I flew to the window and then ran back, crumpling the note in my hand. Of course I could not see anything; he would hardly stand in front of the house waving a lantern. I darted about the room like a mouse trapped in a box. My cloak. I would need my heavy cloak, and clogs . . . My jewels too, they were mine by right, if not by law. Clare should not have my mother's jewels.

After all I forgot the clogs. With my cloak trailing awkwardly from one shoulder and the heavy jewel box under my arm, I ran across the room in my black silk shoes and opened the door into Clare's bedchamber. There was a good fire on the hearth, as there always was, whether he was at home or not. I was halfway across the room when I stopped short, as suddenly as if I had struck a solid, invisible wall.

It must be from such moments that the idea of premonitions and ghostly warnings arise. I felt as if I had heard an actual voice cry out, felt a physical hand catch my arm to stop me.

I went back to my room, not in a wild rush, but walking slowly. The note was on the floor where I had dropped it. I picked it up, smoothed out the wrinkles, and read it again.

This was the origin of the warning—no guardian angel or supernatural message, only my knowledge of Jonathan. I did not know his hand, but there was no need for me to question the writing. He had not written this note.

I grimaced as I reread the stiff, florid phrases. No, Jonathan would never have written like this. He would not have mentioned his life being in danger. . . . Why, the words didn't even mean that. They were ambiguous; they might be interpreted as effusive evidence of an ordinary sordid little intrigue.

Another of Clare's tricks, then; and, like his other acts, this could be viewed in two different ways.

It might be a test, invented by Clare's sick jealousy. Would I have found him waiting, if I had gone down into the rain-drenched night answering the appeal from my supposed lover? A shiver ran through me, and I crept closer to the dying fire. Yes, the note could be a test, and Clare's departure, with his hoodwinked friend, a blind to make me feel safe from observation. No doubt he could creep out of the vicarage without waking either of its occupants.

Bad as it was, I preferred that idea to the alternative.

Someone wanted me to leave my husband. It might be Clare himself, it might be an unknown schemer. Huddled by the fire, I tried to reason out an answer, but I failed—not only because I was too distracted to be reasonable, but because there was no clear answer.

Clare had a motive for murder (now I had thought the word). But had he sufficient cause?

Assuming the worst—that he had married me solely for my fortune, that he found me repulsive, that he wished to marry Charlotte Fleetwood—would a man like Clare commit murder for such a cause?

I could not believe it. He was capable of cruelty, of injustice, of calloused indifference toward suffering. He had all the weaknesses of his class, but he had its virtues as well. The cold-blooded, treacherous murder of a woman who bore his name and was under his protection . . . No, it was not possible.

Nor was it likely that my death was the desired end of whatever plot was afoot. Surely, I thought wildly—surely a murderer is more efficient! The little bottle of laudanum, the rides we had taken together—yes, Clare had had ample opportunity to destroy me without resorting to the clumsy tricks that had been played.

My thoughts went round and round like a treadmill. There was only one thing of which I was relatively certain—only the merest chance had saved me from disaster of some kind that night. The forged note could have no innocent cause, even if I could not guess what the true cause might be.

Chapter 16

I FELT MORE OPTIMISTIC NEXT MORNING, NOT BE-
cause the gray dawn brought an increase of hope,
but because my spirits had sunk so low during
the night there was nowhere else for them to go
but up. I found myself thinking more hopefully
of London. The horrors of the metropolis would
not appall me so much if I were trying to mitigate
them; there might be committees or charitable
groups I could assist. I would not be so cut off
there. Any other climate, however foul, would be
preferable to the actual isolation of winter in Yorkshire. The very sound of the rain here weighed on
the nerves, after days and days of it.

Not until then did I notice the silence. The rain
had finally stopped.

I rose stiffly and went to the window.

The view from my window made me catch my
breath in mingled admiration and consternation.

Never had I seen such a sunrise. Above the black-silhouetted shapes of the trees the whole eastern horizon was splashed with color, as if a mad artist had flung the contents of his palette at a vast canvas. A patch of sullen, crimson, glowing like a dying fire, a bar of palest green, delicate as a patch of new grass, sable and purple streaks across a lavender band. Low on the horizon, blending with the sullen deep gray of the moorland, lay what appeared to be a mountain range, sprung up overnight. The peaks were ragged and barren, like fanged teeth. Even as I watched, one towering pinnacle sagged and broke, and others rose up in its place. It was a huge, menacing cloud bank, and its somber hues suggested more than the obvious threat of bad weather to come; it was like a celestial warning.

Shivering, I turned away from the window. The room was cold; I had been too preoccupied to replenish the fire. I decided it was not worth the struggle to start it again. Despite Mr. Fleetwood's warning, I must speak to Clare that day. I could not continue in this state any longer.

I removed my wrinkled dress and washed it in icy water before assuming my warmest frock, a gray wool trimmed in white, which I had not worn much because it was like one of Miss Fleetwood's favorite dresses. My fingers were so stiff I could scarcely manage the tiny jet buttons that ran from the throat to the waist. All the comfort of the house, with its blazing fires, all the balmy summer days were forgotten; I would never think of Yorkshire as anything but bitter cold.

Some of my courage evaporated in the cold. I had meant to ring for Betty, but could not bring myself to face her smirk. There was no point to calling her, I argued with myself; I could not order her to pack, since I did not know when we were going; and I would not give her the satisfaction of asking her for information my husband had not given me. So I sat in my chair with my cold hands wrapped in the folds of my skirt, and I waited.

It was almost noon before I heard the sound for which I had been waiting. I went to the window. Clare had returned. He was on horseback. I wondered what had become of the carriage.

He came directly upstairs. I was ready for him; and if my heart was beating too fast, the folds of the shawl I had wrapped around me concealed its agitated flutter.

He did not look at me, but cast a disapproving look around the room. Admittedly it was not in good order.

"Call your maid," he commanded; and when Betty had come, he ordered her to straighten the room and pack my trunk.

"Shall I build a fire, my lord?" she asked, with a humility she had never shown to me.

"Certainly. The room is freezing."

"When are we leaving?" I asked.

"This afternoon, I hope; if not, early tomorrow morning. I am waiting on some business matter which must be transacted before I go."

His manner was odd; if I had not known him better, I would have thought he was embarrassed.

Despite the conciliatory, almost gossipy, tone, he still avoided my eyes.

Suddenly he gave an exaggerated shiver.

"You should not be sitting here, it is too cold," he said, bending down to examine a dust spot on a low table. "Will you not come down, until the room is warmer? We are dining early today. The meal will not be up to Mrs. Andrews' standard, but the inconvenience will not be for long, I hope."

"Very well," I said, wondering; decidedly, he was ill at ease. Perhaps this was his way of telling me he was sorry and ashamed. I did not expect a formal apology, certainly not in front of Betty.

He accompanied me to the parlor, but did not speak again. The silence grew awkward. I asked after the Fleetwoods.

"Oh, yes. They left early this morning. Traveling conditions are bad, but Jack would go; he will hear no arguments when he has made up his mind. Even though the chaise he had hired from Ripon broke down upon arrival, he was determined to go. So I sent them in the carriage."

"Oh, that is why you came back on horseback. But then with the carriage and the coach both gone, how will we travel?"

It was an idle question, intended to express interest and a willingness to be agreeable.

"Why must you always question my actions?" he demanded angrily.

"I did not mean—"

"Very well, very well. I—I spoke hastily. The carriage will be back before we must go."

"Then you don't mean to leave today? From Ripon it is—"

Clare flung down the newspaper he had been looking at.

"By God, this incessant questioning—"

"I am sorry."

"I know what I am about," he said more gently. "Try to credit that."

"I do. I am sorry."

A servant came to announce dinner. Clare relapsed into silence, and I did not break it; my efforts at casual conversation had not been strikingly successful. He took the newspaper to the table with him—an act of discourtesy which was not like him—and he read it throughout the meal. It was, as he had predicted, a miserable affair; without Mrs. Andrews' supervision, the cook had taken little trouble. Yet Clare, the most fastidious of men, munched his way through underdone roast and scorched potatoes without comment.

I went back upstairs after dinner. The fire was burning brightly and the room was pleasantly warm now. My clothes and belongings had been tidied away and my trunk, bound with cord, stood in the middle of the carpet. I lay down for a rest. My nights had not been peaceful.

When I awoke it was growing dark. I had dreamed of departures and journeys; I woke with the rumble of wheels still in my ear, and thought what a vivid dream it had been. Then I realized that perhaps the sound had been real. If the carriage had indeed returned, Clare might wish to leave now, late as it was.

I went to the window and looked out. I saw no carriage, but saw something else that made the thought of a night journey even less appealing. It was snowing—great, slow, lazy flakes now, but the skies threatened more. The wind that seeped in through the edges of the window was bitter enough to burn the skin.

I rang for Betty, and then went to get a shawl. She was slow in answering; I rang again. As I waited, my annoyance increased. The girl's behavior was becoming intolerable. I gave the bell rope a sharp tug.

It came off in my hand.

I stared stupidly at the brocaded strip. Everything seemed ominous to me that day, but this incident was especially frightening; it was a symbol of my isolation. Clutching the bell rope, I ran to the door and threw it open. The sight of the quiet hallway reassured me; then I realized the house was abnormally still. I went along the hall to the stairs and looked down.

The first object my eyes fell upon was Clare. He did not see me at first. I had the idea that he had just come in from out-of-doors. His face was flushed, as if with cold, and he kept rubbing his hands together. I shifted my weight; a board creaked underfoot, and Clare started, with a harsh, indrawn breath. He looked up.

I don't know what he saw. It may be that I myself looked spectral, with my pale face and dark hair floating bodiless in the shadows that blended with my gray gown. It may be that he saw, or sensed, something else. Whatever it was, the effect was frightful. He staggered back several steps, the color fading from his cheeks.

Glancing nervously over my shoulder—and seeing nothing but the alternating shadow and light of the hallway—I descended the stairs more quickly than I had meant to do.

"Where are the servants?" I asked. "I rang for Betty. . . ."

I held up the bell rope. Clare had recovered himself; except for that strange habit of avoiding my eyes, he seemed quite as usual. He took the rope from my hand and looked at it.

"Frayed," he said, tossing it onto a table. "The servants are a lazy lot; that ought to have been seen and mended."

"But where are they?" I asked, glancing into the open doorway of the parlor. The rooms were brightly lit and almost too neat, like the stage setting for a play after the actors have gone.

"I sent them away."

"What?"

"Come in and sit down by the fire," Clare said. "You were asleep and I didn't like to waken you; but I thought you knew I had planned to leave today. I keep only a skeleton staff here when I am away; there is no point in paying for services which are not required. Mrs. Williams is in her rooms over the stable, but the inside staff has gone off."

Stupidly I followed him into the parlor and watched as he went to the sideboard and poured out some wine.

"The carriage has returned, then?" I asked, trying to sort out the flood of questions that came to my mind.

"What? The carriage ... yes, yes, it is here. Only—I stepped outside just now, and I really do not like the look of the weather. It would be better to wait until morning. Do you not agree? Do you not think we would be unwise to risk traveling now? You will not be uncomfortable; Mrs. Williams can help you tonight, if you need a maid, and I will see to your fire. It will be quite like an adventure."

He came toward me, holding the wine glasses, and offered me one. I stared at him in amazement. His eyes shifted away from mine, and there was the strangest little smile on his lips.

I took the glass. He drank his wine quickly and went back to the decanter.

"Drink it," he said, over his shoulder. "It will warm you."

I took one sip. It was enough.

There was very little time, and no potted plant—the conventional receptacle for unwanted beverages—anywhere within reach. Needs must, as the old saying goes. I lifted the cushion on the sofa where I sat and tipped the liquid down into the crack between back and arm. When Clare turned, I was holding an empty glass.

My feelings were really rather pitiable. I could not swear that there had been anything in the wine except the fantasy of an overwrought imagination; disposing of it had only been a precaution, which could do no harm—except to the sofa—and might do considerable good. Supposing there had been something in the drink. I did not know how the additive was meant to affect me. Arsenic, if I remembered correctly, produced agonizing pain and considerable internal distress.

I was very near the point where terror runs over into hysteria; for an instant I was tempted to fall to the floor and die with theatrical anguish. Watching Clare drink wine as if it were water, and he an explorer lost for days in the desert, I controlled myself. It could do no harm to simulate drowsiness. Laudanum would produce that initial effect, and laudanum was a drug I knew he possessed.

"I am really too drowsy to sit up any longer," I mumbled. "If you will excuse me . . ."

"Shall I call Mrs. Williams?"

I think I knew, then. False, false—every word, every look shrieked of lies. He had no intention of summoning the head groom's wife from her snug quarters, so safely distant from the house. He would delay and make excuses until I was too sleepy to care, and then. . . .

"No," I said listlessly. "I am too tired for anything but sleep; I just will lie down as I am. We are leaving early?"

"At dawn."

He did not even turn to bid me good-night. His fine white hand, reaching again for the decanter, was trembling visibly.

I went slowly up the stairs. Once inside my room, I flew into action. The cloak, my jewel box—and now I remembered the clogs. I tied them on with hands that felt as if all the fingers were thumbs. The soft hiss of falling snow outside did not daunt me; any atmosphere was preferable to the poison in that house.

I was about to rise from the bed, where I had sat to tie my shoes, when I heard the sound at the door. I cursed my stupidity; of course he would come to make sure I was sleeping. One quick glance assured me that the cloak, flung over a chair where Betty might have left it in readiness for the journey, concealed the jewel box. I threw myself down on the bed, dragging the folds of my skirt down to cover the clogs, as the door started to open.

When the door was open far enough to admit him, Clare stepped in. He stood quite still for a moment; then, in a soft but clear voice, he spoke my name. When there was no response, he came closer. I had been watching, through half-closed eyes; now I closed them completely.

It was dreadful not to see what he was doing. The creations of imagination—knives and nooses, and pillows to smother me with—were more frightening than any visible threat. Then came a sound that literally froze my blood. Yet it was an innocent sound, nothing like the horrors I had imagined—only the familiar creaking whisper of the cushions on my favorite yellow brocade chair. Clare had sat down.

Did he mean to sit there and watch me expire? I was sure now that he meant to drug me, but his watching confounded all my theories. Once the drug started to take effect, there was no danger of my escaping. He need only place the little black bottle on the table, and go; after my erratic remarks to the vicar and Mrs. Andrews it would be assumed that I had taken my own life.

Now that he was seated some distance away, I could open my eyes a slit, and I did so; I had to do something, or I would have shrieked aloud with frustration. He was a black silhouette against the glowing coals of the fire; the slump of his shoulders looked weary, and doubt weakened my fear of his intentions.

I don't know how long the ordeal lasted. It must have been several hours; it seemed, of course, like the unending stretch of eternity. Toward the end of the time I must have lost consciousness.

I came to myself when Clare moved, making the chair springs squeak. In my dazed state I made a small sound, I think, but Clare was too absorbed to hear it. He was transformed; the weary watcher was on his feet, quivering from head to foot with eagerness. It was strange to see a man of his size move so silently, yet without his usual grace; a crouched bulk, he crept toward the door and stood there poised. His arms were close to his sides, and the firelight glittered on his distended eyeballs. All his concentration was focused on the door, which was fortunate for me, because the menace of his movement had so alarmed me that I forgot pretense, and lay with both eyes open wide, watching.

I was slow in hearing the sound that aroused him; but he was listening for it, expecting it. His right arm moved. It took some object from his pocket and then lifted high in the air. I squinted, trying to make out through the shadows what it was he held, and then suddenly the meaning of his pose came to me; I recognized the footsteps in the hall, soft as they were; and I sat bolt upright on the bed and screamed.

The cry was an error; it precipitated the event I hoped to prevent. The door burst open and Jonathan rushed in. I don't think he even saw the danger that waited for him. With a single bound, Clare was upon him; the lifted arm struck, and there was a horrible, muffled sound. Jonathan pitched forward, to lie like a dead man on the floor.

Clare caught me in an iron grip as I scrambled down off the bed. He was cursing, in low, mumbling monotone that rose to a muffled yell as my teeth sank into his hand. He pushed me face down onto the bed. I felt his knee in the small of my back, and his hands fumbling; then he had my wrists tied together. He turned me over, just in time; with my mouth and nose pressed against the comforter I was near suffocating. Before I could draw breath he had tied a kerchief over my mouth and bent to bind my ankles.

He stepped back. He was breathing hard, with his smooth cap of hair disarranged. With an undignified heave, I sat up. That was as much as I could do, and a smile curved Clare's mouth as he contemplated my helpless form.

"I doubt that anyone could hear you scream," he said coolly. "But your howls grate on my nerves. I meant to spare you this; if you had not been so clever about the wine, you would not be uncomfortable now. I don't intend you to be hurt, Lucy—not much, at any rate—so stop writhing, if you please."

I would have gone on writhing, if only to annoy him, but then I heard a muffled groan and saw Jonathan stir. Clare moved quickly to bind his arms as he had mine. I sat still, all my anger and fire drained out of me. He was alive. I had thought him dead. The firelight showed a sticky wet patch on the back of his head, but he lived.

After binding Jonathan's wrists, Clare heaved him up and propped him against the door.

"I know you are conscious, Scott," he began, and then caught the foot Jonathan thrust out toward him. "Ah, I thought as much. I fear you are still slow."

He proceeded to tie Jonathan's feet. Seeing there was no reason for pretense, Jonathan opened his eyes. He looked at me, as I sat perched like a ruffled wren on the bed, with my feet dangling, but he did not speak.

"Now," Clare said, straightening. "I must stop and think. You are early, Scott; I can't risk leaving just yet."

"What are you going to do with us?" Jonathan asked thickly.

"You don't know? You can't imagine—you, with your clever legal brain?"

Clare stood grinning down at his recumbent victim. All the hesitation and unease he had shown toward me were gone. He had some qualms about his treatment of me, but his hatred of Jonathan wiped out any trace of conscience there. He might be delaying for practical reasons which were as yet unknown to me; but one reason for the delay was the pleasure he derived from tormenting the man he hated. He would never forgive Jonathan for overcoming him in physical combat—for holding him on his knees and helpless before me.

"I know more than you think," Jonathan said, lifting himself up. "You're mad, you know. You can't hope to succeed with this."

"Trite, as well as untrue. Who is to prevent me? Not you, at any rate."

Jonathan's head slipped sideways, as if it were too heavy to hold up. His eyes were half closed. He looked like a man in the last coma that precedes death. I saw that he was wearing rough workingmen's attire, with heavy boots and a thick shirt instead of a coat.

Leaning forward, I overbalanced myself and felt myself falling. The feeling of helplessness was terrible. I could do nothing to stop my fall and toppled off the bed, striking my cheek heavily on the floor. Clare picked me up. Seeing that I was choking behind the kerchief, in an effort to catch my breath, he removed the gag and shook me slightly.

"You will do yourself an injury if you do not keep still," he said severely.

Jonathan gave an odd choking laugh. He had pulled himself up again, and his eyes looked less drowsy.

"Your concern is touching," he said. "What do a few bruises matter, if you plan to murder her?"

Clare whirled around.

"How dare you!" he exclaimed. "How dare you suggest I would kill a woman—a lady who is under my protection?"

Jonathan stared at him, openmouthed. He shook his head, and then closed his eyes as if the movement hurt him.

"Incredible," he muttered. "They ought to preserve you, in a cage, as a specimen. The triumph of tradition over intelligence . . . Now then, my lord, don't get excited," he added, as Clare strode toward him. "I apologize for my thoughtless words; your handling of me was a little rough, I fear my wits are addled. May I humbly inquire how you do mean to deal with us, if murder is not on your list of allowable crimes?"

The calm tone had its effect on Clare, who was becoming more and more rattled. He pulled out his watch and looked at it. He grimaced.

"The time goes slowly."

"Only when one is not enjoying oneself," Jonathan said. "Perhaps it would ease your mind to go over your plan of action. There may be flaws you have not seen."

"There are no flaws." Clare seemed not unwilling to talk. "It is simple enough. My—my wife and her lover attempt to flee. Unfortunately the roads are bad; the carriage overturns. In the morning, when I discover she is missing, I send out parties to search for her. They find . . . a situation which cannot be misinterpreted."

Jonathan started to nod, and then thought better of it.

"I see. And the carriage—the hired chaise, which proved unacceptable to our friend the vicar, but which is now repaired—I am assumed to have hired it?"

"It has been stolen from the vicarage stable, where it was left."

I could control myself no longer.

"You do not call that murder? To leave us out in the freezing cold all night—injured, of course, because we would seek shelter if we were able—"

Jonathan gave me a warning glance, and I subsided.

"There is a moral difference between omission and commission," he explained. "At least there is in the mind of his Lordship. He has already arranged several of these little accidents for you. It was he who whistled for your horse that day on the moor; it is no crime, surely, to call a horse. If you had been thrown, or taken a serious illness, well, that would not have been his doing. He dosed you with laudanum in the hope that you might become dependent on it, or sufficiently stupefied by it to do yourself an injury. Would he be to blame if you misused this soothing medicine he was kind enough to procure for you? He has been trying to urge you to run away for quite some time, but you are so disobliging you won't help him. His crimes are of a very weak milk-and-water variety; he must dislike his present course of action intensely."

"Why not hire someone?" I asked sarcastically. "That brute from London looks the type."

"I suspect that was in his mind when he brought the fellow here. But he—or someone—" Jonathan said oddly, "was wise enough to realize that an accomplice in crime is a potential accuser.

His Lordship's conscience is a pretty thing, Lucy, but it is not uncommon. Many people will shrink in virtuous horror from a particular act, but they will accept the fruits of crime so long as they can pretend ignorance of it."

The irony of his speech reached Clare, who had been staring at the hands of his watch as if he were willing them to move. With a scowl he thrust it into his waistcoat pocket and said angrily,

"Again you do me an injustice. If you remain in the carriage and keep yourselves warmly wrapped, you will not even take cold. Why should I wish to harm Lucy? The incident will discredit any statement she might make."

"Divorce?" I said, hardly believing it; and yet his voice carried conviction. If only he would look directly at me. "Is that what you want? You don't need to do this, Clare, you can divorce me; I won't argue with you. It's the money, is it not? I will give it to you. Every penny. Only let us go. Don't harm anyone."

Clare looked at me then, and I wished he had not. If he had sneered in triumph, like a fictional villain, I could have hated him. But he did not. His face had the same look of sick suffering, of weak malice, I had seen in the eyes of a trapped animal.

"I wish I could," he muttered.

"But why not? I will sign anything you give me, I will confess to anything you wish. Divorce will cancel the marriage contract, and I will make Mr. Beam give you the money. Only don't involve Jonathan. Why should his career be ruined? I will name Fernando, or one of the servants—anyone you say. Please, Clare. I give you my word—"

"You might," said Clare. "But . . ."

He gestured toward Jonathan, who was watching him with the oddest look.

"What can he say?" I cried; my hopes were soaring. "If you accuse me, and I confess—if his name is not brought into the case—"

"Lucy," said Jonathan; and simultaneously Clare cried out,

"You don't understand! You don't know! Do you think I would do this, stoop to this, to get your money for myself? I married you because you were ill and fragile. They told me you were consumptive. Damn them! Damn that fat, painted old woman! It is all her fault. She knew you were strong, she knew you would live. She lied to me."

His face was red, and he was panting with passion. It was the final revelation, to see him in a tantrum like a spoiled child, trying to pass the blame for his acts on to someone else. Why had I never seen his basic weakness? Like most of the world, I had been deluded by an aristocratic bearing and a handsome face. The man beneath was still a pampered boy who could not bear to see his wishes thwarted.

Yet it was not Clare's look that crushed the hope rising within me; it was Jonathan's. Whatever the secret Clare had hinted at, Jonathan knew it; there was the strangest expression on his face. Yet I could not give up without a last attempt.

"I don't care what your reasons are," I said. "What do they matter? I beg you—"

"Stop," Jonathan said. "It is useless, Lucy. He can't let me go. So long as I live, your suggestion would be impossible. I know he—"

With one bound Clare was upon him, his hands clamped over Jonathan's mouth.

"Be still, you fool! Be silent! Will you force me to destroy her too?"

He was crouching on the floor by his prisoner; their eyes were inches apart. After a moment Clare seemed to see acquiescence in Jonathan's look. Slowly he lifted his hands, leaving the marks of his fingers printed whitely across Jonathan's cheeks. He was breathing like a man who has been running for his life.

"I can't bear the delay," he whispered, as if to himself. "It is time that weakens me. How much longer must I wait?"

Again Clare consulted his watch; again he thrust it back into its place with a growl of impatience. He pushed Jonathan out of the way, opened the door, and went out. But he was back again almost at once, before I could move. For the next half hour he paced like a caged beast. And then, on what must have been his third trip to the window, he gave a low exclamation, holding the curtains back and staring intently out into the darkness.

Jonathan had turned onto his side and was lying quite still. From where I sat I could see his hands. He was twisting and straining them, trying to loosen the knots on his wrists. I followed suit. It did not take me long to decide the effort was probably futile, but I went on trying; there was nothing else I could do. Then one of my nails broke, down near the quick, and I exclaimed with the pain.

Clare whirled around.

"Hush," he said loudly. "Hush, I must hear. Don't you hear it? What is it . . . Oh, God, who is it coming?"

Then I did hear the sound—hoofbeats, coming quickly, too quickly for the icy, treacherous road.

The horse reached the house and stopped, in a slither of gravel. Then, from Clare's throat, came a sound like nothing I have ever heard, and hope never to hear again. It was a howl like an animal's dying cry; there was nothing human in it. He staggered back from the window, dragging the curtain as if his hands had frozen to it.

Jonathan sat upright, alert and watchful. I too felt that this new development was hopeful; anyone who struck such horror into Clare could only mean good luck for us. I listened, my heart hammering at my ribs, as sounds followed sounds, telling the progress of the unknown through the house. First the heavy front door opened with a crash as it slammed against the wall. There was no sound of its closing. Footsteps followed; slow, heavy, ponderous steps—and with them I began to feel that my hope had been premature. No human rescuer would come like that, all alone, with that dragging deliberation.

Clare stood riveted to his place, glaring wildly; the outstretched cloth of the drapery swathed his body like a pall.

The slow steps came on, up the stairs and down the hall. I thought I would perish of suspense before the unknown came into sight. Already I dreaded his appearance. What would I see in the open doorway?

Chapter

17

IN THE FIRST MOMENT I FAILED TO RECOGNIZE HIM. His face was so darkly crusted it might have been a mask. Then, gleaming uncannily through congealed blood and mud which had hardened with cold, I recognized the gray eyes. His clothes were torn, and stiff with frozen mud.

Mr. Fleetwood glanced at me and at Jonathan; his eyes moved on, disinterestedly, as if we had been pieces of furniture. He looked at Clare, who stood unmoving, with that wild glare imprinted on his features.

"She is dead," the vicar said. "Dead . . . and the child too. The bridge—weakened by floods, and then frozen . . ."

Clutching the folds of the draperies like an antique Roman wrapping his toga around him, Clare was the focus of all our eyes. The vicar's expression was one of shrinking dread, Jonathan's of shock and calculation. And I? Unexpectedly, I felt pity. She had been very beautiful, and he had loved her very much. I knew now what it was to feel for another more than for myself. And the horrible, ironic justice of it—not even I would have planned such a revenge, if I could have done so.

"I am glad you take it so well," Fleetwood said, eyeing Clare apprehensively. "I feared . . . I have been riding for hours to tell you, I did not even wait to have my own injuries dressed. Thank God I came in time."

Then, as Clare still did not move or speak, he turned to Jonathan. He was obviously in great bodily pain as well as distress of mind; even so, I found his words fantastic and, in a sense, more repellent than any others that had been spoken.

"I was in time," he said. "You will remember that, and speak for me, if it should ever come to . . . I knew nothing of this. You believe that? I knew nothing until she told me, as she lay dying. . . ."

Clare began to laugh. It was a great roar of laughter, like thunder, impersonal and quite mad. With one jerk of his arm he brought the heavy draperies down from their bar. They swirled around him like a cloak and billowed out behind him as he strode across the room. He flung the masses of cloth so that they fell half into the hearth and half out, trailing across the carpet.

I was too stunned to sense his purpose, but Fleetwood knew. With a shriek like a woman's scream he flung himself at Clare, and the latter threw him off with a sweep of the arm that sent the slighter man spinning backward until he fell heavily to the floor, where he lay stunned. At that moment the coals caught on to the fabric; a high, white flame sprang up and seized greedily on this dry tinder. Clare reached for the tongs. He swept the fire out onto the trailing folds. Without a backward glance he walked to the connecting door, opened it, and passed through. He was talking—to himself, I suppose. I caught a few words: "—burn. Let it burn." From the next room I heard a clatter of tools, and then a light flared up. Clare's steps went on, out the door and down the hall.

Jonathan was struggling wildly.

"Fleetwood," he called. "Wake up, man! Will you let us all burn?"

The vicar stirred feebly. The fall had stunned him, but had not rendered him unconscious. With a groan he rolled over and then rose to his knees. As his opening eyes fell on the fire they widened in terror. With another of those womanish shrieks he leaped to his feet and ran. I could hear him screaming all the way down the hall; my cries, and Jonathan's shouts, were drowned by his. I don't think he meant to desert us. He was out of his wits with fear.

I sat on the edge of the bed. The carpet had caught and was burning merrily; a row of hungry little yellow flames separated me from Jonathan. He had struggled to his feet, but the effort cost him dear; he was swaying and his face was gray.

"Mrs. Williams will see the fire," I said. I was abnormally calm; I suppose it was shock. I could not credit the reality of the creeping yellow flames.

"By the time someone sees it, it will be too late

for us," Jonathan said weakly. "You must move, Lucy. Hop, roll, but move, out of here. I can't help you . . . can't move. . . ."

I slid down off the bed, barely keeping my feet. Hop? I could do that, yes; but jump across the line of fire with hands and feet bound . . . No, I felt sure that was beyond my powers. There was no escape through the next room. Clare had been more thorough there, or the fire had found more to seize upon; already the scene through the open door was hazy with smoke, red-stained by the flames that produced it.

As I hesitated, Jonathan's eyes rolled up. He dropped to his knees and then fell forward.

The smoke was thicker. I began to cough and could not stop. One hop; then another; and then the coughing made me bend over too far. I fell, prostrate. I could no longer see Jonathan for the smoke and the rising flames. I felt a pang of bitter disappointment. I had had so little, and there was so much waiting. . . .

Something came through the air like a great bird. It caught me up roughly, so that I woke and cried out, coughing still. Again it leaped the fire; I smelled singeing cloth. We were out, in the hall, in clearer air. There was only a faint haze of smoke. I blinked my streaming eyes, and recognized the face of the man who held me.

"Tom," I said. "Where did you come from? Oh, Tom, he's back there . . . get him out. . . ."

"No, my lady," said Tom, clutching me so tightly I could hardly breathe. The tears were streaming down his dirty face; they may have been tears of emotion, but I think it was probably the smoke. "Frank has him; don't fret, my lady, we'll have you both safe. . . ."

Over his shoulder I saw another face I knew—Anna. No sentimentalist, she; she gave Tom a hearty shove, so that he staggered and almost dropped me.

"Run, you —— young fool," she said, using a word I had never heard. "The whole ——ing house is afire."

Clutched like an unwieldy parcel I traveled down the stairs in Tom's arms. It was rather exhilarating. As he thudded across the lower hall I could see a red glow from the drawing room. A great gust of smoke came eddying down the corridor leading to the offices. Then we were out in the bitter freezing night air, and I coughed and choked and strangled on my tears; and Tom stood still, staring at Greygallows House, burning, until Anna came charging up and made him put me down, and started sawing at the ropes with a knife. She had me free, and wrapped in a rough blanket, before Jonathan made his appearance, slung over someone's shoulder like a side of beef, and—I might have expected it—laughing.

I tried to struggle to my feet, but Anna put me down again with a heavy hand. I subsided; and saw, in amazement, that I was in the midst of a sizable crowd. Half the village was there. I recognized old Jenkins first. It was his surly son-in-law who had carried Jonathan out and was now wrapping him in his own blanket-shawl. I saw

Mary Peters and her oldest son, Anna's father and her two brothers . . .

"Please let me get up," I said to Anna. "The ground is so cold."

A grin spread over her face. It looked quite wild, all smoke-stained and black.

"Don't be so impatient, my lady. He'll come to you. Let him come; it's all we women can do, to keep them in their places."

She nodded toward Jonathan. He was on his feet, looking like a clumsy child's toy, with a head atop a shapeless bundle of body. Shaking off the support of Frank's arm, he came toward me.

"Safe," he said.

"Yes. But your head . . ."

"I'm not complaining," Jonathan said, with his familiar wry smile. "It could be worse. Lucy—"

"Not now. I can't think yet. . . . Oh, God, Jonathan, is he still in there?"

The great front door had been left open—by design or accident, I knew not which, but the draft only fanned the flames. All I could see inside was fire, a great orange sheet of it.

Jonathan put his arm around me.

"He has not come out. No, Lucy, don't. I won't even ask them to go in there. This may be the best thing. It is what he wanted, what he meant to do."

"But the house . . ."

"Look," Jonathan said quietly.

There were flames spouting out of the upper windows now, like fiery scarlet curtains blowing;

it made a spectacular sight against the black sky and the slow-falling snow. But it was not the spectacle of the burning house Jonathan had meant me to look at. I turned my eyes toward the crowd of people who stood by.

They stood quite still, all of them—men and women and even a few small children. The flames, which made the nearer scene bright as day, flickered weirdly off the still, silent watchers. As they huddled in their worn clothing, their faces stood out stark and pale; and on all the faces, even those of the children, there was a similarity of expression that made them seem akin. The mobs of peasants who burned the châteaus in France must have looked like this. These people—my people—had not lit this fire, they were not so savage. But they liked to see it burn. I could no more have asked them to fight the flames than ask them to fling their bodies into the maelstrom to quench it.

"Let it burn," I said.

A man standing near us turned as he heard the words. It was old Jenkins. With the wind lifting his white beard and long hair, and the glow of the flames crimsoning them, he resembled an Old Testament prophet.

"Aye, my lady. Let it burn! The place is accursed and has been, from the day the usurper took the land. Let it burn, and its evil master with it!"

He was very terrible, standing there with his arms raised as if in invocation. I looked from him to Anna and saw the same glow in her eyes . . . to Tom, and saw his young face hardened . . . and I knew they were right.

I shivered, despite the heavy blanket, and Jonathan said gently,

"We will go to the village. He must have hidden the carriage somewhere nearby; I'll see if I can find it."

"No. No, I can't go yet."

"Lucy. Must you, too, watch it burn?"

"I keep thinking," I said. "If he should come out, now—what would they do? Would they help him, tend his hurts, or would they—"

"I don't know," Jonathan said. "I cannot tell you soothing lies, Lucy. I don't know what they would do. But he won't come out, not now. He is gone. It is not such a bad death as you may think. The smoke induces merciful unconsciousness long before—before anything else can happen."

We had moved back a little, so that we stood apart from the others. I saw them as still black shapes against the fire which now spouted from every door and window. We were with them, and yet not of them; we could not completely share their emotions, which were compounded of old hatreds and ancient loyalties.

"He has his revenge at last," I said, half to myself. "I wonder if it would amuse him, to know."

"Who? Clare?"

"No," I said. I smiled. "No. Dickon. Richard of Gloucester, king of England. Didn't Jenkins tell you? It was only four hundred years ago. . . . They have long memories here in Yorkshire, long memories and loyal hearts. Oh, Jonathan, is there such a thing as a curse? Can treachery and selfishness be passed on from father to son?"

"No."

"You sound like a solicitor again," I said, leaning shamelessly against him.

"I am happy to be a living man, Lucy, let alone a solicitor. One does not need curses to explain Clare, unless the curse of inherited rank and title can be viewed as such."

"And now you sound like a Leveler."

"I am, and proud of it. Look at these people here. They are rough and poor and untaught. They might fight to keep their children from starving; but which of them would descend to Clare's villainy to keep an empty thing like position? He was not even an honest villain. He could not face poverty, nor relinquish a single thing he wanted, as these men and women have relinquished everything, with dignity and decency. 'When Adam delved and Eve span—'"

"'Who was then the gentleman?' You did not tell me what became of Mr. Fleetwood."

"Your irrelevancies have the ring of cosmic truth," Jonathan said. "The vicar—er—left. In haste. They saw him go, but did not prevent his departure. I fancy that by now he is well on his way abroad. You see, only a few of them know the truth."

"I'm not sure I know it either."

"I hoped you need never know."

"That is no way to begin our new life, not if you wish me to be the woman your mother is. I am so looking forward to your mother. . . . Jonathan . . ."

He looked down at me; the weariness of his

face disappeared as he smiled, knowing what I was about to say.

"Jonathan, you are going to marry me, aren't you? It would be quite dishonorable for you to refuse."

"You are becoming too bold. How dare you propose to me? Of course I will marry you, Lucy, if you will have me."

"I have no shame left," I said. "No regret, no sense of propriety. We should wait a year—"

"No," Jonathan said. "We need not wait any time at all. Had you not suspected the truth? Well, then, what better place or time could there be? We should get it over and done with, all of it, tonight. Then we can move on. Perhaps you can even feel some pity for the poor devil. I see him as doomed by the demands of class and family more fatally than any curse could do. And I believe Fleetwood was the greater villain of the two."

"In what way?"

"Remember them," Jonathan said, his eyes fixed on the soaring flames. "The three of them, young and happy and secure. He loved her and she returned his love. All seemed safe; the future bright; and then came the catastrophe. The late Mr. Fleetwood was a fool and a knave, and he took a coward's way out, leaving his children to disgrace. The old Baron forbade his son the acquaintance of the woman he loved. What would any man of spirit do in such a case?"

The truth began to dawn on me.

"But surely . . ."

"When the old man died," Jonathan went on,

still looking straight ahead, "Clare found he had been doubly tricked. There was no money. Every cent of his inheritance had been squandered, and the estate was deeply in debt. Another man might have faced the fact with dignity, lived humbly— even sought honorable employment. Not Clare. Family pride and old tradition dictated only one possible solution to poverty: a wealthy marriage. Good God, Lucy, it has been the disgusting solution of our upper classes for generations! So Clare went to London in search of a rich bride. I don't know why she allowed it. Perhaps she did not know until after the fact; perhaps she accepted her role of submission and obedience. At any rate, it was done. He told you why he chose you. There were other women, I think, who had as much money."

"He thought I would die. He liked me while he thought that. He was kind and gentle."

"Your aunt doubtless encouraged the idea," Jonathan said grimly. "She would have told him anything he wanted to hear. Imagine his distress when you bloomed day after day! Even your famous limp, which troubled you only when you let it. . . . Now don't purse up your mouth at me, Lucy; how much has it troubled you of late? You can thank Clare for that, at least."

He was trying to make me smile, but I could not; not with the flaming pyre before me. One thing he had said made me especially incredulous, and I returned to it.

"It is unbelievable that Mr. Fleetwood should have been aware of all this from the beginning."

"Did I not say he was the greater villain of the two? Clare's evil came from weakness, from following his whims without thinking of the consequences. At the end, his situation was truly terrible. In his place . . . Well, I know what I would have done; but Clare could not do it, he was trapped by a lifetime of bad habits and false ideals. But Fleetwood! He must have known of Clare's reason for going to London last year. Indeed, he may have urged him to go; he had already learned to dread poverty. He also wished to avoid direct violence so long as there was a chance of getting rid of you by natural means. Didn't he interfere whenever Clare's temper made him forbid you to go to the village, with all its danger of infection? On all but the first occasion, when you happened to glimpse his sister leaving Clare's room, Fleetwood was the notorious White Lady; and a charming maiden he must have made, with his pretty face and willowy figure! Phosphorus, smeared on gauzy draperies, creates quite a weird effect by night. The White Lady plot was typical of their cautious cowardice; the second apparition served no purpose except to remove your suspicions of Fleetwood's sister and, hopefully, to make you nervous and susceptible. Of course at that time there was no special urgency. They believed they could experiment at their leisure, and Fleetwood, at least, must have enjoyed tormenting you. Then disaster struck, and they had to act quickly."

"So stupid," I muttered. "It is so like you men, to ignore the logical, inevitable consequence. . . ."

"That is a vile slander on my sex, and one

which I hope to prove that I, at least, do not deserve," said Jonathan, with a look that made me blush. "After all, nothing did happen, not for several years. She must have learned of her condition early in the summer; it was after that that the plotters became desperate. Clare's attempt to get his hands on the remaining portion of your estate was indeed a desperate expedient. He needed the money for her, you see. If he could arrange a suitable establishment abroad, she could have the child without scandal, posing as a wealthy widow. Money has its own immunity; people do not question the rich."

"I can see that, but I don't understand how they hoped to continue the farce. She could never bring the child here. Did Clare mean to abandon her, or give up his ancestral home? He could hardly keep both."

"You still don't understand Clare. That was his difficulty; he would not relinquish *anything* he wanted. He wanted her; he loved her desperately, in his way."

"And she him. How she must have loved him, to consent to such a thing! I can feel no anger toward her, Jonathan, only pity."

"She must have suffered greatly," he agreed. "We should not grieve for her; this ending, hard as it may seem, was more merciful than many. I am confident she never knew of the danger to your life; she would never knowingly have consented to such a thing. Yet eventually she would have suspected the truth, and it would have ruined her peace."

"And the child . . ."

"That, too, Clare wanted. His son—her son, no other woman's. His acknowledged heir, his ancestral estates handed down—he must have them all. Oh, it could have been managed. It would be natural for a heartbroken widower to go abroad, to forget; equally natural for him to visit old friends there. In five or six years' time Baron Clare would return, with his second wife, and a child whose age could be falsified by a year or two. What a precocious three-year-old it would have been!"

"A year or two, yes," I said, as the enormity of the plan dawned on me. "But no more than that. He had to act quickly, Jonathan."

"He did. It did not take him long to realize how to utilize my unwanted presence. We had ample opportunity to betray him; he saw to that. When we refused, he had to be more direct."

"The note," I exclaimed. Jonathan had not known of that, so I told him.

"Yes. You were clever enough to see through that trick. I was not so wise! You know why I came here tonight, don't you? And if I had not had the foresight to tell Jenkins and Tom some of my plans . . ." He nodded toward the blazing building.

"Thank God you did," I murmured. "Thank God for their courage and affection. . . . But you have not told me why you came."

"Because tonight I found the proof I was looking for. They let me find it, I know that now; I should have suspected, when I found the papers so easily. I broke into the vicarage as soon as it was dark, and there the evidence was, in a box in Fleetwood's study. The box was not even locked! Fleetwood would not have left such a damning thing unless he meant me to find it; no doubt it was part of Clare's task tonight to conceal the thing once again, after he had disposed of us. But it was the one certain method of making me come for you. Once I knew the truth I had hardly dared suspect, I knew you were in mortal danger, and I was free to get you away."

"I don't know what made you suspect. No such idea ever occurred to me."

"It came to me first the day we met her on the moor. I could not help but agree with your assessment of her character. And suddenly I thought: What if . . . At first it seemed to me utterly impossible; but the more I considered it, the more likely it became. It explained so much—even Clare's avoidance of you. It was typical of his strange mixture of principle and villainy that he would not approach you as a husband."

"High principles were not the only reason," I said coldly. "Even Clare could foresee the difficulty inherent in two legitimate heirs. . . . Oh, don't look so shocked, Jonathan! I can pity Clare, but I cannot think well of him; how can I, when he meant to kill you? He allowed you to discover the truth, and because you knew the truth, you had to die. And I—why, he was fooling himself up to the very end. I would not have survived the 'accident.' Divorce was no solution to his problem; he needed my money, and he needed it at once."

"Yes, I think Clare was unable to admit even to himself what he had to do. When the fatal blow struck you, it would have been another 'accident.' How unfortunate that the poor girl should have struck her head on a stone! He had no such qualms with me; I fancy he could have stabbed me cheerfully at any time for the past few weeks."

"And then to leave the proof lying about! I wonder they committed it to paper at all."

"Oh, that was essential. Fleetwood would insist on it, in the case of Clare's death or betrayal."

"I wonder what will become of him."

"He will survive," Jonathan said grimly. "I will do my best to track him down, be sure of that; he has too great a capacity for evil, with that candid face and eloquent voice, to be allowed his freedom. But I have a feeling he has arts superior to mine. It will be a dreadful scandal, Lucy; yet it must come out. You do agree?"

"Yes, of course. You need not fear for me; talk cannot hurt me, not now."

"At least some of your estate is left," Jonathan said, trying to sound optimistic. "The real property—mines and mills and factories—"

"Is that what my wealth comes from?"

"Yes. I thought you knew."

"Those deformed children from the mills . . . To think they might have been my work! Oh, Jonathan, there is so much to be done! You will help me, won't you?"

"To get rid of your ugly mills?"

"No, no, to make them into something helpful instead of evil. Train the men—give them employment instead of the children—shorter hours, free schools."

"You will spend all of your profits," Jonathan said. "I don't think I can marry you after all."

"And the village, here; I can help the people buy their land back, it will go to the Crown now, will it not? New houses . . ."

"I expect you will want to go to Oxford, to complete your education," Jonathan suggested. "I can go on strike with you. We will riot and march, and perhaps attack Buckingham Palace . . ."

"Don't laugh!"

"I am not laughing at you. I only wonder whether I can be worthy of such a woman." Jonathan's arm tightened. "Lucy, you have faced almost all of it now. I took a copy of the paper. Do you wish to see it?"

I reached out my hand—and then stood still, as a long, low cry went up from the watching crowd. In a thunder of sound and flame the roof collapsed. The great chimneys wavered like reflections in water, and then fell into the boiling sea of fire. I thought, for an instant, that I saw . . . But I did not, it was only my imagination. In the fiery light I looked at the paper Jonathan had handed me.

Signed by the Reverend John Fleetwood, of St. Catherine's parish, York, it was a copy of marriage lines—the marriage of Edward Grosvenor, not yet Baron Clare, and Charlotte Fleetwood.